VIGILARE

Where One System Fails,
Another Never Gives Up

Brooklyn James

To Doug, Nice meeting you at Hill Country Bookstore. All my best to you and yours. Thanks for supporting local writers. Happy Holidays! Light & Love, Brooklyn James

Vigilare

by Brooklyn James
www.brooklyn-james.com
Copyright © 2011 by Brooklyn James
All rights reserved.

Edited by Janet Kilgore
Cover design by Steve Richey
Text design and layout by Steve Richey

Published by Arena Books, Austin, Texas
First Edition—November 2011
ISBN 1466402113
ISBN 9781466402119

Printed in the United States of America

To Innocence Lost...

PROLOGUE

Vigilare—to guard, to look out, to keep an eye on.

Perched atop the tallest building in downtown Vanguard,
Night has long since fallen.
My eyes pierce through the darkness, spanning the city below,
Is 'this' my calling?

'This' is what I do,
I sit. I watch. I wait. But, I don't know why.
As autonomic as taking a breath, a divine assignment,
Too compelling to defy.

My sight, something unnatural,
One's thoughts are not safe from me.
Take care evil ones,
You'll answer, eventually.

I see everything,
Some things so beautiful I replay them in my mind.
While others so menacing,
I sometimes wish these eyes of mine were blind.

Who am I?
My steps, quick and light.
A 'Vigilare,' they tell me,
I am the keeper of the night.

CHAPTER 1

Night falls over Vanguard Park as darkness cascades the heart of the city. Fall foliage has begun, causing a colorful array of leaves to float through the air as they make their descent to the cool ground below. Dim pole lights provide those of the aerobic persuasion a set of eyes as they walk off this evening's dinner.

A woman jogs through the park at a casual pace, exchanging glances with the occasional passerby. She gives a wave to a group of Vanguard College students jogging at a healthy pace, determined to escape the ever-threatening *Freshman Fifteen*. But to the six-foot, sandy blonde-haired adonis with the six-pack abs and dimpled chin, she extends a smile, and a second look as her head naturally pivots behind her, curious as to whether the backside is as intriguing as the front. Scanning him from bottom to top, her face blushes coupled with quiet laughter as she meets his eyes, realizing he shares the same curiosity. His image disappearing from her sight as they continue in opposite directions. She is two-miles into her five-mile run as she veers off the beaten path onto a forboding, unpopulated trail that leads to the forest surrounding the east side of the park.

Stay on the main path, she hears her instinct kicking in. She ignores the warning, forging ahead.

Her feet keep time with the upbeat rhythm of a song playing at a high volume in the earpieces of her MP3 Player. Her breath forms faint clouds of moisture in the air as she mouths the words, attempting to distract her thoughts. Her head darts from side to side, scanning the darkness, fighting a feeling of discomfort as she realizes she is alone on the trail.

Oh, quit psyching yourself out already.

She starts down a steep grade along the gravel path, picking up speed to push up the other side. Words once spoken to her in a distant self-defense class flood her memory, "Always be aware of your surroundings. Stay with the crowd."

Spontaneously, her legs move at a full sprint keeping pace with her thoughts. She veers off the gravel path, and with the finesse of a deer, she launches into the woods, ducking and diving until she reaches a small clearing.

What the hell are you doing? Go back, she orders herself, her eyes wide and scared.

Her stomach wound tight with nerves, she pulls the earpieces from her ears, her breath forming condensed mini-clouds, matching the strained rise and fall of her chest. Her heart knocks fast and furious at the little spot in the back of her throat.

"Who's out there?" she demands, spinning fast circles, her eyes peer into the darkness, searching every angle.

Turn around. Go back. Run!

Her body does not obey her mind. She stands still as if preparing for something. The trees overhead seem to encroach on her as her internal feeling of darkness mimics that of the night, black and wicked. She crouches defensively.

"Well, what do we have here?" a male voice sounds behind her. She spins in his direction, backing away at the sight of the unruly man, flanked by two others smiling menacingly at her. The word CONGO tattooed and proudly displayed on the front of each man's neck.

The woman turns to run, only to be stopped by a swift arm around her waist. "Where are you going, sweetheart?" the voice purrs tauntingly in her ear from behind, sending chills to the depths of her bones. The man jerks her around to face their leader, shoving her in his direction. He crushes her torso in his arms while gripping her hands behind her back.

Scream for help. Do something! Once again, her body will not obey. Instead she simply whispers, "Let me go."

The two men laugh, while the leader smiles looking down at her. "This is Congo Territory," he says, while taking his free hand and pulling her hairband from her hair, allowing the auburn strands to fall around her face. "I run the Congo," he adds, winding his hand in her hair. He jerks her head back exposing her neck. Her jugular vein throbs ferociously, *ga-gung...ga-gung...ga-gung,* matching her heart rate. She chokes back a cry as he runs his tongue the length of her neck, now hovering over her mouth. "Everything in the Congo belongs to me," he teases with a smile before crushing her lips with his own.

She meets his mouth with her teeth, biting down for all she's worth as she knees him forcefully between his legs. He yelps, snapping his head back from hers, his lip tinged with blood as he falls to the ground cupping his insulted manhood. The woman turns to run but is intercepted by his two goons, who wrestle her to the cold, grassy soil.

"Hold her down. Stupid bitch," the man spews, spitting blood as he crawls to them, mounting her waist. She tries to kick and punch, but her attempts are muddled by his wingmen. One sits on her thighs, restraining her legs, as the other kneels at her head, her arms outstretched, his knees buried in each palm. The man sits atop her momentarily regaining his breath. He wipes at his mouth. Looking at the inside of his hand, he smiles disturbingly, winds up and blasts her across the face, leaving a smear of his blood along her cheekbone. The woman winces in pain, a quiet cry escapes her. "That's your fault. I tried to be nice," he taunts his hand harshly pulling at the waistband of her running pants, his skin in contact with hers. The woman's body tenses, fear burns in her eyes. "Not so tough now, are we?" He smiles, the other men laugh, as he crouches over her, only inches separating his face from hers. "That's the problem with you bitches. Always have to be put in your place."

Don't do it. Don't do it, she coaches before feeling her lips part, between them passes her own saliva, splatting onto the ugly, harsh face staring down at her. He sits upright, momentarily thrown off guard, swiping at his face. His teeth gritting together, his hand grips her neck, squeezing and shaking.

"You like it rough, baby?" he jeers. The woman struggles against the men, faint coughs muted by the hands squeezed mercilessly around her neck. Her face red, her body exhausted finally lies limp. Her eyes are dark green and helpless, as tears roll from each corner trickling down her temples.

"I'm gonna tear you up, then leave you to the wolves," he says, leaving one hand on her neck and returning the other to the waistband of her running pants, pawing at the material. His wingmen tip their heads back and howl tauntingly. He bends his face to hers, the smell of his breath instantly making her nauseous. She purses her lips together, turning her head from him. He grabs a handful of her hair, yanking her head back into position, bearing down against her mouth with his teeth until he feels a warm spurt of blood.

"Returning the favor," he says, sitting upright he grabs at the belt buckle on his jeans, quickly unfastening it, positioning himself between her thighs.

"Aw shit man, something ain't right. This bitch ain't right," the man at the woman's head warns.

The blood released from her lip feels cool and tingly, the same sensation surging through her entire body. From the tips of her fingers to the ends of her toes her form quivers, electrified and powerful. She lies still, confused, her heart pounding with renewed force, aware of every surge of life blood pumped through her. With each beat, she is sure the life sustaining organ will explode from her chest.

What the hell is going on? What's happening to me?

Her eyes are wide and searching with intent, as if designed specifically to do so. She breathes deeply through her nose, unsure if she could ever acquire enough air to fill her seemingly supersized lungs. Every sound amplified times ten, her ears flood with stimulation.

"Look at her eyes, bro!" the man at her head challenges.

The leader, forcefully hunched between her thighs, does as instructed, leaning forward, unimpressed at first, until his eyes stare into hers. Hers, once complacent, now sparkle like emeralds. She tries to blink, closing her eyes from his. She cannot. They remain wide and steadily searching, as if someone willed them unable to close. The leader tries to look away, move, shut his eyes—something, anything to break the stare. He cannot. Propelled by a far greater force, he remains there, his eyes giving into hers. Images flash in her mind, reflections of the man and the things he has done. The eyes are the windows to the soul. His soul is evil.

With the last image, they disengage. Her eyes close momentarily, releasing their hold on his. He flings himself off of her, staggering to his feet, wiping at his eyes, feeling as if the energy has drained from his body. The other two men follow suit, releasing her, quickly scrambling to their feet, backing away. Instinctively, she arches her back and springs to her feet, assuming a defensive martial arts position. Her hands in perfect form, suddenly aware of the power and lightness of her body, unsure of what to do with it exactly.

"This chick thinks she's Bruce-fuckin'-Lee!" the disbelieving wingman who held her feet pops off, waving his arms and hands around mockingly accompanied by nervous laughter.

"Shut up, man. The bitch ain't right. Look at her!" the other wingman sputters, his head swiveling from side to side and behind him, in search of a clear getaway.

"You scared? You gonna cry?" he jeers, quivering his lip condescendingly at his partner. "Man-up, pussy." The leader remains quiet, shocked, simply staring at her in disbelief.

"I ain't scared of her. I ain't scared of nothing," the man replies, nervously *manning up*. Both wingmen pull out knives and lunge at her simultaneously.

With unparalleled quickness and accuracy, she steps into the men grabbing each one by the wrist, pulling them toward her as she spins them around. Cradling their backs into her chest, she bears down against their hands as the knives meet the flesh of their necks. *Wisht!* The knives sound as she quickly draws them across their throats, finishing with her arms outstretched from her sides. In her hands, she still holds each man's wrist. Their fingers give way to release the weapons as the life fades from their bodies. Her ears hone in on the faint sounds of the blood-tinged blades tumbling end over end, until they find stillness in the grass. Her attention immediately returns to the leader who has taken off in a full-fledged run. Her body moves effortlessly through time and space. Her mind feels disconnected as if she is outside herself looking in, but the speed, the rush, feels astounding. Within seconds she catches up with him, lurching forward she pins him to the ground, straddling him as he had her moments earlier.

"Get off me, you crazy bitch!" he yells, his voice high-pitched. He swats, swings and kicks at her. Each attempt easily combatted, he finally stills, exhausted, his chest heaving up and down for air.

"Not so tough now, are we?" she echoes his own words, a wry smile forming on her lips. Her hand clasps his neck, the way he had hers, applying firm pressure. "That's the problem with you thugs. Always have to be put in your place." She locks her sparkling emerald eyes on his, replaying all the images of his past, the havoc he wreaked in the lives of others. With each new reflection, she squeezes harder. The slideshow eventually extinguished, along with his breath.

THE NEXT MORNING, Detective Gina DeLuca and her partner, Officer Sam Marks, are on duty at the Vanguard Police Department. They have been assigned a new patrol car, the department's first Dodge Challenger Hemi.

"Okay, who's feeling frisky? A car chase, anyone?" Gina asks, her hands caressing the steering wheel with anticipation at how the vehicle might handle when they are not running their rudimentary patrol of the neighborhood—at a safe twenty-five miles per hour.

"Did you see the look on Gronkowski's face?" Officer Marks asks, smiling indulgently. "When Chief assigned the car to us this morning?"

"Can you blame him? Look at that pile of metal he has to shove around on four wheels," she says, referring to Detective Gronkowski's old-school Pontiac Gran Prix.

Officer Marks laughs. "Ah, he's up next for renewal. Wonder what they'll give him?"

Gina smiles. "Maybe a Prius."

"A Prius?" he replies, chuckling. "And I thought you liked Gronkowski."

"I do. I just don't want to fight over who's first in anymore."

He shakes his head, grinning. "Why do you do this job?"

She looks at him perplexed.

"I just mean. Well...you're kinda pretty. You don't need to do a job like this. You got options, DeLuca."

"I like my job. And, by the way, don't ever tell a woman she's *kinda* pretty," she replies through an easy smile. "Why do you do it?"

"Good versus evil. Simple as that. I always wanted to be the good guy as a kid. Well, that and Erik Estrada. He looked so cool in those sunglasses," he says with a charming grin.

"Base to 223," a voice calls over the radio.

"Oh, please be a car chase. Come on, I dare ya," Gina crosses her fingers.

"Base, this is 223," Officer Marks radios back.

"Domestic dispute, the corner of Rio and 25th, possible weapon."

"We're on it," Officer Marks confirms.

"We're in the area, too," a deep voice, that of Detective Tony Gronkowski comes over the airwaves. "We'll take first in. Marks, you take backup."

Gina grabs the radio from Officer Marks. "Gronkowski, we got the call. We're first in. You take backup."

"Drop the ego, DeLuca. Possible weapon. We're first in," Tony argues.

"Ego? Look who's talking," she rolls her eyes, as if he can see her through the radio. "Tell you what, first car there, first in." She hands the radio back to Officer Marks and slams the accelerator to the floor, talking nearly as fast as she is driving. "Why do I do this job? You're right Marks, I do have options!" Her siren blaring, her speed steadily increases as she takes a ninety-degree corner barely on two wheels, throwing Officer Marks to the left. He grabs for the dash. She guns the engine, pulling the car out of its skid. The force pushes Officer Marks steadily back into his seat.

"DeLuca. Gina," Gronkowski calls from the radio.

"Ah, she's a little busy right now," Officer Marks answers him nervously.

"Marks, get DeLuca on the line. Now!"

Gina continues down the street at break-neck speed, blasting through a yellow light, driving up onto the curb to avoid a bicyclist. A combination of roses, carnations and lilies from the flower shop on the corner fly onto the windshield and up over the hood of her cruiser before she gets it leveled back out onto the road. "I guess I do this job to get heckled by some boorish man who thinks I'm too delicate to be first in. Come on baby," she strokes the dashboard of the car, coaxing it on.

As they near the residence from which the 911 call was made, Gina turns the siren off, and pulls up to the curb cautiously, as she and Marks make a visual assessment of the scene. The rundown house sits surrounded by others of the same make and model. The front porch steps creak as they accept the weight of Gina and

Officer Marks. They share an uneasy glance, both putting on supportive smiles as they approach the main entrance. Gina knocks authoritatively, but only a few times.

"Vanguard PD. Detective DeLuca. Open up," she identifies herself, her hand casually but purposefully resting on her gun belt.

After a few moments, the front door opens slowly. Gina scans down from the open space behind the door until her eyes meet those of a child, trepidation written in her expression. A young girl, maybe six-years old, her curly brown hair disheveled and unkempt, steadily wringing one hand in the cotton fabric of her oversized T-shirt, while the other grips a telephone.

"Hi," Gina says, flashing a settling smile at the girl. "Are your parents home?"

The girl's eyes remain locked in on Gina's, as tears form in them. "No," she replies, as her head nods up and down, contradicting her words.

"Maybe we have the wrong address." Gina winks at her. "Since we're here, how would you like to see a real live police car?" Gina holds her hand out. The girl hesitates only for a moment before putting her hand in Gina's, squeezing tightly. Gina looks to Officer Marks. He silently reads the direction in her expression, taking the little girl's hand, escorting her to the safety of the patrol car. Gina maneuvers stealthily inside the front door, her Light Double Action 1911 pistol engaged, her eyes peer through the sights, searching.

"Vanguard Police. We received a call to this house. I can't leave until I talk to someone," Gina coaxes as she clears the living room and kitchen, making her way down the hall. A muffled cry, a woman's voice, is heard on the other side of the door to her right, followed by a shifting of bodies.

The door flies open, Gina quickly backs up to a safe distance, her pistol aimed and pointing at her target.

"I'll cut her up, you come any closer," a male voice pumped full of adrenaline yells, his arm clenched tightly around his victim's neck.

"Please, just leave," the woman chokes through tears as her hands remain locked around her captors forearm, attempting to maintain her balance and keep the pressure of the knife blade off her neck.

Gina flashes her eyes around the room, clear of anyone else. The shattered mirror over the sink smeared with blood matches the bruises and lacerations on the woman's forehead and eyebrow. Her lip is cut open and swollen. Gina swallows hard, curbing her instinct to verbally admonish the man. "Put the knife down. Nobody's in trouble here." She lowers her weapon, reholstering it, her hands palms out at shoulder level, as a sign of good faith. "I'm only here to help. Talk to me. Put the knife down and talk to me."

The man hesitates, his facial expression flashes from desperation to helplessness. His eyes begin to water as he loosens his grip on the knife around the woman's throat. "I didn't. I didn't mean to," he whimpers.

The front door to the house bursts open, startling the man. He tightens his grip, pulling the woman backwards, dragging her to the room behind him. "Liar!" he yells through clenched teeth, shutting the door.

"Nice Gronkowski," Gina growls, as he and his partner, Officer Torres enter the hallway.

The sound of shattered glass echoes from behind the closed door. Detective Gronkowski plants his shoulder into the frame, forcing the lock. Gina pushes past him into the room. In front of her, jagged glass hangs from the window frame. To her left, the woman sits in a corner, her knees hugged to her chest rocking back and forth, holding pressure to her neck. Gina kneels in front of her, inspecting her wound.

"Where's my daughter?" the woman cries.

"She's safe. She's with Officer Marks, out front. Everything's going to be okay, ma'am."

Gronkowski catapults out the window in pursuit of the fleeing man.

"Torres," Gina beckons. Torres exchanges places with Gina, comforting the woman. "Call an ambulance. Stay with her."

Torres radios in, watching Gina successfully launch through the window pane, her feet plant firmly onto the concrete as her knees and lower back take the brunt of the impact. In a full sprint, it takes her a few seconds to catch up with Gronkowski.

"Just can't stand it, can you? Always have to be first," Gronkowski says through labored breaths, maintaining a steady run. "Were you a middle child or something?"

"It's not about being first. I'm not a quitter. This was my call. I started it. I finish it. And, FYI, I was an *only* child."

"That figures," he replies, accompanied by a cough, the cold air stinging as it makes its way forcefully in and out of his chest.

"What's the matter Gronkowski, riding patrol making the lungs soft?" She chuckles. Their pace matched stride for stride, their boots dig into the grass of neighboring backyards as they dodge clotheslines and swing sets.

"Yeah, that's it. It couldn't be the two hours of Jiu-Jitsu training I had this morning."

"Jiu-Jitsu? Nobody told me."

"Don't worry DeLuca. It's not through the department. Kills you to think you might be missing out on something, huh?"

"50 bucks...he goes for the fence," Gina wagers, her words interrupted by her lungs requiring maximum oxygen intake at this rate.

"You're on. Makes more sense to take the alleyway." Tony pauses, catching his breath. "We'll catch him on the fence."

"Because criminals are always the sharpest tools in the shed." Gina playfully thumps the back of her hand off Tony's chest, inhaling and exhaling rapidly, before continuing, "See, there he goes."

"You gotta be kidding me," Tony huffs at the sight, his labored breathing visible in the cool air. "The jackass is going for the fence."

"When opportunity knocks," Gina says, kicking up her pace, outrunning Tony. She lunges forward, scaling the front of the fence, her hands making contact with the man's T-shirt as he is straddling the fence, preparing to jump off the other side. Her hands are now tightly wound in the cotton fabric. "Open the door," she continues, letting her weight fall back to the ground, the man coming with her. His back comes to rest in the cold, dead grass, creating a dull *thud!*

"You had to do it, huh? Had to be the one to take him down," Gronkowski mutters through strained breaths, as he turns the man over, his knee shoved into his back, forcing his hands behind him into cuffs.

"Ow. Shit. Ow! My arms, man. You're hurting my arms," the man proclaims.

"Don't be a poor sport. You get to manhandle him," Gina chimes in, her choppy reply matching the arduous rise and fall of her chest. She grabs her radio. "We got him. We're at the 600-block of Worchester Ave." Pocketing her radio, she continues with a grin, "You're built for brawn. I'm built for speed. We might as well stick with what we've got."

Tony is roughly maneuvering the man to a sitting position against the fence. "This shit hurts!" the man yells into Tony's face.

Tony grabs him by the neck scolding him through clenched teeth, "And you think what you did to your girlfriend felt good? I ought to turn her loose on you, right here. Put a baseball bat in her hand and let her beat your sorry ass to a pulp."

"Tony," Gina lays her hand on his back.

Tony shoves the man backward, bouncing his head off the fence behind him.

"You better be careful hotshot. I know my rights," the man threatens.

"Good. I guess I won't have to read them to you, *hotshot.*" Tony turns to Gina. "Besides, I slowed down so you could keep up, *speedy.*"

The sound of sirens wail as a police cruiser pulls up to their location. Gina and Tony bend on both sides of the man, pulling him to a standing position to be loaded in the car. "Denial...first step Gronkowski." Gina shrugs her shoulders, a smirk across her lips. "Just saying."

Chapter 2

Evening. A woman wheels her grocery cart to her car, exchanging pleasantries with a passerby. With one click of the car remote, her trunk gives way to its latch. She eyeballs her surroundings in front, to the sides, and in back prior to bending into the trunk, offloading her groceries to their temporary resting place. The coast is clear, leaving her to feel comfortable and safe. A conscientious citizen, she returns her grocery cart to it's appropriate corral in the center of the parking lot, gets in her car and drives off. As she leaves the lights of town, she can't help but feel unsettled in her gut, her innate instinct warming up. She searches in her mirrors, scanning the scene around her. Nothing out of the ordinary.

"Oh stop it," she coaches aloud. "Quit being a big scaredy-cat." She smiles at herself into the rearview mirror, flicking the button on the radio.

I always feel like, somebody's watching me. The tune floods through her speakers.

"Geez-us!" she exclaims, quickly hitting the scan button, tuning the dial to a different song. "Someone actually thought that was a good idea for a song? Creepy."

When the working day is done, oh girls, they wanna have fu-un. Oh girls just wanna have fun. Cindy Lauper comes at her through the radio.

"Now, that's more like it." She cranks the volume, shimmy -ing around in her driver's seat. "'That's all they really wa-a-a-ant. Is some fu-u-u-un. When the working day is done. Oh girls, they wanna have fu-un.'"

"I like the last song better," a voice sounds from the backseat.

Her eyes dart to the rearview mirror. A man wearing a baseball cap and full beard sits directly behind her. She slams on the brakes. The car screeches all over the road. She wants to scream, but can't.

"There's no need to cause a scene. Take your foot off the brake. Drive the speed limit. Now!" he demands, brandishing a .38-Special Revolver. He leans up over the seat, nuzzling the snub-nosed pistol into her hair directly behind her ear. The cold, hard steel causes the skin on her entire body to form goosebumps. She pulls the car back into the right-hand lane avoiding a collision with a pair of oncoming headlights, following his instruction. Her hands are visibly shaking as they maintain control of the steering wheel.

The woman's eyes flicker back and forth from the road to the man in the rearview mirror. Her mind races a mile a minute. *Drive into a tree. Speed up. Cause attention to yourself. Do something!*

The man chuckles. "Don't even think about doing something stupid. All that shit you women read about 'fighting the good fight, don't let him take you to a secluded area, make a scene.' It's bullshit. The only way you get out of this alive is do what I tell you. You got it?" He rams the revolver further into her skull behind her ear. "You got it!"

She nods her head, holding back a sob.

After a long, torturous drive, the car pulls up to a remote body of water. The man jumps out of the car, wrestling the woman out of the driver's seat. "Help me! Please somebody help me!" she yells.

"You can scream all you want to now, baby. Ain't nobody around for miles." He grabs a handful of her hair, pulling her in the direction of the water, wielding the pistol in his other hand. "I lied. All that shit they tell you women—turns out it is true. You should've made a scene when you had your chance."

"Why are you doing this!" the woman cries.

"It's the only thing you uptight sluts respond to." He spins her around facing him, grabbing the collar of her blouse, he runs the barrel end of the pistol over the silk material covering her breasts. She winces and pushes against him with the contact. "Night after night. Bar after bar. I tried buying you bitches drinks. Asking you out on dates. A guy gets tired of asking. Eventually, I started taking. Sorry baby, you're not my first," he jeers, forcing her hand to the front of his pants, stroking it over his engorged unit.

Overcome with disgust and rage, the woman bangs her forehead into his face, causing him to release her shirt collar, instinctively tending to his bloody nose. She makes a run for the water. He fires the revolver in her direction. *Bang! Bang! Bang! Bang! Bang! Bang!* She falls to the sand lying on the outer edge of the lake. He makes his way to her, rolling her over onto her back. He scans her body for blood, bulletholes, something...without a trace.

He straddles her, shaking her seemingly unconscious body, "Why'd you fall down? Are you hit? Goddammit!"

She opens her eyes and lets out a deviously provoking chuckle. "You're a horrible shot."

"You think it's funny? I'm some kinda clown to you? Bitch!" He holds his revolver to her temple.

"Click," she exaggerates the sound of an empty gun with a smile. "Unless yours magically holds seven, you're out of ammo *Wyatt Earp.*"

He throws the gun into the sand, pulls her torso up off the ground by her blouse and slams his forehead into her face. She groans with the impact. "How's that feel, funny girl? Not so funny is it!" He lets her head and upper body fall back into the sand.

Her vision is temporarily inhibited by stars of the entoptic sort, surely a side-effect of her throbbing nose, from which blood begins to trickle. Her upper lip tingles at every contact point of the viscous substance. *Ga-gung...ga-gung...ga-gung,* her heartbeat quickens, gaining in strength as if it is supplying a body at least twice the size of hers. With each inhale, her back arches allowing her chest and ribcage the expansion needed to accommodate the massive amount of air her lungs suddenly seem to require. She opens her eyes, scared and startled, breathing laboriously through pursed lips, attempting to slow her rapid breathing rate. The look on the man's face begins to match her own as his eyes make contact with hers, emerald green and sparkling. He tries to look away, she attempts to close her eyes, but the connection has been made. His visions are now hers. She sees the first woman he raped (a college freshman—he slipped Rohipnol in her drink, and left her on the front yard of her sorority house). And the last. He raped her right here on the sand. Held her head underwater, until she quit fighting.

With the last image, the stare is released. They begin to grapple, exchanging positions of domination in the sand, their bodies encroaching on the water.

"What kinda freak bitch are you? You been to the Halloween store or something?" he teases through ragged breaths. The man holds her down, submerging her face under water, which splashes and bubbles as she struggles against him.

His hands losing their grasp on her neck, he digs in with his fingernails, drawing blood. The first drop of the red sticky substance released to the air sends a jolt of adrenaline through her system, shocking in its effect. She lies still momentarily, her body absorbing the impact, then releasing with a surge of supernatural strength as she physically overpowers the man who easily outweighs her. Gasping for air as she comes up out of the water, she locks her legs around his back and neck forming a triangle hold. Her eyes flickering down over his.

"Night after night. Guy after guy," she begins, twisting his previous monologue. "I tried being nice. Asking you schleps to change your lives." She tightens her thigh muscles further, causing his face to turn a bright red. "A girl gets tired of asking. Eventually, I started taking." She releases her legs, pushing his head back into the water. His muffled protests stifled by bubbles. "Sorry baby, you're not my first."

VANGUARD POLICE DEPARTMENT, early afternoon. Chief Robert Burns, a burly middle-aged man with a full head of thick, wavy, salt and pepper hair sits sorting through paperwork at his desk. Quite uncomfortable in his heavily starched uniform shirt his wife insists he wears, he has removed his tie, and released the top button after several *near death* experiences from contact of the tight fabric against his Adam's Apple.

He holds the call key down on his phone, "Bonnie, did you leave those files on my desk this morning? I can't find the damn things."

"Sure did, Chief. Right-hand side, in front of your computer," Bonnie's pleasing and patient tone comes through the speaker.

Frustrated, he continues shuffling through the files haphazardly. A knock sounds from the glass pane separating his office from the main corridor. Detectives DeLuca and Gronkowski poke their heads inside the door.

He motions them in. "Bonnie..." he begins.

"Be right there, Chief," she interrupts.

He hangs up the phone. "Well, if it isn't my little regulators. You two mind telling me what the hell happened out there yesterday?"

"It was my fault, sir," Gina and Tony speak in unison.

Bonnie enters the office. She is a page right out of Mad Men, redheaded and buxom, wearing a professional, yet formfitting blouse with a pencil skirt, fully in charge of her magnetic prowess. Tony, and Gina, cannot help but follow her with their eyes as she enters the room. Gina looks down at her bland navy blue uniform top, feeling uncharacteristically inferior at the moment. Without missing a beat, she reaches over and lightly taps Tony's chin, firmly reconnecting the admirable gape to his jaw. The only person unaffected by her presence is Chief Burns, completely oblivious and happily married for the past twenty-five years.

Bonnie rifles through the files on his desk. "If it were a snake, it would have bit you." She smiles, pulling the file from the exact place she told him it resided. She sets a brown paper bag in front of him. "Mrs. Burns left this for you. She's so sweet."

"Thanks Bonnie."

Bonnie nods her head, a gentle bow of duty. "Anything else, Chief?"

"That'll do it."

"Detectives," she politely recognizes them upon her exit.

"Bonnie," Tony and Gina mumble, swiveling their necks in her direction like two awestruck teenagers. Gina subconsciously touches her hand to her hair, slicked back in a ponytail, as she watches Bonnie's glorious wavy auburn crown bounce and flow with each step, reminiscent of a supermodel on the catwalk.

"Uh-hum," Chief Burns clears his throat, causing their necks to jerk back to him in attention. "Yesterday...what happened?"

"I should've posted for backup until Detective DeLuca gave me her position," Tony says.

Chief Burns clumsily removes a hoagie from the brown paper bag. "It's been a while since I went through the academy, but if I remember correctly, alpha team—Detective DeLuca—should've waited for backup before entering the building."

"She had it under control, until I showed up busting through the front door," Tony defends.

"I should've waited," Gina speaks up.

Part of the filling from the hoagie Chief Burns is desperately trying to direct to his mouth falls from the bun, dribbling down his shirt. "Dammit!"

Gronkowski and DeLuca bite the insides of their lips, attempting not to smile or laugh.

Chief wipes at the hoagie filling with a piece of paper from his desk. Gina leans forward pulling a napkin from the brown paper bag, handing it to him. He swipes it out of her hand agitatedly.

"Thanks. You two are two of the best I've got. I can't have you out in the street, tearing up the neighborhood. It's bad press. I've got citizens complaining you ran through their backyards, tearing down their clotheslines. The flower shop on West Avenue, delivered a bill this morning for five hundred sixty-two-dollars and twenty-nine cents! And don't think I didn't notice the ding on the brand new squad car, DeLuca." He slaps his hand down on his desk, then runs it through his hair frustratingly.

"The guy ran, Chief," Gina says.

"We got our man. Isn't that what counts?" Tony backs her.

"Maybe driving on the sidewalk was a little excessive," she admits.

"A *little* excessive? First day out and you scratch the shit out of it!" Chief Burns stands from his desk, pacing. "I asked myself, I said, 'Chief, what do you do with two detectives who do good work, but work against each other half the time?'"

"Aw, no, Chief," Gina retorts.

"You got it, DeLuca. Hit the hammer on the head. Meet your new partner," Chief announces, his fists pridefully resting on his hips.

Gina and Tony share a puzzled glance, both mouthing, *Hit the hammer on the head?*

"I'm starting to warm up to Marks. Come on, Chief. Gronkowski's been teamed up with Torres for a while now, too. We can't work together." She gestures largely from herself to Tony and back again for effect. "Hell, you see what happens when we end up on scene together, in two separate patrol cars. You can't seriously be thinking about teaming us up."

"No, DeLuca, I'm not *thinking* about anything. It's done. And here's your first assignment." He slaps a folder down on the desk in front of them.

"Chief..."

"Gina. It's done."

Tony smiles at her, a beguiling grin. "Come on, DeLuca. Might be fun. At least we won't be fighting over who's first in." She smirks back at him, crossing her arms defiantly over her chest.

"We have a little problem, boys and girls." Chief Burns opens up the file, shifting through rap sheets that match morgue pictures. "Seems we've got a vigilante of sorts, who's primary targets are rapists and child molesters."

"What's the problem?" Gronkowski asks, in a calloused tone.

Chief exchanges an understanding, yet authoritative glance with Tony. "Thomas Boyd, Victor Peebles, Roberto Moreno, Darius Williams...and the list goes on. All of 'em convicted rapists or child molesters. Rap sheets longer than my arm. They just found another one this morning. A lake outside of town. Drowned."

"People die all the time from accidental drowning," Gina says.

"Now listen, you two. That's enough with the comments. We took an oath to serve and protect...everyone." Chief runs his thumbs around the inside of the waist of his pants, giving them a gentle tug, his neck and jaw twitching momentarily as if the admission pained him.

Tony and Gina watch him uncomfortably.

"What we do know, whoever this vigilante is, he's no amateur. Patterns have been established. Every murder takes place on the *home ground*, if you will, of the perpetrator. Maybe a setup. For instance, this guy here." Chief Burns points to a photo. "Elroy Dawson. Released three-months ago after serving time for child molestation. Hung around the playground of Reagan Elementary. Friggin' *Easter Bunny* baited kids with candy. Found dead, lying under the Monkey Bars at Reagan Elementary last week, bound and gagged with a mouth full of candy laced with enough Mercury to kill a moose."

Tony chuckles. "Gotta give him some props for creativity." He clears his throat, removing the smile from his face after receiving a disgruntled look from Chief Burns. "Just saying."

"Him?" Gina asks. "Do we know it's a he?"

"The only thing we've got from forensics is a few traces of blood, which are defective in their DNA. Some kind of fake, made-up blood type. It's not natural," Chief Burns replies.

"Covering his tracks?" Tony implies. "What is he some kind of scientist, medical professional? Who else knows enough about blood to fool forensics?"

"Any leads? Family members? Witnesses? Who and where do we start?" Gina's wheels start turning, aloud.

Chief Burns turns to the back of the file, and points to a business card. "Dr. Ryan, the department Psychologist. She's had every one of these men in her office at some point. Has all their records. Knows their patterns. It's a part of the State's mandatory rehabilitation protocol. They all have to participate once they're on probation. She's the only link in the string right now."

Gina and Tony share another puzzled glance at his second ill-spoken idiom. Chief takes a bite from his hoagie, successfully keeping its contents within the bun this time. However, that doesn't stop a smear of mayonnaise from residing at the corner of his mouth. Tony wipes at the corner of his own mouth, thinking maybe Chief will pick up on his subtle gesture. He does not. Gina picks up a napkin and timidly reaches across the desk.

"Missed a spot, Chief." She smiles coyly.

Chief swipes at his mouth with the cuff of his shirt, foregoing the napkin. "Alright then. Get to it."

Gina picks up the file and turns swiftly to exit the room.

"I need a report on my desk by week's end," Chief says, tapping his desk with his knuckles.

"I'll have my secretary get right on that. Huh, DeLuca?" Tony pipes up, grinning.

She slaps the file against his chest as she walks by him, maintaining its possession. "I'll have him in a dress and heels by the end of the week, Chief. So he looks real pretty when he delivers that report." The sound of her shoes echo down the hall.

Chief laughs heartily. "Gronkowski, you've got your work cut out for you, in more ways than one."

"Don't I know," he says, shaking his head as he walks from the room. Stopping at the outer edge of Chief's office, he peeks his head back inside the doorway. "Uh, Chief. For future reference...it's 'hit the *nail* on the head,' and 'link in the *chain*.'"

"I know. That's what I said." Chief wads up a piece of paper and wings it at him. Tony catches the paper ball with swift reflexes. "Get on it, Gronkowski."

Gina and Tony take separate paths. Tony casually meanders to his station, while Gina makes a beeline for Dr. Ryan's office. Her door is open. Dr. Cynthia Ryan sits at her desk, head down, writing. Gina stands outside and knocks lightly on the door casing.

Dr. Ryan does not look up as she responds, "It's open."

Gina enters the room slowly. Dr. Ryan finally looks up acknowledging her guest. "Detective DeLuca. I've been expecting you. Please, have a seat."

Gina sits down in the chair in front of Dr. Ryan's desk. "Busy day, huh?" She attempts to make small talk.

"Ms. DeLuca, I know you didn't come here to talk about my busy day." Dr. Ryan lays her pen down and removes her glasses, looking sharply at Gina. "I know what you're here for, and I must regrettably inform you, you're not going to get much information. Even therapists who work for Vanguard PD are held accountable to patient confidentiality. You're wasting your time, Detective. And mine."

"The department doesn't consider investigating a string of murders a waste of time."

"I see," Dr. Ryan says, sitting back in her chair, crossing one leg over the other, her hands primly pressed together in her lap. "There are innocent people murdered in this city every day. Instead of finding justice for them, the department has chosen to focus its time and manpower on tracking down the murders of convicted rapists and child molesters. My thanks to the city for having their priorities in order."

Gina looks at her quizzically, slightly thrown off. "I understand your distaste for the situation. However, I have a job to do. Unfortunately, it starts with you." Gina opens the file in front of Dr. Ryan, displaying photographs of the victims. "Do you recognize any of these men?"

Dr. Ryan remains distant, her back against her chair, her eyes fixed on Gina, purposely refusing to look down at the photos. "I've already told you my relationships with clients are strictly classified."

Gina sighs and responds sympathetically, "Dr. Ryan. You know there are ways the department has of getting around confidentiality. Please don't make this any more difficult than it already is."

Dr. Ryan leans up on her desk toward Gina, her body language intense. "Difficult? Let me tell you about difficult, *Detective DeLuca,*" reiterating her name sharply. "Pretend for a moment that you are me, and I am a client. I stroll in here and tell you how I met a fifteen-year-old girl online. Convinced her to invite me over when her parents were out of the house. And how I held her down on her bed and raped her because, of course, she wanted me to. And that I may be proud or indifferent of that fact." She takes a moment, transitioning from feeling to detachment. Her body language softens. She leans back into her chair, fidgeting with a pen in her hand. "Then you have to explain my actions, make me feel like I'm actually human. When what you really want to do is hang me up by my balls in the middle of town square so the entire world can see what a heartless, guiltless animal looks like." The pen snaps in her palm.

Gina sits speechless.

"My files are closed." Dr. Ryan leans forward closing Gina's file and hands it to her. "Maybe yours should be too."

Gina gets up to leave, responding as she walks to the door, "I'll be back."

Dr. Ryan busies herself with paperwork. "I'm sure you will."

EARLY EVENING. VANGUARD Police Department. Gina walks the long corridor to her desk in a frustrated state. She has been following leads for hours, coming up empty-handed. As she rounds the corner, she spots Tony kicked back in her chair, his feet propped up on her desk, sorting through a pile of paperwork.

Oh great, she thinks.

Upon seeing her, he flashes a lavish smile. "How'd it go *partner?*"

Gina smacks his feet down off of her desk. "Don't get too comfortable. You'll be back at your own desk before you know it." She sits down across from him, burying her head in her hands.

"Not so well I take it?" He throws a stack of files her way, grinning. "Here. Have a look. See what you come up with."

She looks at him, annoyed by his playfully handsome demeanor. She opens up the first file, leafing through it eagerly, looking to Tony in disbelief. She shuffles through the other files. Each one a detailed account of every murdered rapist's history, including psychological evaluations and victim statements. "How'd you get these? *Where* did you get these?"

"My charm, DeLuca, my charm." He leans toward her, his hands nimbly assembling a piece of paper into a paper football.

"Are they legal?"

"The *documents* are legal." He smiles.

"Gronkowski, are these files admissible? Can we use them to build a case?" Gina whispers, closing the manila folder, she looks around suspiciously.

"Don't sweat the small stuff, DeLuca. The bottom line—we need information to establish a pattern. We figure out the puzzle, we catch our vigilante in the act." He flicks the paper football in her direction. It lands on top of her stack of files. "You got the pieces right there. At the end of it all, it won't matter how we acquired them, just as long as we got 'em."

She gets up from her chair, pushes the paper football off the documents, loading them into her brief case.

"Come on DeLuca, don't be such a stickler. Do you know how many strings I pulled to get those? I thought you might show a little gratitude."

"I'm not an ingrate. I'm simply smart enough to take these elsewhere before I tear off into them." She flings her briefcase over her shoulder and talks in a low voice, "What are the chances you could get some info on Dr. Ryan?"

Tony's ears perk up, the tenacity returning to his face. "Now you're thinking." He slaps his hand affirmatively on the desk.

"Shh." Gina looks around surreptitiously.

"I can probably swing that. She give you a vibe?"

Gina doesn't answer, continuing to gather her stuff.

"Where you going to look those over? You wanna grab some coffee?"

"Home. There's a hot bath calling my name," she replies.

Tony smiles mischievously. "You need someone to wash your back?"

"I think I can handle it." She returns his smile. "I'll call if I need any help." She zones in on the paper football lying on the table with intense concentration, biting her lip for increased focus.

"You don't have my number." Tony continues to play.

She flicks the paper football in his direction, its destination perfectly resting half on, half off the side of the desk. Touchdown. Her eyes trail back up to Tony's. "Exactly," she says.

He watches her walk away, shaking his head, unable to rein in his admiration.

CHAPTER 3

Late evening. Detective Gina DeLuca's house. Her place smells of cucumber melon bubble bath and scented candles. On the coffee table in the living room, files are scattered about, accompanied by Sticky Notes outlined in bright red ink and diagrams attempting to make sense of the chaos within each manila sleeve.

Music blasts from the radio, Sheryl Crow's *C'mon C'mon* album, track eight *Lucky Kid.* Gina dances down the hallway in a black bra and matching panties, her hair soaking wet, her aroma good enough to eat from her bubbly indulgence. Her body keeping time with the music, she makes her way to the kitchen pulling a whiskey bottle from the top of the refrigerator.

"'Oh-oh-oh-oh-oh, you're a lucky kid,'" she sings along with the radio as she drops a few ice cubes into a short glass, topping it off with the high-octane oak-colored liquid. Tipping her head back, her lips part, her mouth wet, her throat warms with the contact.

"Hmm," she groans, a pleasurable smile forming. She moves methodically to her coffee pot in preparation for her five-thirty wake-up call.

Knock! Knock! Knock! The urgent sound coming from her front door sends her into alert mode. She quickly throws a robe on over her attire, scooping up her handgun while in transit. She stands warily to the side of the door casing, "Who is it?"

"Tony."

Tony? She mouths the name perplexingly to herself. "How'd you get my address?" she asks absentmindedly before fully considering who she's talking to.

"Uh, gee, it's this little thing called my job. *Detectives*...they're supposed to be good at finding things. Come on, Gina, I got something you are going to love."

"Typical," she says dryly, releasing the deadbolt. "That's what all the boys say." She peers through the chain, scanning Tony up and down through the tiny crack, a wry smile forming as she sees him standing there, fidgeting. It's obvious he can hardly contain himself, a file tucked securely under his arm.

"Come on, Gina. Quit playing." He looks from side to side, "This is it," he says jockeying the folder from under his arm.

"Alright, alright." She releases the chain, pulling the door open for him, as she uses it to hide her nighttime attire.

Tony busts in, slaps the file down on the island in the kitchen, the adrenaline in his system responsible for his choppy pacing. Gina closes the door behind him, holstering her pistol in its rightful place, her breadbox.

"Take a look," he says, his knuckles knock on the file, as he props himself up against the counter.

Gina opens the file to find Dr. Patricia Ryan's name and a much younger picture of her staring back, a graduation picture from West Point, Class of 1985. "Wow. She was beautiful." Under the picture is a New York State rape report. The pieces coming together as Gina looks up at Tony, stunned.

"She was raped her senior year at West Point. Date rape. Frat party. She knew the guy."

"Most of them do."

"The police were out looking for him the next day, after she filed the report. Got a call from Campus PD. They found the guy dead in his dorm room. O.D.'d on Special K."

"Karma's a real bitch sometimes," Gina defends, shrugging her shoulders.

"Karma Schmarma, Gina." Tony paces, his eyes diverting from

the file to Gina, distractedly. "The guy was an athlete. Star running back. Full scholarship. It doesn't make any sense."

"Oh, because jocks always make the best sense. I see where you're going with this Gronkowski, and I don't like it. She's a psychologist with the department. You realize where you're going here? When you start blaming your own? That's dangerous territory, Tony, and you know it."

"Dammit, Gina. Yes, I know that." Frustrated, he slaps his hand down on the counter top. "But we can't ignore the possibility just because she's one of us."

Gina makes her way around the island, preparing a drink for Tony, as he seems to need one.

"His teammates reported they were due to be tested two days after the party. Why would the guy do Special K when he knew he was up for testing?"

"I don't know. Why would the guy go on a drinking binge when he knew he was up for testing?" She slides the drink in front of him. "We could go tit for tat on this all night."

He takes a swig from the glass.

"What about his previous drug tests? Any of them come back positive?" she asks.

"Nope. Clean as a whistle. I'm telling ya, I just got this feeling, Gina."

"Ahhh," she exhales frustrated, winding her hands around the back of her neck, her head tips up toward the ceiling, as she spins in circles. Tony watches her, his mind momentarily pulled from the task at hand.

"I got this other feeling, too. That maybe you should put some clothes on."

She stops spinning and looks to him annoyed. "You come to my house uninvited, shake up my relaxation time, and think you can tell me how to dress?"

"You're distracting." He takes another drink.

She follows suit, meeting her mouth with her glass, deliberately running her tongue over her top lip slowly removing any remnants of the toxic substance. "Get over it, Gronkowski."

He shakes his head, smiling.

Setting her glass down, she paces from one end of the kitchen island to the next, pondering Tony's suspicions. "So, you're implying the overdose was not an overdose at all. Do you really think she would have had the knowledge or the wherewithal as a college student to get her hands on Ketamine and know how to administer it at a lethal level? The kid was a football player. How would she have overpowered him to get the stuff in his system? That's a stretch Tony. We're talking Gumby here." She holds her arms extended from her sides for affect.

"I know...it sounds a little far-fetched. But get this, Dr. Ryan's uncle was a Chief at Highland Falls PD. The case was in his jurisdiction. Her father was tight with Daniel Pinkard, Chief of Police for NYPD at the time. They came up in the same neighborhood, roomed together in college. Suicide, Gina. They dismissed the case. Said the kid committed suicide."

"So now, you're not only questioning one of your own. You're questioning the integrity of two other police departments and their chiefs?" Gina takes another drink, shaking her head. "You gotta have more than a hunch to make that kind of accusation. I don't like it, Tony. At least now I know what to get you for Secret Santa this year. Some brass ball paperweights...big ones." She chuckles. "God Gronkowski, do you hear what you're saying?"

"I know. I know. But you can't tell me all of these guys coming up dead...every single one of them has been in her psychological care at some point and time...that's not a coincidence, DeLuca. Maybe it's not her, directly. But whatever the hell is going on, it's connected to her somehow." He pours himself another drink, sitting down at her dining room table.

"Don't get too comfy." She looks at the clock, a quarter 'til ten.

"You got fifteen minutes before my bedtime."

"Oh, are we going to bed?" He jumps up, downs his drink and playfully grabs at his coat for removal.

"Ha," Gina quips, as he makes his way to the sink, rinsing his glass. "If it'll make you feel any better, I'll go see her again tomorrow."

"You already struck out with her today. We'll send in a new hitter tomorrow. Gotta get our RBIs up." He walks to Gina.

"What are you up to?" She looks at him quizzically.

"Thanks for the drink," he ignores her question, slipping his hand around the back of her neck, his thumb rests on her jawline. He bends his head to hers, meeting the fullness of her lips with his own. Her mouth warm, she tastes of whiskey. She moans with his contact, leaning into him, before pulling away.

She backs up toward the counter, needing it to hold herself up. "What the hell was that?" She pulls the back of her hand to her mouth, slowly sliding it across her bottom lip, attempting to extinguish the tingling sensation.

Tony smiles. "Just feeling you out, DeLuca." He knocks playfully on the kitchen island, a knowing grin displayed. "If you didn't like it, I'd be picking my ass up off your kitchen floor."

"Pretty risky move," she replies coolly, retaining her power.

Running his teeth over his bottom lip, his smile dissipates. "Some returns outweigh the risk." He pivots, walking to the front door.

"Are you okay to drive? You can take the couch."

"See, one kiss and you want me to stay," he teases. "I cabbed it over. I'll cab it back."

"Who are you sending to Dr. Ryan's office tomorrow?"

"No one who isn't already on her books."

"Gronkowski?"

"Can't stand it, can you?" He chuckles. "Always gotta be in control. First in." He shakes his head, letting himself out. Gina makes her way to the door, as it pops back open. "Silver," he says, poking his head inside.

She looks at him perplexed, her mind working, swiftly coming to its own conclusion. "Ah. Let me guess, brass isn't your color."

His face lights up. "We're getting there. Only took ya a few seconds. The same wavelength. Pretty soon we'll be finishing each others' sentences. Happens to partners all the time."

She puts her hand over his smiling face, gently pushing him out of the space between her door and its casing. "Your *wavelength* is a rare and precious thing, Gronkowski. Better kept to yourself."

"Lock up," he reminds her as she shuts the door.

MIDNIGHT. AUBREY RAINES sleeps in her bed. A stack of law books lie scattered around her, after a rigorous week of studying for her Bar Exam. Having nodded off prior to her intention, the bedside lamp burns dimly, and the sheer sky-blue curtain shadowing her windowpane blows in the breeze. Her boyfriend has scolded her before about leaving her bedroom window open to her first floor apartment.

"You're too trusting Aubrey, baby. People suck," he has said.

"If somebody really wants to get me, my window isn't going to stop them anyway. You're sweet to worry though," she consoles.

Her boyfriend is out of town this weekend, and she dwells in her apartment alone. A fact all too familiar to the man, a so-called friend, who has been watching her every move for the past two days, compiling the patterns. A real freak show, this one. He stands over her dressed in black from head to toe, accessorized with a Michael Myers mask. He runs his finger up the inside of her thigh, startling her from her sleep. Aubrey opens her mouth to scream, but before the sound comes out, her lips are met with a rag soaked in Chloroform. She resists, attempting to ward the man off, but is overpowered, as he sits atop her, waiting for the anesthetic to take affect. Her body gives in, falling limp beneath him.

She wakes groggily, her vision slightly blurred, tuning into her surroundings. Her bedroom lamp no longer burning, her room is dark. One ray of light streaks through her open window and bounces off the adjacent wall. Her arms and legs feel heavy, as she attempts to pull them back to her core. They will not give. She is bound to the bed, each limb securely tied to its respective corner by nylon ropes. A cool breeze pushes through her window raising goosebumps on her skin, alerted to the fact she is completely naked. Her only air exchange, fast and labored, is through her nose, her mouth secure with duct tape. She lifts her head, which seems to weigh a hundred pounds, to find the man kneeling between her thighs, stroking himself. Her eyes pop, startled, frightened. She pulls and kicks against the nylon restraints, her nostrils flaring. Her throat burns as she attempts to make noise, muffled by the tape covering her lips. He watches her through his ridiculous mask until her body relaxes, giving into the muscular exhaustion her struggle has caused.

"It's about time you woke up, baby. I was getting tired of waiting." He strokes the side of her face. "I want you to remember everything."

His vile touch causes her to jerk her head away from his hand, exhausting her body once more fighting against the restraints. Her chest heaves up and down, attempting to fill her lungs with air. An impossible task having only her nose to breathe through. Physically incapable, she appeals to him with her eyes, tears forming in them, releasing down the sides of her face. *Please don't do this.* She shakes her head from side to side.

"Don't cry, baby. You don't need to be afraid of me. I love you, Aubrey." He removes his mask, leans his face down to hers and kisses the duct tape covering her lips. "I'm gonna make sure you enjoy every minute of it."

Sick in the pit of her being and furious upon recognition of her so-called friend, she rears her head back and slams it into his face.

Her forehead makes contact with his lip, causing it to bleed. Again, she pulls frantically at her restraints, her frustrated cries audible now in the back of her throat, as her attempt yields no result.

He raises his hand as if he may slap her across the face. He does not. He wipes the blood from his lip, momentarily and sits back on his heels. He laughs, a low, sinister chuckle, rubbing the inside of her thighs with his cold touch. "I should've known you would do that. Always fighting what you want. I see the way you look at me, every morning at the coffee shop. You want me as bad as I want you." He rubs his unit against her. "You make me so hard, baby," he groans.

She closes her eyes, tears continuing to fall down her temples, attempting to take herself to a distant place mentally. Her wrists and ankles feel on fire as the unforgiving nylon rubs against her soft skin. The white rope encompassing her left wrist turns red in places, as it cuts into her flesh, drawing blood. Her mind delivering, finally, she feels out of her body. Opening her eyes, they now sparkle emerald green. She stares at the ceiling, the image of a young boy running toward her with a smile on his face, his arms outstretched. Her hearing, somehow incomparably keen, she hears distant footsteps, quick and light approaching. Unable to track the sound with her eyes, they are fixated on the ceiling, the imagery above. Her smile reciprocates that of the child.

"Ah, shit. Fuck me!" the man squawks, jumping off the bed at the sight of her eyes glimmering up at the ceiling. "What the hell?" He grabs at his pants pulling them up around his waist as he backs away toward the window.

"Going somewhere?" a voice sounds behind him.

He spins around to find a woman crouching, in black from head to toe, emerald green eyes staring him down. "Jesus! How'd you do that?" he cries, whipping his head back in the direction of the bed, as if he believes Aubrey to be the woman moving impossibly through space and time. Aubrey remains in the bed, tied up, her eyes locked in on the ceiling. Slowly he pivots back to the window, the woman remains between him and the square opening. Frantically, he jets for the bedroom door.

She tracks him, dropping her shoulder into the back of his knee, an affective chop block, causing his leg to give out beneath him. "Ugh!" his lungs forcibly emptied of air with his abrupt contact to the floor. He lands on one of his nylon ropes, tucking it into his hand. The woman makes her way up his back, as the two begin to grapple.

"Now, if you'd calm down, this would go much smoother...and faster," she taunts between labored breaths.

The man takes the dominant position, outweighing her. He hurls the rope around the front of her neck, jerking the slack tightly. "You don't want to do this," the woman warns, her voice a whisper, the nylon ever-tightening. "Don't make me bleed."

"Crazy bitch! You and your friend are gonna bleed out of every hole when I'm done with ya."

Her body goes limp momentarily as her blood is exposed to the air. She lies on her stomach, the man crouches over her, pushing his pants down around his ankles. He resorts to his same bit, stroking himself as he pulls at the back of her pants, fully intending to rape her from behind.

Her ears ring and the pulse in her head feels so strong, rhythmic like a drum as her senses heighten to a supernatural level. With each beat of her heart and every consecutive breath requiring more oxygen than the last, her body begins to awaken, feverishly hot, aching for release. In one fluid movement, she pushes off the floor, spinning herself around underneath the crouching man. Her foot connects swiftly and severely to his throbbing unit, kicking him off of her, catapulting his body across the room into the adjacent corner. He whimpers with the contact. With the speed of light, she covers him with her paranormal frame, winding the same piece of nylon rope he used on her around his neck, rapidly concocting a slipknot at the end for more efficient use.

She crouches over his debilitated body, surely in shock. "Do you know what happens to a woman when a filthy pig like you touches her? Do you!" She tightens the cord, smiling down at the fear in his eyes. "She loses her soul. It dies a little more each time she has to shower to wash your filth away...and every time she wakes from a nightmare with the image of your sweaty body leaning over her... until one day she can't find it anymore."

He closes his eyes, tears trickle down the sides of his face.

"Oh, you're going to try the crying bit," she bites sarcastically. "Did Aubrey's tears stop you? How many souls have you taken?"

He remains quiet, his eyes squeezed shut.

"What's the matter, cat got your tongue?" She roughly pats the side of his face. "That's okay. You don't have to answer. I'll find out soon enough. Never ceases to amaze me how mouthy you guys are when you've got the upper hand, and how passive you become when you're in their position. Doesn't feel so good, does it?" She pulls tightly on the cord. "Open your eyes."

He shakes his head.

"It's retribution time my friend. I'm here to take what's left of your soul. Let's see if you have one. Open your eyes. Open your eyes!"

Startled, he does as she commands. At first contact with hers, emerald green and sparkling, he's locked in, physically unable to close his eyes or divert them in any way. Image after image, her mind and heart take a beating, reliving all the nauseating deeds he's done. Bodies abused, souls left scarred and broken, he has left his mark. With each innocent face that flashes before her, she tightens the noose until the life leaves his body. His soul finally extinguished. Retribution delivered.

Her eyelids close heavily, her body exhausted. She pushes off the man's chest, even standing proves a laborious task. The circle of emerald green light and imagery on the ceiling evaporates in a flash from Aubrey's vision. The woman opens her eyes, the sparkle is gone.

CHAPTER 4

Early morning, downtown Vanguard. Detectives DeLuca and Gronkowski wait for their coffee from a local, well-known street vendor, Stavros.

"Tony...you not look, ah, so good this morning," Stavros remarks. "You, ah, have woman last night?" He smiles.

"Something like that," Tony refers to the 2:00 a.m. wake-up call he and Gina received to investigate the murder at Aubrey Raines' apartment. Both of them are moving at an unusually slow pace this morning, in much need of a caffeine pick-me-up.

"And my Gina," Stavros greets her with a kiss for each cheek, wherein lies a dimple, an attractive trait when she smiles. "You look, ah, beautiful, as usual. She's easy on the eyes, this one," Stavros nudges Tony, making his intentions clear. He cups her face with his hands. She smiles at him, her dimples exaggerated. "You blessed two times. The dimples. The mark of angels, they kiss you at birth."

"Remind me, why don't I come here more often? This is the way to start a day," she stands, her arm around Stavros' waist. They look at Tony, who is rolling his eyes. "Oh, don't be so sour. The angel kissed you, too." She traces his dimpled chin with her thumb.

"I thought that's, ah, where the doctor drop him," Stavros cracks himself up, his round belly jiggling with his laughter.

"I can go down the street," Tony playfully rebukes, flinging his arm toward the neighboring vendor.

"I joke. I joke." Stavros makes his way behind the cart. "You look, ah, good, Tony. Strong, like bull." He makes a fist, pumping his arm, conveying virility, as he pours them each a cup of coffee.

"Alright, alright," Tony ends his bid of flattery. "You're still going to get a tip."

Stavros chuckles, setting the cups in front of them, the steam rises, visible as it contacts the cool morning air.

Gina reaches into her pocket. Tony gently suppresses her arm. "My turn. You got the last round." He wads some cash into Stavros' tip jar.

"Chivalry too," Stavros comments, smiling at him, raising his eyebrows. Tony pulls out a few more ones, shoving them down into the glass container. Gina snickers, winking at Stavros, as she and Tony walk away.

"It doesn't make sense. I had them cross-reference Dr. Ryan and the woman from last night. Nothing," Tony says.

"Aubrey?" Gina helps him with her name.

"Yeah...Aubrey and Dr. Ryan."

"Why would you think they have to be connected?"

"DeLuca, that woman...Aubrey, knows more than what she's saying. So does Dr. Ryan. It's all too close." He takes a drink of his coffee. "Holy, God." He shakes his head at the strength of the beverage.

Gina laughs. "If you don't have hair on your chest, wait a few minutes," she jokes. "You're lucky he actually removed the grounds. Greek coffee is a stout brew."

"Whew!" he exclaims, continuing to choke the coffee down. "You mean to tell me, a woman gets tied up to her bed, sexually assaulted...the man winds up strangled on her bedroom floor, and she doesn't recall anything? I say bullshit."

"Sparkling emerald green light...she remembers that."

"Yeah. Sparkling emerald green light. What the hell is that? Maybe she needs a drug clearance. Sounds like some psychedelic leprechaun bullshit. Maybe she likes recreational hallucinogens. Sparkling emerald green light, my ass."

"You ever been tied down against your will, Gronkowski?" Gina asks defensively. "While some pig rubs his dick all over you?" She takes a drink of her coffee, swallowing hard at the bitterness. "His pre-ejaculate DNA was all over the inside of her thighs and on her stomach. Sick bastard. The friggin' douchebag slumped in the corner with his penis hanging out of his pants." She pauses momentarily, the thought sickening. "And you mean to tell me you can't fathom how she wouldn't remember every detail. Has it escaped your mind that maybe she's chosen to block it out!" She stops, thrown by the rise in her voice and emotion.

"Sorry. Shit Gina, I'm sorry." He looks at her as they walk along, she avoids eye contact with him, slightly embarrassed by her outburst.

"No, I'm sorry. I don't know where that came from. It's this damn case. The pure ethics of it all."

"Maybe you have a point. We see it all the time. People experience something horrific, and the details vanish. What's that part of your brain...that controls that? You know that built-in defense mechanism thing?"

"The amygdala," she answers.

"Yeah...what you said. Maybe that's what happened to her. And maybe I want to crack this case so bad I'm willing to dig for anything, making up my own conclusions." He lightly kicks at a pebble on the sidewalk. "You remember the Rubik's Cube?"

"Yeah." She smiles with the childhood memory.

"I remember getting one in my stocking for Christmas. Do you know I sat with that thing for hours? Wouldn't put it down until I had it conquered. Guess you could say I get a little obsessive about figuring things out."

"You don't say," she chuckles, throwing her near empty coffee cup into a garbage can conveniently taking up space on the sidewalk. Tony hands her his, nearly full. She grins, throwing it in the trash. "But, what do you do with a case like this? I mean, what exactly do you do when you get it figured out?"

They walk in silence, the wheels of their minds spinning restlessly.

"Did we get anything from the scene? Evidence? Something concrete?" she asks, hopeful.

"Maybe some DNA. Skin from the rope. Looks like there's two different strands. His, and the perp's."

"The perp's," she says flatly. "He's the rapist, yet someone else is the perp." She shakes her head, biting her bottom lip, a smug grin on her face. "Now that right there...that's concrete evidence. Getting caught with your hand in the cookie jar." Gina points to the window of a convenient store on the corner.

A young man, wearing a hooded coat, stands nervously behind the counter next to the clerk. The clerk is visibly shaken up, digging through the drawer of the cash register. Gina and Tony wear black fatigues today, no uniforms, unthreatening to the young thief as he quickly glances out the window in their direction.

"I got the front. You go around back," Tony says.

"I saw him first," Gina rebukes, as they approach the store. The young man agitatedly hurries the clerk along.

"DeLuca..."

"Fine. Have it your way." She casually departs down the side alley until she is out of sight, picking up her pace, hoofing it to the back of the convenient store.

Detective Gronkowski continues calmly into the front entrance of the store. The young man grows edgy at the sound of the jingling bell hanging from the doorstop. He moves closer to the cashier, one hand in the pocket of his oversized coat. The cashier looks up, coyly diverting his eyes, an attempt to alert Tony.

Tony lays a hundred dollar bill on the counter "Can you make change for a hundred? I need a pack of Marlboro Lights." He points to the cigarettes behind the young man's head.

The young man uses his free hand to pull a pack from the bin.

Laying them on the counter, he nudges the cashier, who quickly counts out Tony's change.

"Thought it might be convenient for you, since you've already got the register open. And just exactly why is that when there's a customer behind the counter?"

"I...I work here," the young man stammers.

"You don't want to do this kid," Tony warns. "Forget about it and walk out the door, right now."

The young man simultaneously grabs the money and pulls a 9-millimeter Glock pistol from his coat pocket. Wrapping his arm around the cashier's neck, he points the gun at his head, backing away from behind the counter, facing Tony.

"Call the police!" the cashier pleads.

"Shut up old man," the thief rams the gun into the side of his head.

"Where ya going, kid? What's your name?" Tony gets his attention, taking a few steps toward him.

Gina makes her way stealthily through the back of the store, coming up behind them.

"Stay back!" the thief warns, his eyes darting frantically from the cashier in his grip to Tony.

"Call 9-1-1," the cashier cries.

"Put the gun down. You don't want to hurt anyone, kid."

"I will if I have to." He continues backing up, dragging the cashier with him.

"Please don't," the cashier begs. "I have two children. My wife. Please."

Gina appears from around the corner, swiftly aiming her side arm at the back of the thief's head. He stops abruptly as the cool steel makes contact with his skull.

"Vanguard PD. Lower your weapon," she speaks calmly.

He spins around, away from her, maintaining his grip on the cashier, positioning himself as the point of a triangle between Gina and Tony. He flings his handgun around, first at Gina then at Tony, holding it sideways, gangster style. "Cops don't shoot kids. You won't shoot me," he rehearses as if he is convincing himself.

"You're right. I don't want to shoot you. But I can't just let you walk out of here. Put the gun down," she coaxes.

A customer walks in the front. The bell on the doorstop sounds, beckoning ears and eyes from the back of the room.

The thief throws his gun down, pushes the cashier away and bum-rushes Gina for the backdoor. She quickly holsters her weapon to avoid shooting him. Using his momentum, she grabs his shoulders when he comes at her and goes to the ground, landing on her back with effortless agility. She sticks her legs into his stomach, catapulting him up and over onto his back while she holds onto him, thrusting herself to roll over with him, coming down on top of him astraddle his waist. He swings, connecting with her left eye. Instinctively, she wants to return his contact, her fists in position. Refraining from doing so as she looks down at him, just a kid. She simply deflects his punches, working with Detective Gronkowski to turn him over, cuffing him.

"Goddammit, Gina. I'm sorry," Tony sputters, checking out her eye, his knee in the delinquent's back holding him down on the tile floor.

"Comes with the territory," she dismisses, standing. She takes hold of the kid's arm by the elbow, waiting for Tony to do the same with the other side.

"You can add battery to your list of crimes, punk," he spews through gritted teeth, jerking the kid into standing position.

"Ow! Ah shit, that hurts," the young man cries at the pressure of the unforgiving handcuffs gripping his wrists.

"Gronkowski," Gina scolds. She helps steady the young man on his feet.

"You think it's okay to hit women?" Tony jerks him around.

The kid shakes his head shamefully.

"You wanna be a big man? Hold guns to people's heads...take their hard-earned money. Get a goddamned job!" Tony advises, briskly walking the kid to the front of the store.

"Central to 223," Gina's radio sounds.

"223. DeLuca," she identifies herself.

"Chief wants you and Gronkowski. 4300-block of MLK. Fast as you can get there."

"We need a pick up. Got one for booking," she replies.

"You got it. 301's in your neighborhood. Dispatching now."

"Copy." Gina clips the little black box back onto her belt.

"Make something of yourself. Contribute to society. Buncha punks," Gronkowski continues. Gina follows behind, smiling, shaking her head, knowing in Tony's anger is genuine concern for the misguided youth. "Take, take, take...you think you're entitled? You big? You bad? You're entitled, alright. Your ass is entitled to remain silent. Anything you say, can and will be used against you..."

MOMENTS LATER, DETECTIVES DeLuca and Gronkowski pull up to the 4300-block of MLK Boulevard. The scene surrounded by patrol cars, police and numerous onlookers. Yellow caution tape blocks the alleyway where a body lies lifeless. They pile out of their squad car, challenging each other with each stride. Even when they arrive together, the mindset still remains, 'Who's going to be first in?'

"Took ya long enough," Chief Burns chirps upon noticing them.

"Tell me about it," Gina replies. "Gronkowski insisted on driving. My grandma drives faster than him."

Chief walks to her, positions his hands on the sides of her face, tipping his head down to focus his eyes over his bifocals, inspecting her left eye. "And just exactly how do you propose to drive with a bruised-up eye?"

"Exactly," Tony says.

"Marks," Chief Burns calls. "What are you drinking there?" He refers to Gina's previous partner, Officer Sam Marks' tall plastic cup with the words *Big Gulp* slathered all over it.

"Coke, Chief. Hey DeLuca!" He greets Gina with pleasant surprise.

"Pour that out. Save the ice. Grab one of those latex gloves out of the console of my cruiser," Chief orders.

"Yes sir." Marks makes quick work of his task.

Tony rolls his eyes at the two officers huffing and puffing, tending to Gina's eye.

"It's alright, Chief. Just a little bump." Gina gently persuades his hands away. "What's going on here?"

Officer Marks returns with the ice inside the latex glove. "See... you were much safer working with me." He smiles at his conclusion, before turning to Tony. "Not even a little scratch." He winks, walking away.

"Yeah, must be some kind of danger...handing out parking tickets. You're one step away from security guard, Marks. Come talk to me when your name tag says detective." Tony flips him the bird.

"As soon as these two divas are done flexing their egos, I'd be happy to tell you," Chief answers Gina, shaking his head, watching the interplay between Gronkowski and Marks. He puts the iced glove in Gina's hand, gently suggesting she hold it to her eye.

She winces with the contact of the cold compress.

"Might be related to your case. Found a body in the alleyway this morning. Pulled the rap sheet on him, and he's got three priors... one sexual assault...two rapes."

Chief's voice is overshadowed by a rising commotion around the alleyway.

"Thomas Knightly," he continues talking louder, as they all three make their way toward the crowd. "Liked to hold his victims at knifepoint. What do you know, he ends up in an alleyway, his neck slit ear to ear, with his own knife."

"She makes a statement with every murder, huh," Tony concludes. "Always some irony in it."

"She?" Chief Burns asks.

"Hey lady, get out of here. This is a crime scene. What do you think you're doing?" A cop challenges a young woman who has pushed through the crowd, breaking through the caution tape.

She stands over the corpse, physically shaken. "You weren't supposed to die. Bastard!" She kicks the lifeless body.

"Lady, come on." The cop approaches her, grabbing hold of her arm.

A hand encases the cop's, swiftly removing it from the woman's arm. "Keep your hands off my daughter. Give her some closure," her father, standing six-foot-four-inches, with shoulders and a chest out to there, eyes the cop, backing him up. "Back off!"

The cop reaches for his billy club. Other officers come to his defense, swarming around the man.

"You use that thing, it'll be your badge, Rookie," Chief Burns warns, approaching the scene. "Back up. All of you."

"Death is too easy for you," the young woman laments, looking down at the deceased. "You should be in some dirty jail cell, rotting away one day at a time." Tears surface in her eyes. She looks to her father, helpless. His eyes reflect her pain. "I want you to suffer like I do, every day."

She begins pacing around the corpse, slowly. Gina and Tony look to each other, then to Chief Burns, who holds them at bay with his expression.

Sirens wail, people move to and fro, but the young woman hears only her heart throbbing in her chest, as time stands still. "My father brings me here every morning. To this spot. Where you held a knife to my throat and...raped me," she says, whispering the last part as if it still hurts to say so. "He's trying to help me." She glances at her father, a faint smile for his efforts. "He thinks if I come here every day, the pain will eventually fade, and I will find peace."

She squats beside his body, wishing his eyes open. They remain closed, as he lays perfectly still, restful, peaceful. "Peace? You took that from me three years ago." She closes her eyes. "I close my eyes and I still feel your hands on me." Her body shakes. "Disgusting waste of human life. Piece of shit, fucker!" her scream rings through the alleyway. Her legs give out and she falls to her knees. "I hope you rot in hell," she seethes through clenched teeth, tears streaming down her face. She grabs two hands full of her own hair, pulling sharply until the physical pain numbs the emotional.

Gina pushes past Chief Burns, kneeling in front of the young woman as she pulls her into an embrace, shielding her from the gathering crowd. The young woman sobs uncontrollably as Gina rocks her in her arms.

"Get these people out of here," Chief Burns orders to the officers witnessing the scene.

The officers turn toward the onlookers, their arms outstretched, backing them up away from the caution tape. "Nothing to see here. Back up people."

"Get your hands off her," the father orders, approaching Gina.

Tony gulps before grabbing the large man by his arm. "She's only trying to help."

The man jerks his arm away from Tony. "I didn't see any of you *trying to help* three years ago." He throws his arms out to his sides, a large reach. "You're a joke. The whole system's a joke!" He chuckles mirthlessly, quenching the urge to cry. "He raped my baby. My baby!" He pounds his chest with his fist. "I'm supposed to protect her." He regroups, shaking off the emotion. "Lord knows the system won't. Three years in jail with early probation on account of good behavior." He shakes his head, disgusted. "We don't want your kind of help."

"You tell 'em!" a lady shouts from the crowd. "I'm sick and tired of all these scumbags roaming our neighborhood. I don't even dare to let my children out of the house to play."

"Our kids don't stand a chance, between the drug dealers and the pedophiles. I looked online. Do you know we have more sex offenders per capita than any other neighborhood in the city," a man joins the lady in her protest.

"'Stick 'em over there on the Eastside,'" the lady continues mockingly. "You don't want them in your communities. Well, we don't want 'em, either!"

The crowd begins applauding the protestors. Random outbursts are interjected as the scene plays out. 'Cops suck.' 'The whole damn system's broke.' 'We're not gonna take it anymore!' 'If you don't stop it, we will.'

"Take it up with the city folks," an officer persuades, as he attempts to quiet the crowd.

"Yep. Get a permit, then you can protest all day long," Officer Marks chimes, herding people away.

The young woman's father gently pulls her from Gina's embrace, up off the ground. "It's all over now, honey," he coaxes. Eyeing Gina directly with disdain, he continues, "Justice has been done."

Gina remains kneeling on the concrete in the alleyway beside the corpse of the rapist, her thoughts scattered. Tony walks to her extending his hand. "He's right. You know he is," she says, shame flooding her expression.

His hand outstretched, he nods at her, prompting her to pull it together. She shakes her head, taking his hand. He pulls her into standing position. "I know," he admits, an afterthought, falling into cadence behind her. She has recovered. In full detective mode now, she heads in the direction of the man and his daughter, knowing she must insist they cooperate for questioning.

THAT AFTERNOON, DR. Patricia Ryan is in session with Randall Barnes, a registered sex offender with a persuasion toward young boys...and girls. Any minor, really. He has served two prison sentences, one for a year, and three years for the second count. Currently on his tenth month of a four-year probation, mandatory psychological counseling is added to his curriculum. The bill for such services, another strain on the local taxpayer, in addition to the thirty thousand dollars for every year he spent incarcerated. What's another hundred dollars an hour for his psychological well-being?

Dr. Ryan's room is dim, the shades pulled, an attempt to make her clients feel at ease. Light seems to cause them great discomfort. Dr. Ryan sits in her chair. Randall Barnes across from her, lying casually on the leather sofa, one leg kicked off onto the floor, his arms relaxed above his head.

"How are you doing with the temptations, Randall?" Dr. Ryan cuts right to the chase.

Without hesitation, he answers, "Not good."

"Have you tried implementing the positive coping techniques we discussed last session? Diversionary tactics? Exercise as a means of exertion? Creativity for mental stimulation to override excessive physical desires?"

He sits up on the couch, rubbing his hands together, grinning. "If you consider jacking off while watching my girlfriend's daughter sleep a positive coping technique, then yeah, I've tried it."

Dr. Ryan shifts uneasily in her chair, while maintaining a controlled body language. "Last time you were here, you told me your girlfriend didn't have any kids. Does she know you're a registered sex offender?"

He stands from the couch, pacing around behind it. "Yeah, she knows. She trusts me, though." He smirks, shaking his head. "It's her fault you know, picking me over her kid. The same way my mom did with my stepfather. Stupid bitch."

"How old is the child?"

"She's fifteen." He props himself up on the back of the sofa. "A ripe fifteen," he continues, miming a full, voluptuous frame with his hands.

Dr. Ryan clears her throat, reframing her initial urge to respond negatively to Randall's probing. "Can you identify with the daughter? Empathize with her, the position she is in? The same position your mother put you in with your stepfather?"

"Sometimes. Other times, I want so bad to feel her insides." He physically moans, causing Dr. Ryan's skin to break out in goosebumps, instantly nauseated. "Maybe her innocence could replace the innocence I lost." His eyes stare straight forward, momentarily reliving a moment in time.

"The innocence your stepfather took from you? You want to do that to another human being?"

"Sometimes."

"You've already done that, Randall, twice," she refers to his previous sentences. "Their innocence did not replace yours. What makes you think another victim will?"

He mocks her condescendingly, "Why, Randall? How does it make you feel, Randall? How are you coping, Randall?" He slaps his hand against the back of the couch as he starts in pacing again. "You ask too many questions, lady."

She sits back, her arms resting casually on the arms of the chair attempting to maintain an open body language. "That's my job, Randall. Without questions, you have nothing propelling you to explore your feelings and actions. The more understanding you have of the things you do, the better equipped you will be to control the negatives and nurture the positives."

"I'm sick of this shit! I've served my time...paid my price. Now I gotta come in here and talk about my feelings with you. Screw this!" He walks toward the door.

"You've paid your price?" Dr. Ryan asks, annoyed, getting up out of her chair. "I was unaware you could put a price tag on a child's innocence."

Randall turns toward her, away from the door, his finger pointed accusingly in her direction. "You have been mindfucking me from the first session. You wanna fuck, Dr. Ryan?"

He moves threateningly close to her. She stands her ground, unwilling to be intimidated.

"I bet you have a price tag, don't you *Patricia?* Or is it Patty?" He circles around behind her, uncomfortable with the eye contact she is maintaining. He runs his fingers through her hair and down the back of her neck. "Tell me, how much does it cost to get between your thighs?"

Dr. Ryan remains firm in both her stance and vocal presence, "Nice technique Randall. Attempting to assert your power to make me feel cheap and inferior."

"Don't try your quack shit on me. If you know me so well, you'd know better than to egg me on." He grabs a handful of her hair, his face pressed against the side of her head, continuing menacingly into her ear, "If I was asserting my power, believe me, you'd know it. I'd have you pinned up against the wall with your skirt up around your neck..."

The office door swings open as Detective Gronkowski enters, a subpoena in hand, meant for Dr. Ryan, calling for a release of her records. Upon entering, the scene becomes quite apparent. Within milliseconds, Tony has Randall Barnes backed up against the wall by his shirt collar.

"Care to elaborate on what the hell I walked in on?" Tony probes Randall.

"Nothing, man, nothing. I...I was just talking with Dr. Ryan."

Dr. Ryan approaches Tony, her hands rest encouragingly on his shoulders. "Really, it's fine, Officer. Sometimes therapy sessions get a little heated."

"Heated? Really." Tony pulls Randall away from the wall, spinning toward the doorway. "I'm taking him down for prints."

"No. That won't be necessary," Dr. Ryan says.

"I think it's necessary." Tony shoves against Randall. "Move!"

Dr. Ryan positions herself between them and the door. "He's

making good progress with therapy. The only thing another arrest would do is set him back even more. Let him go, Officer."

"Detective," Tony corrects her on her second reference to him as Officer. "Are you sure, lady?"

"Doctor," she corrects him. Touché. Nodding her head, she extends her hand toward the door.

Tony heaves Randall's frame out of Dr. Ryan's office. Randall spins, a sinister grin forming on his mouth. He takes off running down the hallway.

Dr. Ryan sits down at her desk, resting her forehead on her hand momentarily.

"You okay?" Tony asks.

Aware of the vulnerability in her body language, she quickly recovers, sitting up straight as a pin, reorganizing the already militaristic formation of her desk. "Yes. I am fine. Detective?" She rises, extending her hand to him.

"Gronkowski. Tony Gronkowski." He meets her handshake firmly. "You know, *Dr*. Ryan," he accentuates Doctor, acknowledging her previous declaration. "You really shouldn't be alone with these creeps. Why aren't their sessions supervised?"

"They open up more when it's one on one," she dismisses. "Gronkowski? You wouldn't happen to be Detective DeLuca's partner, would you?" She eyes him suspiciously.

He smiles, handing her the subpoena for release of her records. "I happen to be such a partner."

She stands, her arms folded one over the other across her chest, refusing to take the paperwork.

Tony winks, dropping the forms to her desk. "Guess I should see myself out."

IN THE MEANTIME, Detective DeLuca sits at her desk, covered in files. The phone rests on her shoulder. She's got one on the line and one on hold. She sees Detective Gronkowski approaching, something mischievous and satisfied in his manner. Officer Marks waits for her on line two. She clicks over.

"DeLuca, you got company. A Father Trahern," he informs.

"Father?" she questions, her wheels spinning. "Alright, send him back."

"DeLuca, put one right here," Tony says, bending at her desk offering up his cheek for a kiss.

Gina shrugs away from him, forcefully patting the side of his face. "Pull yourself together Gronkowski. Can't you see I'm covered up here."

"I'd like to cover you up," he smirks. "Seriously, you are going to want to slip me the tongue. I just delivered Dr. Ryan a subpoena for release of all her records."

"Hold it together, *Frenchy*," she pipes back, referring to his aforementioned form of kissing. "We already have her records."

"Now, they'll be legal. Completely admissible in court."

"If I didn't know any better, I'd think you have it in for her," Gina huffs, filing her paperwork."

"A hunch, DeLuca. Got a feeling." He inspects her eye, the bruise at the corner darkening. "Geez. You need to ice that thing again."

She swats his hand away. "It's fine." Looking up, she notices a priest walking toward them. "And I got a feeling, you better move. I don't need any lightning striking my desk."

Tony turns in the direction of her eyeline. "Ah, Christ," Tony says nervously.

"That would be the man he works for." Gina smiles as she stands beside him.

Tony fidgets, further tucking his department-issued black fatigue sweater into his black BDU's. He turns to Gina, breathing into her face. "I had a few more drinks last night after I left your place. Can you smell anything?"

"You're fine Gronkowski." She grins. "Although a breath mint wouldn't hurt."

Tony holds his hand to his lips, breathing into it.

"Will you relax," Gina mutters out the side of her mouth, elbowing him.

A short, yet stately man approaches, wearing black dress pants and a black button-down shirt with a white clerical collar inserted behind the top button. Gina extends her hand. Tony awkwardly puts his hands together palm to palm, bowing his head. Gina chokes back a giggle, as the priest takes her hand in his. "Gina DeLuca."

"Father Trahern. St. Francis Catholic Church," he introduces himself.

"This is my partner, Tony Gronkowski." Gina pats Tony's hands down from their prayer position. Motioning toward a chair across from her desk, she says, "Please. Make yourself comfortable."

They all sit.

"Where is St. Francis?" Tony asks cordially.

"401 East Hampton Boulevard."

"Huh?" Tony expels. "You keep some rough company over there," he refers to the numerous pawnshops and its infamous reputation as *Prostitution Central.*

Father Trahern nods.

"So, ah. What brings you in?" Gina kicks things off.

"I find myself in a bit of a dilemma." He sits forward in his chair, his body language displaying his internal discomfort. "As a priest, I am restricted in discussing confessions. However, when someone is in danger or poses a threat, I feel obliged to speak out."

Tony lights up. "Did someone confess a murder or something?"

"Not exactly," Father Trahern quickly interjects.

Gina eyeballs Tony, willing him mute. "Go on, Father."

"Yesterday evening a man came in. He was asking questions about taking justice into his own hands. An eye for an eye, things of that persuasion. He wanted to know if people were forgiven if they took care of wrongdoers themselves." Father Trahern clears his throat. "Pardon me for insinuating such, but he made mention that when the *system* fails, civilians are left with few alternatives."

"Vigilante justice," Tony declares.

Father Trahern nods. "I didn't think much about it until I heard what happened over on MLK Boulevard this morning."

Tony picks up the phone, speaking into the receiver. "Marks, get me everything you got on William Truly," Tony refers to the father of the young woman they met on scene in the alleyway of MLK.

Father Trahern watches Tony intently. Gina comforts him. "Standard operating procedure."

"Now, I don't know who the man is. Confessionals are confidential. No names, no faces. I am unable to identify anyone," he speaks nervously.

"You've done everything you can do, Father. More than enough. Now it's up to us to put the pieces together," Gina councils.

Tony hangs up the phone.

"But there's more." Father Trahern takes a deep breath. "He said the revolution is coming. That he's not the only one who feels this way." He shrugs his shoulders. "Then again, I'm not sure he's even mentally stable. He talked of unreal things...a *Vigilare,* I believe was the word," Father Trahern sifts through his memory bank. "And a green sparkling light..."

"Sparkling emerald green light," Tony and Gina mouth the words together. The explanation Aubrey Raines gave them in the wee hours of the morning.

"Here Sarge," Officer Marks interrupts, flopping a file down in front of Tony. He eyes the priest. "Interrogating men of the cloth now, DeLuca?" He smiles, nudging Tony. "Don't mess with this one. She's tough as nails, boss." He winks at Gina, to which she responds in kind, as he walks off.

"Well, if that's all, I must be going," Father Trahern asks before standing from the desk.

Tony and Gina quickly follow his lead, rising to their feet, extending their hands once again. "Thank you, Father," they speak in unison.

He ducks his head somewhere between a nod and a bow. "You kids come see me sometime, won't you?"

Gina and Tony glance to one another, knowing full well they cannot fib to a priest. "We don't get down to your area of town much," Tony replies.

"But, if we do, we'll stop in," Gina adds politely. Tony elbows her in the side.

Father Trahern smiles and walks away.

"What'd you say that for?" Tony mutters.

"I didn't want to be rude."

"That's just great, DeLuca. Now we have to." He picks up the file from her desk.

"Like it would kill either one of us."

"Obviously you've never been to confession."

"Maybe not. Or maybe I'm not as bad as you." She smiles.

"Now where's the lightning going to strike?" He sidesteps her, purposefully giving her a wide berth, as he heads toward the exit.

"Where are you going?" she calls after him.

He spins around, holding the file against his chest. "Turns out William Truly's an ex-Navy Seal. The training he must have," Tony responds determinedly.

"Let him have this one, DeLuca," she coaches herself, resisting the urge to accompany him, compete with him, rather. She sits down at her desk, her hands laced behind her neck, eyes on the ceiling, contemplating the hectic events of the day, wondering just exactly how it all ties together...if it ties together at all.

The sound of women's heels clicking on the tiled floor interrupts her thoughts. A purposeful, flawless cadence, *click-click-click-click*. *Oh great,* she mumbles internally, while presenting a smile to Dr. Patricia Ryan who stands before her in a perfectly tailored designer pantsuit, accessorized with commanding four-inch heels. Her poise flawless. Gina refuses to speak first, causing Dr. Ryan to do the honors.

"May I?" she asks, gesturing toward the chair across from Gina.

Gina nods, her body stiffening from its previously relaxed state. She sits upright. "Help yourself."

"Looks like this case has you covered up, Detective," she refers to the mounds of files and paperwork on Gina's desk.

Gina props her arms up on the bulky pile. "Nothing I can't handle."

Dr. Ryan scopes out her black eye. "Isn't helping your beauty regimen, either."

"What do you want, Dr. Ryan?"

"So much for pleasantries." She smirks, meeting Gina's ante, propping her arms up on the desk, her body language leaned forward and intense. "I know what you're trying to do."

"Do tell." Gina leans into her further, looking around, and continues with a sarcastic whisper, "That way I'll know too."

"You and your *boy*. The department is coming down on you for answers. You need a fall guy for this case. Who better than the psychologist? 'A bitter woman who is subjected to the vile scum that is a rapist. Poor lady, has to sit day in and day out listening to the truths of those pigs hearts, until she can't take it anymore. Until she is forced to take justice into her own hands.' Is that the way it's going down? Does that about sum it up, *Detective* DeLuca?"

Gina crosses her hands one into the other. "Ya know, *Dr.* Ryan, sounds as though you could use some psychological counseling yourself. Does the word delusional mean anything to you?"

"You want to play word games? Okay. Incompetent. Buffoon. Washed-Up. Mean anything to you?"

"I'd love to sit here and exchange civilities, but I'm afraid I have to highly recommend you leave." Gina's tone has turned icy, her jaw twitches. She files some paperwork, slamming the drawer to her desk shut. "Now."

Dr. Ryan smiles. "Well, Detective DeLuca, seems you have quite the temper. Tell me, how do you feel about rapists?"

Gina ignores her goading.

Dr. Ryan eyes her thoroughly, focusing on her neck. Her hand subconsciously following her train of thought, she reaches out pulling at the mock collar of Gina's black fatigue sweater, revealing what appears to be rope burn. "Where were you last night?" she provokes.

With catlike swiftness, Gina places her hand over Dr. Ryan's, pinpointing localized pressure to a reflex area, causing it to open unwillingly. Dr. Ryan winces, a smile forming on her lips. Gina loosens her grip. Dr. Ryan pulls her hand to her lap, massaging it briefly.

"Bodies coming up dead. No solid evidence. Guess work and speculation. Resorting to blaming your own. I feel a panic coming on, Detective DeLuca. Something tells me this city's on the brink of a witch hunt." Dr. Ryan stands, pushing her chair in. "Unless you have an affinity for fire, you may want to take care of that neck." She winks furtively before turning to walk away.

Chapter 5

Late night. One seedy apartment complex after another. This side of town is dark and dreary, even on the most luminous of days. Randall Barnes wears a hooded, bulky winter coat, his hands tucked deeply in the pockets of his ill-fitting jeans. He carries himself cautiously, his posture stooped, eyeing every corner and alleyway for what may be lurking there. He enters his apartment building, taking an old-school freight elevator to his unit. He holds his finger over the UP button. The elevator takes off, making it to the tenth floor before coming to a screeching halt.

"Goddammit," he mutters, jamming the palm of his hand against the UP button.

"I see you, Randall."

His head cranks upward in the direction of a muffled, distorted voice. Glaring fluorescent lights cloud his vision. He shades his frantic face, holding his arm above his forehead, searching for someone, anyone. "Who's there?" He turns circles.

"How does it feel?" the voice echoes out of the speaker box in the elevator ceiling.

"What...what are you talking about? Who's there!" The whites of his eyes protruding, his chest heaves up and down.

The voice laughs lightly. "Do you remember Rudy Sangino?"

Recognition displays itself in Randall's expression. He says nothing.

"What's the matter, Randall? Cat got your tongue?"

He panics, pushing and punching the UP button until it breaks loose. His breath heavy with adrenaline, his mouth is dry as cotton from the massive endorphins released by his sympathetic nervous system...fight or flight. He bangs on the door of the elevator.

"Five years ago, you dated Rudy's mother. She trusted you with her little boy. Dark black hair, big brown eyes, sweet smile...infectious laugh. Remember him?

He backs up in the corner away from the speaker box, his arms clutching the walls of the elevator. "What do you want from me!"

"'The one who sows to please his sinful nature, from that nature will reap destruction,'" the voice quotes from the Bible, Galatians 6:8. "It's your turn to reap the fruits of your harvest, Randall."

The elevator lights flicker as it begins to drop. Randall slides down the wall in the corner, hiding his head between his knees. With a hard jolt, the square box stops midair, clanking and clacking. The pulley above creaks, as it rocks back and forth.

Randall jumps up, raging and punching at the walls of the elevator and at the vent above him. "Let me out of here!" he screams, frightened to the point of tears.

"Not so fun, is it, Randall? Being caged up like an animal against your will. How do you think Rudy felt? Every time you picked him up from school and took him home to his mother's apartment. Telling him the elevator was the *Buddy Box*. A secret place, only for you and him. How many times did he ask you to stop? When you touched him, made him touch you. Did you? Did you stop, Randall? You had no mercy for him. I have no mercy for you."

"That was a long time ago. I'm a different person now. I swear I am. Please!" he cries, his hands pressed together in prayer formation. "Let me go!" He sobs.

Laughter purrs out of the speaker. "A leopard never changes its spots, Randall. You have a new girlfriend. With a fifteen-year-old daughter. You think I don't know what you're thinking every time you look at her? You swear you're a different person. Let's test psychological theory. Does rehabilitation work on the mind of a pedophile? A rapist? I'm not gambling with those odds."

"Somebody help me!" He bangs frantically on the elevator door.

The flickering lights in the elevator go to black, complete darkness. Randall screams, pleading and begging for help.

"You guys make me sick. You push, and you prod, and you threaten...little kids, women...rob them of their lives, their sanity. But when pushed back, you scream and cry and flail about. Pathetic mother-fuckers."

The sound of the pulley screeches, giving way. The elevator drops furiously, its destination the concrete below. The shimmying causes Randall to fall into the corner. He is rolled up in the fetal position. The sound of the pulley zinging off the rope rings through his ears, as he covers them with his hands.

"'Yea, tho I walk through the valley of the shadow of death, I will fear no evil...'" he recites.

The elevator stops a floor from the concrete, lurching from the momentum, creaking and clacking. The lights flicker, finally burning full and bright.

And again a soft, delightful laugh flows out of the speakers. "Now you're a Christian? Love that about you guys. You always seem to find God after you have taken so much from Him in the souls and spirits of His flesh. Get up!"

His rapid breathing the only thing audible, he scurries from the floor, facing the elevator door, hopeful.

"Death is inevitable for you, Randall Barnes. It's a matter of when and where. I will be lurking in the shadows. Hell, maybe I'll even check in on you from time to time as you sleep. Creepy, huh? That's how Rudy felt. Knowing it was coming...you were coming, again and again...simply uncertain of when. Now, you will know the same fear."

The elevator dings. The buttons light up. Randall throws himself in front of the doors as they begin to open. Grasping at the edges with his unsteady hands, he pries with all his might, fleeing from the large metal box.

"Be seeing you, Randall," the voice echoes behind him.

DETECTIVE DELUCA'S HOUSE, midnight. She traipses to the door, assembling a black silk housecoat to cover the black silk nighty she wears underneath, having been disturbed from a perfectly wonderful sleep by her pesky partner, Detective Gronkowski. He knocks impatiently. She expects him this time, as he has been *blowing up* her phone for the past two hours.

"Why did I give him my number?" she scolds, shaking her head. "I'm coming."

He knocks again for good measure.

She whips the door back. "It's twelve o'clock in the freaking morning," she whispers with an underlying roar. "You trying to get me thrown out of the neighborhood?" She motions him in hurriedly. "You ever dealt with the Homeowners Association? We're talking more powerful than the mob." She locks the door behind him.

"William Truly," he says, with his one-track mind, proceeding to the archway between her kitchen and her living room. He rests his arms above his head, gripping the sturdy pull-up bar Gina has rigged to the archway. "Nothing on the guy. I got nothing, Gina. Except wasted hours." He peers up at the pull-up bar. "You use this thing?"

"Nope. Just there for decoration." She rolls her eyes, making her way into the living room.

Tony follows, his senses instantly bombarded with heat, wood scent, and flickering light dancing on the tops of several large pillar candles. An instant feeling of comfort, and desire, pummels his system as he sees a pile of faux fur blankets and pillows lying in front of the fireplace. Gina stokes the fire, feeding its vibrant flames with a few more pieces of wood.

"You got company?" Tony asks, suddenly wondering if he is out of place.

"Yeah." Gina giggles. "He's waiting in the closet until you leave."

Tony grins. "Just looks like you were expecting someone."

"Maybe I am," she says, looking at him momentarily as if he is the last piece of Godiva left in the box. Quickly recovering, she changes the subject. "Nothing. No records on an ex-Navy Seal. We both know what that means." She shivers, kneeling in front of the fireplace for warmth.

Tony watches her, instinctively wanting to warm her up. He idles in position, safely across the room. "Black Ops. Confirms the guy was some kind of badass."

"They work outside the spectrum of the law...all the time. That's why there's no records of their existence. No records. No existence. Deniability. But think about it, Tony. Doesn't make sense. Why would he wait three years to kill the guy who raped his daughter?"

"Why not?" He removes his coat, his body warming intensely, and not simply from the fireplace. "Perfect timing. All the other murders happening. This one fits right in, looks like it's one of ours. He gets away with it."

"Do you think he may be linked to the other murders?"

"At this point, Gina, I don't know what to think." He paces, running his fingers through his hair.

Gina watches him. In this moment, after a long stressful day, she is aware of his closeness, his maleness. He's handsome with his dark hair, dark features, light eyes, and five o'clock shadow. Very masculine in his build, broad shoulders, narrow-waisted, long-limbed—the perfect mix of brawn and brains. She blinks. *Snap out of it, DeLuca.*

"This case. It can't be that mysterious. We have to be missing something. One little piece of the puzzle. We're so close. I can feel it," he says, knocking his fist against the tightness of his abdomen.

"Remember that game? 'You're getting warmer,'" he refers to the childhood game where an object was selected and participants were gauged by how cold, warm or hot they were in guessing its identity. "I am so freaking hot right now, I just can't put my finger on it."

"Maybe it's the fireplace." She chuckles.

He looks to her annoyed, at first. His expression quickly changing as he takes her in, her auburn hair full and wavy, cascading around her face, accentuating her dark green eyes in the glow of the fireplace. The bruise at the corner of her left eye reminds him of his position, her partner—work partner. He pulls his stare from her, checking out her mantle. One piece of art accessorized with a few candles. Quite clean and stoic in its presentation. No family pictures. No present connecting Gina to a past.

"Where's your pictures?" he asks. "Family? Friends?"

She hesitates. "My parents died in a car wreck when I was sixteen." Clearing her throat, she continues, filling the silence. "No need to hold onto something...someone who's gone. Keeps you in the past. Life's about the future, so they say."

"Sorry," he speaks softly.

"No need for apologies, pity." She sits back on the blanket. "I'm a big girl. Shit happens. I don't have a very good memory anyway. I don't recall a lot from my past. Maybe I blocked it out." She yawns, stretching catlike—arching her back, her arms overhead. Tony eyes her, all too aware of her every move. "And with this job, I don't have time for a social life, hence the exclusion of friends."

The curve of her breasts have him locked up momentarily. Forcing his way upward, he scans over her neck. Walking to her, almost subconsciously as if pulled by some kinetic force, he kneels beside her. She sits upright from her stretching position, pulling her housecoat closed, purposely attempting to withdraw from his effortless affect. "What's this?" He gently traces her neck with his finger.

She watches him, genuine concern in his expression. "Krav Maga training. We were learning how to get out of choke holds."

"Looks like rope burn."

"It is."

"Does it hurt?" He rests his hand on the back of her neck, a gentle massage.

Gina moans faintly at his contact, kneading her tense muscles. Her eyes close, she wets her bottom lip with her tongue. "Not really," she replies, her dark lashes open slowly to find Tony sporting a sexy smirk.

"Ms. DeLuca, where were you the night before last?"

"If I told you, I'd have to kill you," she replies playfully. "You sound like Dr. Ryan."

"What do you mean?" He indulges her now with both hands rubbing her neck and upper back.

Her head pivots to the side, pure bliss evident in her expression and in her vocal tone. "She came to see me today. Very suspicious of my injury."

"You know what they say about blame. Deflection of guilt." He bends his head into her neck, physically unable to hold it upright any longer, his resilient exoskeleton turning to mush in her presence. The warmth of his breath trailing her neck, followed by the cool, wet sensation of his mouth sends chills through her body like tiny shock waves. Each nerve ending teased, yearning to be touched. He kisses her softly over the length of the rope burn, graduating to a more arduous, urgent response once he reaches healthy, unscathed flesh.

Gina bites her lip, holding back a moan, but her body voluntarily reacts, arching her back into him.

"You like that?" he teases.

"Don't get cocky, Gronkowski. Anybody would like that. We shouldn't be doing this." She pushes against his chest, turning her head away.

"Doing what?" He cups her chin with his hand, gently turning her face back to his. "This is medicine. Healing. That's all that's going on here. Just think of me as the medicine man." He grins and with the same sweetness he lavished the rope burn, he *doctors* the bruise over her left eye.

"It's all well and good until you pull out the *penis-cillin,* medicine man," she says, causing them both to chuckle. Gina transitions to serious mode, lightly patting the side of his face. "This is elementary, Tony. Work and play don't mix."

"There is nothing elementary about you, DeLuca." He guides her mouth up to meet his. Wondering which is warmer, the fire at her back or the fire at her front, Gina melts into it, matching him effort for effort. "You're the freaking PhD," he growls, pulling away from her, wiping his mouth on the back of his hand. His chest rising and falling at a labored rate, he pivots to stand. "I better get going."

Gina grabs his wrist firmly. He smiles, thinking to himself, *Well played.* "Oh, no you don't. You can't walk in here, turn me on, then leave me to turn it off. It's like team sports. You finish what you start, Gronkowski."

"Gladly," he says, turning to her. She meets his mouth with her own, playfully biting down on his bottom lip before releasing it. He guides her body back onto the plush faux fur blankets beneath her, simultaneously releasing her robe. She smiles at his prowess with the material, returning the favor. His fully sculpted body now hovers over hers in the raw. With one swift movement, she flips him onto his back as she settles in astraddle his waist. His eyes grow wide with excitement.

"I have this thing about being on top," she purrs.

"Just when I thought you couldn't get any sexier." He smiles mischievously, pulling her down to him.

CHAPTER 6

City Hall. Early morning. Downtown Vanguard has awakened. The sun is on the rise, the pavement is teeming with the hustle and bustle of those living the dream—working, playing, and living hard. The streets are filled with the sounds of engines purring, horns honking, some friendly and not-so-friendly morning exchanges between passersby. The city is alive. News vans have swarmed City Hall. The steps leading up to the building are over-crowded with rowdy patrons and some passive onlookers.

Detectives Gronkowski and DeLuca arrive on scene, jumping out of their police cruiser. Both are disheveled, tucking in shirttails and tidying themselves as they take two steps at a time, swiftly working their way through the crowd. Partially distracted by last night's activities, and thoroughly tuckered out as pleasure trumped sleep, over and over again. Every step, every movement requires deliberate effort. Their scene assessment skills piqued one after the other with the onslaught of chaos.

"Take back our city!" a group of picketers chant, while a more peaceful congregation paces back and forth, holding signs that read, *Viva Vigilare!*

A news reporter stands between two citizens, interviewing them for the local television news. "It may not be legal, but it's just," a woman comments into the reporter's microphone.

The man across from her makes his rebuttal, "Murder is murder. We can't have some vigilante running around killing people."

"The hell we can't. I'm just glad someone is finally doing what our justice system won't," the woman leans into the microphone.

"But you can't have people taking the law into their own hands," the man snatches the microphone away from her. "It's madness!"

She snatches the microphone back. "You wouldn't say that if it was your wife or daughter. Or even you. Men get raped, too, ya know!"

The reporter reclaims the microphone, looking into the camera for a quick sign-off. "Obviously a controversial subject. And we want to hear your thoughts at KVEN.com. Vigilante justice or cold-blooded murder? For KVEN, I'm Samantha Storm."

The assault of Tony and Gina's senses continues as they near the top of the steps.

"The sonsabitches got exactly what they had coming to them," a superbly dressed man with salt-and-pepper hair speaks authoritatively to a newspaper reporter. His wife nods approvingly.

"Citizens of Vanguard," a familiar booming voice sounds over the crowd. William Truly stands at the makeshift podium in front of the doors to City Hall. His six-foot-four-inch frame large and commanding. The rumble of the crowd simmers as attentions turn to the ex-Navy Seal. His daughter, Emily Truly stands to his left, Aubrey Raines to his right.

Tony and Gina share a perplexed look at Aubrey Raines' association with the Truly's.

"We gather here this morning to celebrate a hero. To unite. Finally standing up for what is right...what is just," William Truly speaks, a beacon to the crowd, they applaud and whistle. "Beside me stand two brave young women. Both victims of sexual predators. One saved, and one avenged. If you ask Vanguard PD, they'll tell you this *vigilante* is dangerous...unfit to mingle in society amongst law abiding citizens. Law abiding citizens," he repeats, something between a smirk and a grimace lining his lips. "Aubrey Raines, law graduate, future attorney, and rape victim advocate knows a thing or two about law abiding citizens," he introduces Aubrey. The amped crowd cheers.

"These so called *law abiding citizens*...rapists...break the law, time and time again, and walk away with a few years in jail and a slap on the wrist. Only to be released, so they can find their next victim. We, taxpayers, house and feed these animals in the correctional system. Prison sentences for the possession of a minute amount of marijuana, a naturally-grown plant, mind you, often far exceed those of rape and sexual assault."

The crowd riles to a frenzy, booing and hissing with her sharp commentary.

"I am ashamed!" Aubrey continues forcefully, feeding off the crowd. "To be part of a justice system that's aware a woman is raped every two minutes and thinks current sex offender legislation is appropriate. This *vigilante*. The one Vanguard PD would have you believe is dangerous...murderous." She looks directly to Detectives Gronkowski and DeLuca. The crowd eyes them disapprovingly. "Is a hero who saved my life and has avenged the souls, the lives of many others. This vigilante is no vigilante at all, but rather a *Vigilare*—one who watches over." She slaps her hand down on the podium, quickly raising it above her head in a fist as she shouts, "Viva Vigilare!"

Her enthusiasm propels the crowd into an active chant, "Viva Vigilare! Viva Vigilare! Viva Vigilare!" Their clenched fists pumping in the air.

Gina and Tony stand amongst the rowdy crowd, feeling as though the space between is spinning, a surreal feeling. The clouds, ample and gray in the morning sky, cast a dreary hue over the city.

"Did we just step into a comic book?" Tony asks, still disbelieving of the scene as it unfolds. "Good, evil...Vigilare?"

Gina shakes her head, prodding him with her elbow. "If so, here comes the Riddler." Encroaching upon them, a svelte Dr. Patricia Ryan beams smugly.

"*Officers* Gronkowski and DeLuca," she greets them.

"Detectives," Tony corrects agitatedly. Gina says nothing, maintaining hard eye contact, accompanied with brash body language.

"Quite the crowd," she says, completely discounting Tony's response. "With such a display, seems to me your case just took a serious nose dive. And they say, the public has no voice."

"Separates the strong from the weak...adversity," Tony says. "I like the pressure." He grins, crossing his arms over his chest, leaning into Dr. Ryan. "Kinda turns me on."

She returns his repartee. "Looks like something, or someone else," she eyes Gina, "turns you on, too." Her vision falls to his neck, where a slight small hickey resides, unbeknownst to him or Gina. "Vampires and Vigilares. We've become a regular Gotham City."

Tony now aware of the mark on his neck, mentally talks himself out of the urge to cover it, his hands forcefully resting across his chest. Gina remains stoic, unyielding and unaffected by Dr. Ryan's taunts.

"What's the matter *Detective* DeLuca, cat got your tongue?" Dr. Ryan continues to jab at her.

Cat got your tongue, the words echo in Gina's head taking her memory to a haunted place. She is on her back, held down against her will. Her eyes frantic and searching, she struggles. The cries of a young boy to which she cannot respond propel her fight instinct. Her breathing is labored, her heart seemingly pounding out of her chest. She kicks, screams, attempts to free her wrists from the unforgiving hands crushing them to the bed beneath her. A masked man leans over her, a spider web tattoo on his neck. Removing the mask, his long greasy hair cascades over his unkempt facial scruff, causing him to remain unrecognizable, momentarily. The man smiles. Gina's recognition kicks in, rendering her mute. "What's the matter, cat got your tongue?" he says, a wicked laugh escaping his disturbed soul.

Dr. Ryan watches Gina come back to reality, a contented grin surfacing.

Gina's jaw twitches, her initial instinct to attack, and not with her words. Tony, assessing her body language, readies himself to intercept should she come unleashed. *Woosah,* Gina exclaims internally, taking her mind-over-matter approach. Her balled up fists at her sides come to rest as she reciprocates Dr. Ryan's instigating smirk. "Maybe you should let something or someone turn you on, Dr. Ryan." Gina eyes her stifling pinstripe pantsuit, perfectly tailored, her blouse buttoned all the way up to her neck. "There's a prescription for being uptight. It's called getting laid."

Dr. Ryan chuckles affectively, diverting her attention from Gina to Tony, with a quick return, "Do you have a card, Detective Gronkowski? Seems you have a very satisfied customer." She smiles, wickedly. "I never do anything without a referral."

He gives her no reply.

She reaches into her briefcase, pulls out a business card and hands it to him. "Just in case you're passing out free samples." She leers at Gina.

"Guaranteed to satisfy," Gina meets her tit with a tat.

"A pleasure, as always." Dr. Ryan nods at each of them before walking away.

Tony shrugs his shoulders throwing his hands out to his sides. "Now you're my pimp?"

Gina grabs his arm pulling him down the steps toward their ride as the crowd around them continues to rally. "Oh, don't act like you're not flattered. I gave you high marks. Besides, isn't it every man's fantasy to have two women fighting over him?"

Tony thinks a moment. "Depends on the women." He continues thoughtfully as they take the steps swiftly to the squad car. "A pillow fight, that's sexy. Maybe a little hair pulling. A little scratching. But you two? That would be a knock-down, drag-out fisticuff."

"I can only hope," Gina scoffs as she makes her way to the driver's side.

"Hey," Tony calls, standing by the passenger side door looking over the hood at her. "What was that? Back there?" he references

Gina's momentary suspended state. "You okay?"

"Yeah. Blanked out for a bit. Bad dream, I guess." She slips into the driver's seat, firing up the Hemi, a pleasant sound to her ears as the RPMs settle into a formidable purr.

Tony shuts himself inside. "She gets under your skin...Dr. Ryan."

"You could say that," Gina confirms, heading for the police station at a rather urgent rate of speed.

"Do you believe me now?" Tony slaps his hand on the dashboard. "She's in this up to her eyeballs, Gina. I can feel it."

"Feel this," she hands him the radio. "You better give Chief a heads-up. After the news hits, the station phones are going to be on fire."

VANGUARD POLICE DEPARTMENT. Tony and Gina walk through the front entrance, making a beeline for Chief Burns' office. The station is busy. Phones are ringing, people moving to and fro.

"I'm the Vigilare," says a portly man in a black wrestling suit adorned with a matching black cape.

A perfectly physically fit woman wearing a tight black leather bodysuit from head-to-toe, her long jet black hair coiffed into a polished ponytail, her features stunning, stands across from the man challengingly. "I'm the Vigilare."

"Ha! The Vigilare can't be a woman," the man scoffs.

She spins in a large circular motion, executing a flawless martial arts butterfly kick, essentially a slanted aerial cartwheel. Her feet replant firmly in the space where she first left the floor, standing across from the man. She reaches out to him, pulling the black face mask away from his eyes and cheekbones. The rubber band stretches. She lets go, causing the mask to snap back against his face. "Let's see you do that, chubs." She smirks, folding her arms over her chest.

[76]

Officers Marks and Torres approach.

"I'll take Batgirl. You take Butterball," Marks orders.

"Flip you for it," Torres wagers.

"I called it first." Marks smiles, continuing under his breath, as the woman becomes clearer to his vision, "Hello, Batgirl."

"You suck, man," Torres whispers out the side of his mouth.

"We got another Vigilare on line three," a dispatcher yells out from her cubicle.

"What the hell is going on?" Gronkowski mumbles as he and Gina walk through all the commotion, approaching Chief Burns' office.

"Everybody wants to be a hero," Gina sighs.

She and Tony stand at Chief's open door. He preps in front of a mirror, unsuccessful in his attempt at assembling his necktie. "God-dammit," he sputters.

Gina and Tony elbow one another, holding back the urge to chuckle. Tony knocks on the door casing. Chief's neck swivels to them, he motions them in urgently, while holding the call button down on his phone.

"Yes, Chief?" Bonnie's sweet sultry voice answers.

"I could use some assistance," he admits self-consciously.

"Be right there, Chief."

"What the hell is going on down at City Hall?" he asks, continuing his attempt to make his tie cooperate. "The department Media Relations Manager called me, all in a panic. Said we need to beat this story to press. She said they're about to riot down there." He rips the tie from around his neck, slapping it down on his desk. "And what the hell is a Vigilare? Everybody and their mother wants to be the Vigilare."

"And their brother," Tony speaks absentmindedly. "Everybody and their brother."

"You say brother, I say mother," Chief sputters. "That's not the point, Gronkowski. What the hell is happening to this city?"

"It's Italian Chief. Derived from Latin. Means to look out for, to watch over," Gina says. "You know, like a superhero."

"Superhero?" Chief paces, running his thumbs around the inside of the waist of his pants, hitching them up. "When did we become the bad guys? You know how many calls we've had this morning from irate citizens, cussing out my officers, swearing up a storm, demanding we leave this *Vigilare* alone? The system is a joke, they say." He flops down into his chair, his arms overhead, hands intertwined against the back of his neck. "If the system is a joke, we're a joke boys and girls. DeLuca, why do you do this job?"

She looks at him quizzically, quickly providing an answer with the rise of his eyebrows. "Help people. Put away the bad guys. Maybe a little personal anger management, too," she admits.

Chief nods his head. "Gronkowski, when you were growing up, who were your heroes?"

He answers with his head held high. "Soldiers, Firefighters, Police Officers."

"Exactly!" Chief slaps his hand down on his desk. "Why did you become a police officer?"

"I wanted to be a hero," Tony systematically deduces.

Chief leans forward across his desk, his hands uniting intensely over a stack of files. "Then how in the hell did we get here? Protecting rapists and pedophiles." Deafening silence rings through the room as the three of them look to one another and at the floor beneath them.

The clicking of heels outside in the hallway interrupts the stillness. "What's up, Chief?" Bonnie asks sashaying into his office, carrying a suit coat with her. She smells divine, her scent filling the lungs of Gina and Tony as she passes by them to Chief's desk. She wears a chic sailor inspired navy blue and white silk jumpsuit with red accessories. The image uplifting and pleasing, suitable for mass production—a regular pinup girl.

Gina and Tony subconsciously perk up in their chairs against the wall. If they were canines, their ears would have certainly given away their curiosity. Chief is the only one oblivious to her charms.

"I hate to call you in here for something so trivial," Chief says, embarrassed. "I can't get this damn thing tied." He holds his necktie in his hand.

Bonnie smiles, sitting on the edge of his desk, taking the tie from his hand. "Well now, that's an easy fix." She flips the collar of his shirt up and begins assembling the necktie. "You have to address this Vigilare thing, huh?" Chief nods disapprovingly. "I think it's kind of exciting."

"Not you, too." He scowls.

"Oh come on, Chief. You have to admit, it gets the imagination stirring." She tidies her strict execution of the knot, flipping his collar down into place. "All set. Now put this on." She hands him his suit jacket.

"The only thing it stirs in me is my blood pressure." He pats the beads of sweat from his forehead with his handkerchief.

"I just think it's captivating. The possibility that superheroes really do exist."

"Heroes exist. Not superheroes," Chief says firmly.

She shrugs her shoulders, standing from his desk. "Makes for great people watching. Did you see that girl in the black leather outfit? She was doing flips and kicks, and everything." Her voice on the rise with excitement, falls back to its low soothing tone. "Until they drug her off in handcuffs." She smiles at Gina and Tony. They smile back simultaneously, both fully entertained with her presence. "Oh geez, what happened?" she exclaims, walking to Gina. Kneeling before her, Bonnie inspects her eye and her neck.

"Burglary arrest," Gina answers quietly, pointing to her eye. "And Krav Maga training," she continues, uncharacteristically smitten.

Bonnie's eyes light up with admiration. "You know how to do that stuff? That's so cool!" Her hand falls onto Gina's knee.

"Wouldn't that be awesome if the Vigilare was a woman? Can you imagine?"

"That's enough Vigilare talk," Chief reprimands, while reading over his approved and prepared statement to the public. "I don't want to hear anymore about that damn Vigilare." He slaps the paperwork down on his desk. "This doesn't even sound like me. Political mumbo jumbo."

Bonnie winks at Gina. "Maybe you could show me some moves sometime." Gina nods, quickly confirming her willing participation in such an event.

Tony's eyes are luminous, locked in on the two women and their interplay, assessing their body language. They're already *sparring* in his mind.

"Let me run and get my makeup bag. I've got something that will cover that right up." She glances at Tony, a grin gracing her full pouty lips, eyeing the hickey on his neck. "I'll get some for you, too!" She giggles, exiting the room.

"What was that?" Tony teases.

"What?" Gina defends.

"You know what. All that touchy-feely, ogling stuff. Did you two just have a moment?" He wishes.

"You're about to have a moment, Gronkowski." Gina eyes him. "Pull it together." She looks down the hallway as a herd of footsteps and simmering voices call her attention. "Chief, you ready? The cavalry's coming." She and Tony rise.

He walks from behind his desk, pulling at the tails of his suit jacket. "The sooner this dog and horse show starts, the sooner it ends."

Gina and Tony share a bewildered glance at yet another botched expression. Gina grabs Chief's handkerchief from his suit for one last brow dab, clearing his forehead of any residual sweat beads. She neatly tucks the square back into his pocket.

"Thanks, DeLuca."

"Go get 'em Chief." She winks.

Tony pokes his head out the office door, unable to contain himself. "Hey Chief."

Chief turns his attention back to Tony.

"Pony...dog and *pony* show," he says sporting a super-sized smile.

"Chief Burns, Pamela Ward from KTEN News." His attention pulled back to the crowd and microphones barraging him as he makes his way down the hall.

"The man is preparing to address the city, and you're correcting him on his idioms," Gina rags Tony as they walk from Chief's office headed in the other direction.

Tony chuckles. "Ah, just helping him relax."

"I thought I'd follow up with Aubrey Raines," Gina gets back to business. "Find out what her motivation is."

"She's motivational alright. Did you see the way she got that crowd fired up this morning?"

"Gronkowski, you got a visitor," Officer Marks calls to him in passing, moving at mach speed.

"What's your hurry, Marks?" Tony smiles knowingly. "You got another Vigilare?"

"Ah...yeah. This one's wearing a Wonder Woman costume." He slaps his hands together, generating friction between his palms. "And to think, I almost called in this morning. Thank you, Jesus!" Muffled laughter is heard throughout the station.

"Make sure you take pictures," Tony calls after him.

Gina grins inquisitively. "What are you so happy about?"

"I saw *Wonder Woman.*"

She wrinkles up her nose. "That bad?"

"Worse." Tony cracks up laughing.

As they approach their work space, Randall Barnes sits at the desk in Gina's chair, wringing his hands nervously.

"What the hell is he doing here?" Tony growls.

"Who?" Gina is confused.

"Officer," Randall calls to Tony upon seeing him, standing from the chair.

"Detective," Tony sharply corrects.

"I need to talk to you. To someone. Last night. In the elevator. They're after me," Randall rambles incoherently, his eyes shifty, fearful. "Who's this?" he asks, referring to Gina, quickly extending his hand, a hint of interest in his expression.

Tony slaps his hand down. "Don't worry about it." His anger rising as he remembers his run-in with Randall in Dr. Ryan's office a few days ago. The thought of him ever having contact with Gina causes his stomach to knot up instantly. He lunges in Randall's direction, grabs him forcefully by the collar of his shirt and slams his back into the wall. "You touch her, you're a dead man," Tony seethes.

"Gronkowski," Gina scolds.

Her voice causes Randall's eyes to track in her direction. Tony slaps his face away from her. "Don't even look at her, man." His body fully amped, he stands nose to nose with Randall, his voice low and profane, "Keep your fucking eyes off her, if you wanna keep 'em in your head."

Randall nods vigorously in full agreement.

"You want to talk to me, you sit down in that chair and turn your back to her." Tony hastily assists Randall into the chair, who, of course, doesn't turn around fast enough for Tony. "Turn around!" Randall scurries his feet, winging the chair in a semicircle, his back to Gina.

Gina looks to Tony and throws her hands in the air, as if to say, *What the hell was that?*

Tony gently takes her by the arm leading her in the opposite direction. "Not so much as a peep, Randall," Tony reiterates as he walks with Gina. "That's the guy I caught in Dr. Ryan's office. The other day. When she wouldn't press charges."

"Oh," Gina connects the dots. "Why'd you go all crazy back

there? I'm your partner, Gronkowski. You don't have dibs on me. I'm not yours to protect." She stops in the middle of the hallway, annoyed. "What does he want? I think I should be in on this conversation. If someone's after him, maybe it's our Vigilare. You don't think that concerns me?" She crosses her arms over her chest, the toe of her shoe agitatedly tapping against the tile floor. "You spend one night with me, and now you're my keeper? It was sex, Gronkowski. SEX. And it's not happening again," she clarifies.

He smiles, knowing his best move to diffuse this situation is humor. He speaks slowly and sultry, exaggerating every enunciation, "Mind-blowing, toe-curling, make you wanna slap yo' mama SEX." He nudges her affectionately, looking around for eavesdroppers, keeping his voice low, "How many times did we do it? I lost count after three. Didn't know you had it in ya, DeLuca. You have to feed an appetite like that."

Her belly growls, timely. She pats it. "Right now, the only appetite I have is for lunch." She throws her arm in Randall's direction. "Have it your way, Gronkowski. He's all yours. I'll follow up on Aubrey Raines. You want me to bring you something from The Fish Market?"

"What are you having?"

"My Oh Mahi Fish Tacos."

He grins at the name.

"What?" Gina holds back a smile, rolling her eyes. "Do you want something, or not?"

"Dozen oysters on the half."

"What! I'm not bringing oysters back to the station."

"Gotta keep my libido fed," he teases, shrugging his shoulders.

"Why? So it can keep up with your ego. God knows that thing's always full." She turns, walking away.

"I'll eat whatever you bring me," he calls after her.

"That's what I thought." She stops momentarily, turning back to him, holding up her hand, exhibiting five fingers. "Five times,

Gronkowski. Wouldn't want you short-changing me." She pivots with military precision, proceeding on her way.

Tony watches her, zoning in on the easy confidence she displays with each effortless step.

Officer Marks, an eyewitness to the scene, in passing Tony in the hallway can't help but comment. "Might as well forget it, Gronkowski. That one there, she's all work, no play."

Tony clutches his chest, over his heart melodramatically, ragging on Marks. "You get any pictures of Wonder Woman?"

"Nope," Marks dismisses him.

"What's the matter? Afraid she'd break your camera?" Tony chuckles, following after him, making his way back to Randall Barnes.

Marks says nothing, never losing stride. He simply raises his hand over his head, flipping Tony the bird.

"Hey don't be sore, man. I hear they're bringing Catwoman in on a crane," he yells after him as Marks disappears around the corner. He continues his quiet, self-entertaining banter until he makes it back to the desk. "Alright, you can turn around now." He takes a seat across from Randall.

"Is it true? The Vigilare? I saw it on the news this morning," Randall questions, his leg bouncing up and down with the jitters.

"What happened last night?" Tony asks with deep-seated annoyance in his tone, ignoring Randall's inquiry.

"Someone's trying to kill me. I think it might be that Vigilare. Do you think that thing has superpowers?" Randall continues to fidget, rolling a pen between his fingers.

"What's the matter? Feel out of place for you...being the prey?" Tony leans across the desk, his hands firmly folding one into the other.

"Is there someone else I can talk to?" Randall grows agitated.

"Nope. My case. My terms. My rules." Tony leans back in his chair, satisfied. "You've got five seconds to tell me something that captivates my interest."

"Someone tried to kill me last night."

"You already said that. I don't find that particularly interesting or surprising. Five, four..."

"They're trying to get even," Randall blurts, pausing before warily continuing. "I was in the elevator. In my apartment. They shut the whole freaking thing down. Turned the lights out and everything. Dropped my ass from fifty feet in the air."

Tony smiles. "Sorry I missed that."

"This is bullshit, man!" Randall jumps up from his chair. "I thought you guys were supposed to help people."

Tony kicks his feet up on the desk nonchalantly. "What did you do? For them to get even?"

"It was years ago. Doesn't matter what I did. I have rights, you know. You have to help me. I'll sue." He paces.

"I don't *have* to do shit. And if you want to sue, take a number. Either you start talking, on the level, or get the hell out of my sight." Tony scuffs his feet off the desk quickly, beginning to stand.

A startled Randall flops himself into the chair across from Tony. "Okay, okay. Years ago, I was arrested for molesting my girlfriend's son." He looks around, ducking his upper body lower to the desktop, maintaining a mild voice. "In the elevator, when I would bring him back to the apartment after school."

Tony's jaw twitches involuntarily.

Randall picks up the pace of confession, attempting to spit it all out before Tony unleashes on him. "Last night...this distorted voice...someone was in the elevator shaft. They knew about the little boy."

"The voice. Male or female?"

Randall's eyes shift to the right with his thought. "Male. Maybe. I don't know. It was distorted. Deep, heavy breathing."

"Darth Vader's trying to kill you? Seems a little far-fetched," Tony taunts, unable to contain himself.

Randall rolls his eyes, continuing. "Said they were there for my soul. It was just a matter of time. They're gonna kill me. This isn't funny!" He slams his fist down on the desk.

Tony shrugs his shoulders as if to say, *That's debatable.*

"Bible quotes," Randall remembers. "They quoted the Bible. Reaping what I sow. Some really freaky shit. Cat got your tongue. Taunting me. Like they got off on it."

Tony repeats aloud, "Cat got your tongue...cat got your tongue. Where did I hear that?" His memory searches, snapshots and voices quickly assemble until he hears Dr. Patricia Ryan's voice from the City Hall protest earlier that morning. *What's the matter, Detective DeLuca, cat got your tongue?* Her words echo repetitively in his mind. "I knew it!" He jumps up out of his chair with renewed satisfaction and confidence in his initial instinct that Dr. Ryan was somehow involved in the string of murders. "Get up," he barks at Randall.

"Where we going?" Randall stands attentively.

"We're not going anywhere. You're leaving." He takes off walking at an intense pace. Randall follows, of course.

"What are you going to do? Can I get some kinda police protection, or something?"

"Ha! Yeah, that's going to happen," Tony dismisses.

"You can't leave me alone. You have to do something. Can't you put me in a cell for the night? Something? Until you catch this murderer."

Tony turns around sharply. Randall follows so closely behind, he runs into him, stumbling backward. Tony's finger pounds into Randall's chest, scoldingly. "You spend too much time with shit, it's bound to rub off. You're shit. Toxic excrement, a waste of human life." His teeth gritting together at this point. "I don't like you. You're right, I have to do something. Sadly, in this case, I'm bound to uphold the law. But I don't have to do a goddamned thing for you." He pulls himself together, retracting his finger from its intrusive encounter with Randall's chest. He smiles contentedly, breathing heavily and deeply with great audibility, displaying his best Darth Vader impersonation. "I'm in no hurry to find Vader. Hope *she* gets to you before I get to her." Tony winks, pushing past Randall.

CHAPTER 7

At the top of the bell tower I wait,
Streets lined below, believers rush in,
Praying for their salvation at Heaven's Gate.

My eyes green and quiet in the night,
Weary for the innocent, sleep, sweet baby, sleep,
With one drop of blood, a shining emerald light.

Images of faces flash like a timeline,
A man, a boy, so close I keep them,
The feeling that once they were mine.

Why do I do this, only time will tell,
Am I a hero, a savior?
Or no better than the evils that I quell?

Did you hear that? From down below evil speaks,
He paces, justifying his desire,
He is one of them, the soulless that I seek.

Randall Barnes paces, his shoes squeaking with each turn on the linoleum kitchen floor in his girlfriend's apartment. He mumbles to himself, a mix of fear and anger. "Stupid cocksucker, pointing his finger in my chest. I should've punched his lights out." He lightly taps his fists against the counter, connecting the second time with a little more force, testing his own bravery. "Nobody wants to help me. This is all that damn doctor's fault...Dr. Ryan. I should've spread her legs when I had the chance. Stupid bitch."

"Night, Randall," Tessa, his girlfriend's fifteen-year-old daughter calls to him as she walks from the bathroom to her bedroom.

"Night, Tess," he speaks up, making his way to the living room, ogling her as she walks away from him. Her long dark hair pulled back in a ponytail. She wears pink cotton pajamas. He circles the living room couch, his thoughts racing. "I asked for help. Nobody wants to help me," he reasons. Shifting his eyes intermittently to Tess' bedroom. "Maybe I'll help myself."

Tessa turns her light out, pulling the blankets up around her body. An eerie feeling sweeps over her, as she jerks her head up from her pillow, eyeing the doorway. "Randall?"

He smiles coyly as he stands, leaning up against the door casing. "Thought I'd tuck you in."

"I'm good," she says quickly. "G'night." She grips her covers in her hands, holding them tightly across her shoulders.

Randall walks to her, sitting down beside her on the bed, he puts one arm across her waist. With the other hand, he strokes her hair back, away from her face. "You're so pretty, Tess. So innocent. The world hasn't ruined you, yet."

She shies away from his hand, edging closer to the wall. The look on her face is painfully fearful.

He smiles. "You don't have to be afraid of me, Tess. I would never hurt you. I just want to be close to you." He pulls her body away from the wall, toward him.

Her heart feels as if it will jump out of her ribcage. Her palms instantly turn sweaty.

"You ever been with a boy, Tess?"

She shakes her head, holding back the urge to cry, pursing her lips together.

Randall strokes her face, allowing his hand to come to rest on her neck, inching its way toward her chest. "You're a good girl, Tess." He runs his hand ever so slowly over her breast and down her stomach, continuing until he settles over her thigh, massaging her. "You wanna be with me? I could show you how to do it. It might be good for you. Then you'd know what to do when you found a boy you wanted to be with."

Again, she shakes her head, vehemently. Her voice mute. Tears escape, streaming down over the apples of her cheeks.

"I know, baby." Randall wipes at her tears with his icy hand. "It's scary, huh? But it feels amazing. I'll take my time with you." He smiles. "You're gonna love it, baby."

ON THE STREET below, Detective Gronkowski and Officer Marks enjoy a stakeout, purposely concocted to follow Randall and inadvertently anyone who may be following him. Their police cruiser is filled with protein bars and energy drinks.

Marks bites into his chocolate peanut butter protein bar, his taste buds instantly disappointed. "Aw yuck! Come on Gronkowski. Where's the donuts? Coffee? Something?" He searches for something to wash it down.

Tony chuckles, handing him an energy drink. "You beat cops, man. You're soft. How do you expect to rise to the occasion with all that sugar and caffeine in your system? That shit makes you slow and fat." He talks in between bites of his protein bar, seemingly unbothered by the taste.

Marks cracks open the energy drink. "Yeah, because this doesn't have any sugar or caffeine," he ridicules, taking a swig. "Aw God," he spits and sputters. "That shit tastes like cough syrup." He coughs, opening his door, pouring the drink out onto the concrete.

"Close the door," Tony barks. "You'll draw attention to us."

Marks pulls the door back, throwing the can on the floorboard. "And again, just exactly why am I here? You have a partner. She'd be pissed if she knew you were out here on this case with me."

"She needs a night off. We've had a rough couple of days."

"DeLuca didn't take the night off. She doesn't know you're here, does she?"

Tony wads up his wrapper, throwing it over his shoulder into the backseat. "No, she doesn't. And don't go running your mouth, Marks. Did you see her eye and her neck? All this Vigilare drama. She's been put through the wringer. She needs a night off." He tunes the radio to a different station. "Nothing she could do here tonight, anyway."

"She's getting to ya, isn't she?" Marks smiles. "Ah, Gronkowski's got the hots for his partner." He slaps the dashboard fully satisfied with his conclusion.

"Whatever, man." Tony chugs down some of his energy drink, formulating his thoughts. "It's sheer respect. She deserves...needs a night off. I'd do the same thing for you."

"Shit!" Marks laughs. "No you wouldn't, or I wouldn't be out here with you right now. I need the night off, too, but it sure didn't hurt your feelings to ask me. You're so full of shit."

Neither one of them speaks momentarily.

"Can't say I blame ya, man. The girl is fine." He uses his hands miming the curvaceous flow of a woman's body. "I'd let her kick my ass, and like it. Whew!"

"You strange. Something's wrong with you, man." Tony purposely turns the focus away from Gina to Marks.

Marks' eyebrows raise with enlightenment. "You hitting that, Gronkowski?"

Displeased with such reference, Tony's eyes dart in his direction, a cool warning to maintain respectful mention of his superior, the woman who outranks him.

Marks throws his hands up at shoulder level, a sign of apology, no harm meant. He smiles, shaking his head. "You and DeLuca? Didn't see that one coming."

"You talk too much," Tony quips as he spots a black silhouette scaling the apartment building. "That's why you don't ever see anything coming." He bails out of the car.

"Where you going?"

"Stay put. I'll call if I need backup." And he's off into the night.

"NO. PLEASE," TESSA begs, sitting up against her headboard, pulling the covers with her, snugly around her neck. "I don't want to do this."

"Tess, you can trust me," Randall coaxes, moving closer to her.

"Please, don't!" she cries, shaking her head.

Randall grabs her by the backs of her arms, shaking her. "I'm not going to hurt you," he consoles contradictingly through gritted teeth. She winces, a distraught moan escaping her mouth. He quickly loosens his grip, apologetically stroking her hair. "Trust me, Tess. I'm going to take care of you." He sniffs the air around her. "God, you smell good. I can't wait to see how you taste," he continues, his mouth moving in toward hers.

"Oh, Randall..." a voice beckons him from behind.

He freezes, warily looking at Tessa as if she can help him. "Who's there? Who's behind me, Tess?"

She says nothing, her attention frozen on the individual standing behind Randall, clad in all black from head to toe.

Randall grabs the lamp off her bedside table and wings it, running out of the bedroom. The Vigilare ducks, the lamp shatters into pieces against the wall.

"Lock the door," she orders Tessa, fleeing the bedroom in diligent pursuit of Randall.

Tessa does as instructed, jumping off her bed and locking the door. She piles in the closet, hiding under the stack of clothing. Her cell phone in hand, she sharply dials 9-1-1.

Randall dashes for the front door, his grand escape. Vigilare grabs the first object she sees, a clothing iron, as she rounds the linen cabinet outside Tessa's bedroom. She heaves the iron with precise accuracy. *Thud!* the sound echoes off the middle of Randall's back, causing him to fall to his knees.

Knock! Knock! Knock! "Vanguard PD. Open up."

"Help me!" Randall screams. "It's here. The Vigilare. Help me!"

Detective Gronkowski, amped by the thought that he has finally made his mark, shoves his shoulder into the unforgiving door.

Vigilare's flight instinct kicking in, she jets to the window in the kitchen, where she first made her ascent. *Shit!* she exclaims to herself, remembering Tessa in the closet. She can't leave her.

Gronkowski backs away, pivoting his body as he lines up, delivering a few solid mule kicks to the area over the deadbolt. The door gives, swinging open. He charges the room, his department issued 1911 handgun drawn, the hammer cocked.

"It's in the kitchen," Randall chokes out, grabbing Tony's leg as he swiftly walks by him.

Tony shakes him off. "Get up," he orders. Randall hovers on his knees, grabbing at his back. Tony quickly and cautiously clears the kitchen, no Vigilare to be found. Doubting Randall, he drops his gun to his side. "You seeing things now, Randall?"

"Boo!" she whispers from behind him.

He spins facing her, pulling the gun from his side. As he raises the weapon, she swiftly intercepts it, twisting the gun around trapping his finger in the trigger pull. She follows through, his finger snaps, releasing the weapon into her hands. She quickly discards it into the trashcan beside them.

Tony is mesmerized momentarily by the fact that this *thing,* the Vigilare, actually exists. And he is doubly smitten by the fact that *it's* a *she,* who took his gun away from him. Her eyes and lips, dark green and full, the only things visible among her black attire. "I don't know whether to be alarmed or turned on," he gulps, a smile forming on his lips.

"Either works for me," she quips, grabbing him by his shirt collar. With great momentum, she twists their bodies, throwing herself gently to the floor on her back. She takes Tony with her, planting her feet into his stomach, propelling him like a springboard with her legs. His body flies end over end until he comes down like a brick, flat on his back onto the living room floor. She gathers her arms and legs underneath her, preparing a perfectly executed backflip, landing on her feet astraddle Tony's hips.

"Umph," he groans. Grabbing her ankles, he sweeps her legs out from under her. And there they go, grappling on the floor.

"You sure you want to take it to the floor?" she teases. "You've seen my work."

"It's worth the risk," he pants. "Especially if I can get you in the north-south position." He chuckles.

"Go for it," she challenges. "Just know that I fight to win, even if that means dirty." She escapes his grasp, reversing to the dominant position once again. "You might not like having your *golden nuggets* anywhere near the vicinity of my teeth," she continues through choppy, labored breaths.

Randall crawls on his hands and knees around to the backside of the couch, removing himself from their direct path as they continue to tumble across the living room floor.

"Seriously," she says. "I'm going to have to choke you out real soon. So let me give you the lo-down."

"Oh," he crows. "Please do." Disbelieving her threat.

"There's a girl in the bedroom," she continues between pants. Both of them breathe heavily, getting a full workout from the grappling. Their bodies hot, fully charged and propelling the other. "Tessa. Randall's girlfriend's daughter." They stop momentarily, a truce. Chests heaving, hearts pounding. "He would've raped her. In her bed. Sick prick. I showed up. Don't leave her." Tony attempts to take advantage while her focus is distracted. She counteracts, using his momentum to secure her position on top of him, setting him up for a nice blood choke hold. "Lock his ass up for violating his probation," she says as she applies the hold.

Randall scurries around to the kitchen, rummaging through the trashcan.

"Shit, that feels funny," Tony confesses.

She smiles down at him. "Little pressure here. You just close your eyes. When you wake, I'll be gone."

Bang! the sound rings through the apartment. The gun drops from Randall's hand as if he stunned himself by pulling the trigger.

Vigilare moans, her right shoulder instantly hot like fire. She arches her back. Blood begins to trickle from the wound. She closes her eyes, focusing on her breathing, attempting to maintain. The rhythmic drum starts up in her temples, it pounds fast and steady as she feels her pulse surge through her body.

"Goddammit! You stupid son of a bitch!" she hears Tony's voice, reprimanding Randall. The words seem as though they're spewed in slow motion inside her head, the change within her body causing her to question whether the scene is even real.

The scent of blood—hers, and of man—the one beneath her, send her searching, gasping for air. She breathes in deep, and with one glorious exhale, her body has delivered a complete transformation. Her senses, her reflexes, her muscles, pristine and unmatched. She opens her eyes.

Tony is awestruck, somewhere between wanting to look away but too mesmerized not to meet her stare. "Sparkling emerald green light," he whispers in disbelief. The very notion he mocked Aubrey Raines about days earlier. "Oh shit," he quickly exclaims as her grasp on his neck becomes more aggressive with her glare. He wriggles about unsuccessful against her seemingly superhuman strength.

She tilts her head in confusion. Locked in on his gaze, she can see his soul, everything, good and bad that he has done. *How is it there is nothing punishable?* A few dirty mags as a kid, some illegitimately retrieved documents as a cop, his first time with his girlfriend in the backseat of a classic 1969 Chevrolet Nova, but nothing worth taking his life over. *Isn't this what I do? An eye for an eye? Who is this man? Why is he here, in my assignment?* She loosens her grip with the realization that he is one of the good guys.

Randall scuffles behind them on the floor, his hands fumble nervously with the gun. He accidentally hits the clip release button causing the clip to drop from the handle. "Shit!" he stammers, his hands busily attempting to reassemble the weapon.

Vigilare whips her head in his direction, a smile forming on her lips as she sights him in. *Bullseye!* With incredible speed, she pushes off Tony, lunging at Randall. Her hands viced around his neck, she jerks him to his feet, throwing him up against the wall. He screams, his eyes wide open, providing her the perfect vantage point. She locks in. He is unable to pull his stare from hers. With each evil image, her right shoulder twinges in pain, the gunshot wound coupled with her rampant heart rate causing ample blood loss. Tony gathers himself from the floor. Vigilare's hands on Randall's neck turn cool and clammy. Her pulse, once loud and rhythmic grows weak, her breathing rapid and shallow. She attempts to steady herself, purposely focusing, her eyes seemingly unwilling to maintain. Her grip loosening, the room begins to spin, the emerald green light flickers, vanishing. She faints, falling to the floor. Randall slides down the wall gasping for air, his nearly limp body unable to sustain itself upright.

"Vanguard PD," the identifier bounces off the walls of the hallway, accompanied by the sound of heavy boots.

Tony rushes to Vigilare, rolling her over onto her back, he applies pressure over her right shoulder.

Four officers enter the apartment, cautiously, stealthily, followed by Tony's stakeout partner, Officer Marks. "Gronkowski?" one of the officer's recognizes Tony. He motions with his hand, a signal to those following him that the scene is secure.

"Tried to tell them you had it under control, Sarge," Marks

chimes.

The officer instantly on the defensive. "Look. We got a call to this address. We gotta answer that call."

Tony nods, waving them toward the closed bedroom door. "She's in the closet. Fifteen-year-old female."

"Tessa," Randall gasps, his breath returning to his body.

Tony hatefully points his finger at Randall, seething, "Get this mother-fucker out of my sight before I kill him." He wipes at the sweat over his brow, exchanging hands over Vigilare's shoulder wound to maintain good pressure.

"I saved your life," Randall defends.

Tony lunges for him. Marks pulls him off, with the help of another officer. "You take him down to the station, and you hold him. I'm booking this piece of shit." Tony is fuming, nearly spitting with every word. His focus delivers, he returns to Vigilare.

Marks pulls Randall up by his shirt collar, handing him off to two officers who happily escort him from the premises.

"Marks, I need an ambulance, yesterday," Tony says.

"You got it, Sarge." Officer Marks paces, near Tony and Vigilare radioing dispatch for medical assistance.

The other two officers have cleared Tessa's room and are taking her statement in the kitchen as two more cops arrive on scene. "We were in the neighborhood. Heard the call. What do ya need?"

"Tess! Tess!" a woman's voice cries down the hallway. Tessa's mother enters. "Oh my God," she exclaims, her hand covering her mouth upon her initial assessment. "Tess, baby." She continues to the kitchen, embracing her daughter.

The apartment is busy. People coming and going, voices all abound. Tony is used to such chaos. Why is it then, that he is having problems focusing on anything but the lifeless body he hovers over? He palpates her carotid artery—pulsing, but faint. His hands bare of gloves, he picks the right one up off the wound where he holds pressure. He stretches his hand out, extending his fingers away from his palm, a small cut visible. Unaware of how or when he acquired it (must have been when they were sparring), it is now soaked in her blood, and tingling. A clot forms at the juncture of his cut, where her blood meets his. His curiosity beyond piqued, he grips the ski mask at her neck and slowly begins to peel it up over her face. Her lips familiar, surely his eyes play tricks on him. His heartbeat enhanced, he continues. With each new facial feature, the chatter in the apartment grows more distant, an ominous feeling befalls him.

"Sarge, ambulance is pulling up out front," Marks reports, encroaching over his shoulder.

Tony attempts to block Marks' view by leaning over her, but it's too late, her auburn hair gives it away.

"Gina?" Marks expels from his lips, his expression deeply disconnected.

Tony identifies with the surreal feeling.

"Pinch me, Sarge," Marks exclaims with serious intent, offering up his arm. "I gotta be freaking dreaming."

Tony hangs his head, wishing such was the case. "Tell them to pull up out back. We're not taking her out the front. You got it?"

Marks nods, his body inert.

"Now!" Tony barks, causing him to move to action.

The other officers hear the rise in his voice, two of them start in his direction, "You need something over here, boss?"

Tony holds his hand out to them, firmly. "I got it." His body language crouched over Gina is protective in every assertion.

They look to one another, eyebrows raised, throwing their hands up to their shoulders in retreat. Tony eyes them until they return to the kitchen. The wheels of a medical stretcher approach from the hallway.

"What'cha got?" the paramedic at the head of the stretcher inquires, guiding his crew to Tony.

"Gunshot wound. Right shoulder. Cool, clammy skin. Rapid, weak pulse. She fell out...fainted."

"Get me a line started. Both ACs. 18-gauge. Fluids, fast and furious. Possible shock," the medic orders to his partner. "You comfortable doing a 12-lead?" he asks the student rider. She nods. "Need to ask you to give us some room." He pats Tony on the shoulder.

"Sure." Tony jumps up. "Just fix her, man."

"That's what we're here to do," the medic affirms.

Tony paces, hovering over them, running his fingers through his hair, watching them work diligently.

"1, 2, 3," the medic counts as they hoist her onto the stretcher for departure to the local trauma center.

"I'm going with her," Tony states.

"Got a student rider. No room, hoss."

"She can ride with him," he points in Marks' direction. "I'm not leaving her. She's my partner, goddammit!" His eyes begin to sting, quenching the urge for emotion, he breathes deeply, calming his voice. "Do you mind riding with Officer Marks?" he asks the student.

She eyes Marks, handsome and tall. "Not at all," she says with a smile.

Tony grabs Marks, pulling him along as they accompany the stretcher. "You call Chief. Have him pull whatever strings he's got with the hospital. I want her room ready before we get there. Somewhere secure and out of the way. Two heavily armed officers better be outside her hospital room waiting to greet us. No media, no visitors, no one gets near her. No one."

"You got it, Sarge," Marks consoles.

CHAPTER 8

Vanguard General Hospital. Tony sits at Gina's bedside. She rests in the Cadillac of hospital rooms, safe and secure from the rest of the ward. As per Detective Gronkowski's request, two armed guards monitor the hallway and entrance to her room. She is listed as Jane Doe, in accordance with hospital confidentiality adherence with Vanguard Police Department in the event of an officer shooting.

She lies still, restrained in the oversized hydraulic medical bed, to which she is shackled at every joint on her body, a safety precaution upon report of her superhuman strength. She is stabilized after the medical team worked on her for half the night. It is now four in the morning. A hematologist lurks in the room, Dr. Godfrey. He is a short, thin man who wears a white lab coat suitably adorned with a pocket protector. His bifocals, way overdue for an adjustment, cause him to continuously scrunch his nose to keep them at an appropriate level to his eyes. His rolling metal desk contains a plethora of slides, tubes, and other blood testing paraphernalia. He loads a slide with a smear of Gina's blood onto his microscope, peering through the tiny lens.

"How come you guys have been taking so much blood from her?" Tony asks. "Thought you were trying to replace that. And are the shackles really necessary?" the disdain resonant in his tone.

"The most peculiar thing," Dr. Godfrey answers. Lifting his head from the microscope, he peers over his bifocals at Tony. "She is a mystery."

You can say that again, Tony thinks to himself.

"Her blood is undetectable. Most humans have one blood type accompanied by one Rh-factor. O, A, B, or AB, and Rh-positive or negative. Her blood registers as none of the above. Yet, when it's broken down to its most basic of components there are traces of O-negative, AB-negative, and B-negative. That is unheard of. Come have a look." He motions Tony to the microscope.

Tony squints with his left eye focusing his right down the barrel of the eyepiece. "Doesn't look like anything, doc. All I see is a bunch of circles."

"That's it. Those are her blood cells. You see how the center of those little discs are clear?"

"Yeah."

"Notice how the cells move around within their own space, gently bouncing off neighboring cells, but never sticking to them or overlapping?"

"I guess," Tony answers, focusing on the tiny round discs as they move under the microscope.

"That's indicative of healthy blood. The *terrain* of her blood is good. The *toxic load* is slim to none. Unhealthy blood, symbolic of an illness or depressed immune system would be sluggish in its movement. It would stick to the other cells, sometimes overlapping."

"So, this is live blood? How can blood survive outside the body?" Tony suddenly feels like he is ten years old again, in his grade school biology class.

"Oh yes. Blood can survive outside the body for several days. A *hearty* little thing—blood." He chuckles at his own dry humor.

"Yeah," Tony says with a weak smile, unimpressed.

Dr. Godfrey clears his throat. "Back to my point." He takes the slide out from under the microscope, replacing it with another. "Now, see here."

Tony peers down into the lens, acquiring an instant headache with the task of keeping up with the amount of little round discs and the momentum with which they move. A faint, sparkling emerald green hue reflects through the glass. He jerks his head up from the microscope, rubbing his eyes. "What kind of blood is that?"

Dr. Godfrey pats him on the back, smiling. "That my friend, is inhuman. Not of this world. Super blood."

"And that's her blood? Gina? My partner?" He returns to his chair beside her bed, sinking down into it, sitting forward his elbows resting on his knees, his head in his hands. "But I thought you said the first slide was her blood. How can she have two different kinds of blood?"

He waves his hands in clarification. "She has only one *kind* of blood, as we all have only one. What makes her unique is that she has three components, three different traces of blood types in her one *kind* of blood," Dr. Godfrey attempts to keep his explanation layperson-friendly. "The last slide is her blood, as was the first slide. The key, oxygen." Dr.Godfrey's eyes light up, excitement exudes out of his every movement, unable to contain his imagination. "When her blood is exposed to oxygen, external oxygen, that which is outside the body, something magical happens."

"Super blood," Tony states flatly. "Like Superman. Superhuman. Don't tell me you believe all this shit about Vigilare." He gets up out of his chair frustrated and pacing. "I've known this girl for almost a year. She transferred to the department from Chicago. She's a hell of a detective. Not some Vigilare, super freak. She's a goddamn human being!" He kicks the side of his chair.

Dr. Godfrey walks to Tony, gesturing for his right hand. Reluctantly, Tony turns his hand palm side up. "You held pressure to her shoulder while waiting on the ambulance?"

Tony nods.

Dr. Godfrey notices the cut on Tony's palm. "You know the term blood brothers? Native Americans started that tradition. They would cut into the flesh of their palm and press it against another, believing that if they were blood brothers their blood would mesh, smoothly, one into the other. No reaction. No clotting."

Tony pulls his hand from Dr. Godfrey, dissatisfied with the topic.

"The clumping that occurs when Rh-negative blood mixes with that of Rh-positive is visible to the naked eye. Did your blood react to hers? Clump? Clot?"

Tony's mind flashes back to the scene at the apartment when he pulled his hand from Gina's shoulder, tingling and covered with blood, a mixture of his and hers, and how tiny beads clumped together at the incision site of his cut. "What's that prove? That we're not *blood brothers?* That I don't carry the gene for 'super blood,'" he accentuates with air quotes, fully annoyed. "Since when did compatibility come down to blood types?"

Dr. Godfrey smiles. "Ah, I see. Your relationship to Vigilare, far exceeds that of work partner."

Tony turns swiftly to him, grabbing him by the collar of his lab coat. "Don't call her that."

"Gina," he quickly corrects.

Tony releases his grip, walks to Gina, and looks her over limb to limb. Her exposed arms display goosebumps. He pulls the blanket up over her, tucking it in around her body. "What's Rh-negative and positive?"

Dr. Godfrey is silently pleased with his question, proof that he has an interest, even if it battles with his pride. "Rh is a blood factor. The type of protein found on red blood cells. Most of us are Rh-positive, meaning we have that blood protein. Eighty-five percent of the world's population is Rh-positive. The term Rh stems from the Rhesus Monkey, linking us to primates."

"Evolution," Tony says.

"Exactly!" Dr. Godfrey excitedly walks around the other side of the bed, across from Tony. He looks down at Gina, as if she is some priceless, rare thing. "But what evolution has yet to explain is the remaining fifteen-percent of the population who have Rh-negative factor. Like our Gina here."

"What's to explain? If Rh stems from a monkey, we're all descendants of primates, right?"

"Rh-positive factor links us to the primate. Rh-negative factor has yet to be scientifically determined. Rh-negative blood is of unknown origin. Not one scientist can give a single reason for its existence. Other than to speculate it is a mutation that occurred tens of thousands of years ago."

"What does it matter, really? In the grand scheme of things? Blood is blood." Tony paces at the bedside. "When do you think she'll wake up?"

"If all mankind evolved from the same ancestor, their blood would be compatible. Where did Rh-negative factor come from?" Dr. Godfrey makes his way back to his rolling metal desk, firing up his centrifuge, its purpose to separate blood densities. "Rh-negative blood is found nowhere in nature, except in humans. It nearly acts as though it doesn't belong here. And, consider this scenario: When an Rh-negative mother is pregnant with an Rh-positive fetus, her body builds antibodies to get rid of that fetus, as if it's a foreign invader to her body, an alien so to speak."

"So, now we're bringing aliens into the mix. Superheroes, super blood, vigilares, aliens...what's next, predators?" Tony scoffs.

"Why would a mother's body reject her own offspring? The only place in nature where the same scenario occurs is in mules—a *crossbreed* between a horse and a donkey."

"Ah man." Tony interrupts. "You're reaching here, doc. Go ahead. When she wakes up, feel free to tell her she's kin to a jackass. See how far that gets ya?" He shakes his head, chuckling.

Doctor Godfrey laughs heartily, scrunching up his nose, causing his bifocals to come to rest nearer to his eyes. "My point...that fact alone says there may be a distinct possibility that two similar yet genetically different species were crossbred creating the Rh-negative factor in the blood. You see, when breeding livestock, animals of any sort, really, some believe crossbreeding creates an optimal breed, a hybrid, if you will. Taking the dominant traits of one species and crossing them with the dominant traits of another, you get the best of both, creating a stronger, more intelligent, elite species."

"Well, Gina is all those things. Cream rises to the top," Tony agrees. "But it's not because of her blood. It's her attitude, her heart, her try. That's just who she is, Doc."

"But imagine the possibilities," he says, intrigued, his mind racing. "No one has ever been able to explain where Rh-negative people come from. What is their origin? Is it a true mutation? Or do they descend from a different ancestor? If so, who? Take it back to the Native Americans."

"Back to blood brothers," Tony huffs, throwing his hands up in the air, sitting down in the recliner beside Gina's bed.

"They declared their ancestors were of cosmic origin," Dr. Godfrey continues. "Were they the *ancient astronauts*? The missing link between the earth and the stars? The missing link between primate and extraterrestrial? The hybrid man, or woman," he motions in Gina's direction.

"Extraterrestrial? Extraterrestrial?" Tony squints, attempting to make sense of this highly educated individual standing in a hospital room justifying aliens. "You're comparing my partner to E-fucking-T?"

"Well, yes, that might be a good example," Dr. Godfrey indulges. "Not exactly, but take for instance the premise that his finger glowed. Remember he touched it to Elliot's cut, and the cut healed?"

Tony shakes his head, disbelieving and disturbed.

"Now, here me out. That one scene from a science fiction movie has some truth to it, and has in fact propelled the research and use of light therapy in modern medicine. OLEDS (organic light-emitting diodes) are effective in treating skin cancer." He puts his pen down from which he has been making aggressive notes on Gina's blood and its components. "It's just as easy to believe there is some truth to ancient lore as it is to believe it is untrue."

Tony remains quiet, pondering Doctor Godfrey's opinions. Chills run down his spine as he remembers the sparkling emerald green light cascading from Gina's eyes in the apartment. Locked into his gaze, rendering him incapable of closing his eyes, or pulling them from hers. He kicks his ankle up over the knee of his other leg, settling back into the recliner. "Alright, Doc. What else you got?"

"Crossbreeding. Some hypothesize the Neanderthals were a completely separate species from modern humans...guys like you and me, said to be descendants of Cro-Magnon Man. Legend has it Neanderthals were bigger, stronger, maybe a little dense. Whereas Cro-Magnon was more civilized, of regular stature and intellect." He continues his work effortlessly while theorizing with Tony. Tony watches him, quietly impressed. "Now, consider the Basques in Western Europe, believed to be descended from Neanderthals. Some scientists will argue Cro-Magnon. Or quite possibly a crossbreed of the two."

"Your hybrid," Tony concludes.

"Exactly. The elite species. Do you know the Basques have the highest percentage of Rh-negative blood of any human population? They do. In addition, they are a physically distinct group—early maturation, bigger, fairer, large eyes, high foreheads, some are even born with extra vertebrae—a cauda, or 'tail,' if you will. A reptilian trait. Are you a Christian, Detective?"

Tony stammers a bit. "I...I guess."

"Some believe Basque could have been the original colony on earth. The original language of the book of Genesis." Dr. Godfrey shrugs his shoulders. "Blood is symbolic in Christianity, often of purity, and it's mentioned in most versions of the Bible over four hundred times. There are theories circulating that Jesus Christ could be the true descendant of the ancient astronauts. Far-fetched? Maybe. Then again, to believe, one acknowledges that He had powers beyond those of mortal man. Which brings me back to Rh-negative factor. It is also believed that Jesus had AB-negative blood, found on the Shroud of Turin. *The blood of the gods.* The rarest blood type, representing only one percent of the world's population."

"So, you're saying everybody who has AB-negative blood has superpowers. If that's the case, then why don't we have superheroes? Why do Superman and Wonder Woman only exist in the pages of a comic book?" Tony challenges.

"One percent of the world's population may seem very minute, but it is staggering. The global universe is such that one percent of the world's population is over sixty-seven million people. We can't have sixty-seven million super humans," he answers so matter-of-factly.

Tony chuckles. "Well, go ahead. Why don't you warp the logistics. Bend it and mold it, until it suits your imagination." He kicks his foot down off his knee, sitting forward in the chair, resting his forearms on his thighs. "You can't have it both ways, Doc. Either it is or it isn't."

Dr. Godfrey smiles, pleased with Tony's participation. His curiosity engaged, the wheels of his mind in action. "Now you're thinking." He raises his pointer finger in the air. "Therein lies the problem. We spend so much time and resources researching things that are concrete, proof positive, that we have no understanding of the unknown."

Tony looks at him confused, wincing his eyes as if to say, *Isn't that the reason it's unknown? Because we don't have proof?*

"You think I'm talking in circles." He pauses for a moment. "Maybe I am. My mind's not quite as sharp as it used to be." He smiles. "Soak up your youth, my friend. Get it while you got it, ya know. Anyway, where was I? The unknown. Yes. I'm simply stating that we, as humans, have this magnificent thing—a brain. Within that center, all other bodily functions are controlled. The mind controls all things. It's just that some of us don't know that. We don't know how to tap into that resource. Take the psychic for instance.

They hone in on their powers, welcoming such a distressing diversion from what most of us consider reality. The olympic athlete. Sure, they train, preparing themselves physically for phenomenal feats. But it's with their mind, their mental control that they rise to such an occasion. They have a *super* ability, if you will, strict mental resolve to make the physical happen."

"So, based on that assumption, super humans walk among us every day, without knowing they're superhuman because they haven't nurtured it, haven't tapped into it," Tony reasons, remaining skeptical.

"Eureka!" Dr. Godfrey claps his hands together. "By George, I think you've got it!" He walks to Gina's bedside, assessing her monitors, looking over her with great admiration. "Then, every once in a great while, you stumble upon a true gem. Something or someone with all the factors, all the attributes to make magic."

"You know all this sounds kind of...Dr. Frankenstein-ish, right? Do you really believe all these theories? And surely you don't expect others to believe them?" Tony rubs his hands together. "Really, you probably shouldn't talk about this stuff to just anybody. You might end up losing your medical license, or on the tenth floor of this hospital reenacting *One Flew Over the Cuckoo's Nest*." He smiles, nervously.

"Did you know O-negative blood is the purest blood in the world?" he continues without missing a beat. "The universal donor. A person with O-negative blood can donate to any other blood type, but they cannot receive from anyone other than their own type. It's incompatible with life. You think there is nothing unique about that? It has no relevance?"

Tony is silent momentarily. "I would say it makes them vulnerable...weak. If they can give to everyone else but can't receive, then they're dependent on their own kind. What's so *super* about that?"

"Match point," Dr. Godfrey credits. "So you argue, maybe O-positive blood type is superior? O-positive is the universal recipient. This blood type is the only blood type that can receive from all others and maintain compatibility with life. Also, an Rh-positive female can bare a child with an Rh-negative male, however the reverse is incompatible in the natural selection of things...without medical intervention." He wrinkles up his nose, once again hoisting his bifocals in the direction of his eyes. "Alas, who is superior? The age old question, is it better to give or to receive?"

Tony stands from the recliner, stretching his hands up over his head. "I've had all the science, hypothesizing, theorizing, aliens, superheroes, mumbo jumbo I can take for one day, Doc. All I want to know...when is she going to wake up?"

"That's up to her. She's good and stable. See here," he points to the monitor measuring vital signs. "Heart rate, blood pressure and body temperature in check. Within normal limits."

Tony notices her blood pressure is 105/72. "I thought 120/80 was normal?"

Dr. Godfrey smiles. "Rh-negative blood types usually have lower heart rates, lower blood pressures, and lower body temperatures than normal."

"Back to this again." Tony grabs a pillow and a blanket out of the linen closet, tossing them into his recliner.

"The protein in Rh-positive blood types allows them to be cloned. Rh-negative blood types lack that protein, whereby arming them with resistance to cloning. They cannot be cloned. A true original." Dr. Godfrey tidies up his work area, assembling his rolling metal desk for departure. "They also have higher than average IQs, the most reported paranormal occurrences and psychic abilities."

Tony rolls his eyes, hunkering down in the recliner. He fluffs the pillow behind his head and pulls his blanket up over his face. "Could you catch the light when you leave, Doc."

"Many are red-haired with green eyes, like our Gina." He rolls his desk to the door. "Oh, and did I mention, many Rh-negatives have keen hearing and sight. *Vigilare*—to supervise, keep an eye on." Dr. Godfrey pulls the light switch down, dimming the room. "Goodnight, Detective." He exits the room. The large steel door closes behind him, *Clink.*

Tony pulls the covers down from his face, his eyes momentarily wide with wonder, reminiscent of his youth when he would hole up in his tree house with the latest edition in the *Captain America* comic book series, his mind fully open to the possibilities. He shakes his head, nestling back into his pillow. "Get a grip, Gronkowski." He closes his eyes, drifting off to dream.

CHAPTER 9

A large, French colonial style home awaits a young woman as she pulls into the long, elegant drive. A feeling of safety and security flashes over her. Fully content in her surroundings after a long day's work. Turning the air off in her Mercedes Coupe, she relieves the engine, grabbing her briefcase from the passenger seat. As soon as her lungs are exposed to the outside air, she is reminded of the suffocating heat a Louisiana summer delivers.

"Mama!" a gorgeous six-year-old boy calls to her, running in her direction from the verandah.

A smile graces her lips. "Hey baby," she greets, catching him in her embrace, planting a kiss on his cheek.

He giggles, wiping at his cheek. "Did you leave that smoochy stuff on there? That stuff you always leave on Daddy's cheek when you kiss him goodbye in the morning."

"No baby. That loses its shade throughout the day. You know how you bite your lip when you're concentrating?"

He nods his head, cupping her face in his hands.

"Mama does that too."

"You eat your smoochy stuff? Euw!"

"Euw," she mocks, gently rubbing noses with him, an Eskimo kiss.

He returns the gesture, smiling. "I'm so glad you're home. Daddy and I waited for you all day. Daddy said it's prelobsterous they make you work on a Sunday." She carries him in her arms as she makes her way up the steps to the elaborate French doors.

She giggles at his pronunciation of preposterous. "Yes, it is *pre-lobsterous*," she concurs, nuzzling his neck, causing him to laugh.

"We made you dinner," he says proudly, pushing her hair back off her shoulders with his hands, as he has watched his father do often.

"You did!" Her expression pleased. "You're such a good boy. What'd you make?"

"Lobster."

She tips her head back, chuckling. "I should've known."

"Hey sugar," a darkly handsome man with a thick Southern accent greets her. A regular Harry Connick Jr. He leans into her for a kiss, a dishtowel thrown over his shoulder, elbow deep in lobster meat and butter sauce.

The *tap tap tap* of little paws resonate off the vintage hardwood floors. "Bou Bou!" short for Boudreaux, the little boy calls to the dog, scuttling down from his mother's arms. He scuffs his hands against the long fur of the black and white Border Collie, whose tail is without containment, winging from one side to the other.

"Ah, that smells incredible, baby." She takes in the succulent looking fare with all her senses, laying her briefcase down on the counter. "What can I do to help?"

He smiles at her. "You can shuffle off to the bathroom where a warm bubble bath and chilled watermelon wine need some company."

She moves to him, running her hands through his hair and down around his neck, softly taking his lips in her own. The little boy giggles, hiding his face in Bou Bou's fur. "And later, you can shuffle off to the bedroom where a warm-blooded woman will most definitely need some company," she whispers in his ear before heading off to the bathroom.

He snaps the dishtowel against the counter with a smile of victory and begins to sing, "'I see trees of green...red roses too... I see 'em bloom...for me and you...and I think to myself...what a wonderful world.'"

"Not that song again," the little boy jeers.

His dad hoists him up in his arms, dancing him around the kitchen, encouraging him to join in on the singing. "'I see skies of blue...clouds of white,'" they continue with their best Louis Armstrong impersonations. Bou Bou performs his own dance moves, jumping up around them, and chiming in on the singing with a howl here and a bark there.

The woman is within earshot and chuckles to herself. She pulls the crucifix from under her shirt collar, planting on it one solitary kiss, a grateful gesture.

SIX-POUNDS OF lobster, one family-friendly movie, one hot bath, and one hotter session between the sheets later, the roomy house hums quietly as its inhabitants rest in the dark, peaceful night.

"Mama?" the little boy calls from the door of her bedroom in his Superman Underoos.

She sits up in bed immediately with the sound of his voice. Her husband groans, reacting to the absence of her body next to his. "What is it, baby?"

"Bou Bou can't sleep. He keeps pacing in front of my bedroom window."

"Come here, love." She pulls the sheet back from her side of the bed.

Her husband, Lon, rolls up on his side, pulling her back against his chest as the little boy climbs in nuzzling his back against her chest. "That's what I'm talking about," Lon whispers contentedly.

The little boy giggles, pulling his mother's arm snugly around the front of his body, holding onto her hand. "Now you're the cheese, Mama," he refers to their bodies making a sandwich, in which he is usually 'the cheese.'

She chuckles sleepily, kissing him on top of his head. The moon, large and full, shines in through the bedroom window. The clouds accenting its eerie pattern, a perfect werewolf moon.

"Goodnight moon," the little boy says, closing his eyes.

"Goodnight stars," his mom finishes, their bedtime ritual.

The sound of glass shattering jolts Lon from his slumber. Bou Bou barks and growls ferociously at the heavy stomps flooding up the stairs. *Cha-chink,* the action bar of a twelve-gauge shotgun sounds before its blast resonates through the house. Bou Bou's growls are replaced by whimpers.

"Bou Bou!" the boy screams attempting to go to him. His mother grabs him tightly.

"Go to the closet!" Lon orders as he busies himself searching through his bedside stand for his .38-Special Revolver. The bullets disassembled as a safety precaution with a child in the house, he opens the cylinder.

"Hey pretty boy," a deep, gruff voice sounds from the bedroom door. Lon turns toward the voice, only time for one bullet in the chamber. *Bang!* he fires the revolver as he turns, stunning his attacker. Another man charges the room, bashing Lon in the face with the butt of his shotgun. Following him to the ground, the man continues ramming the gun into the back and side of his head. Blood seeps from his nose, mouth and ears.

The woman and the boy hide in the back of the closet, sitting Indian style on the floor up against the wall. She holds him in her arms, her hand over his mouth attempting to camouflage his sobs. The light from the moon reveals a dark shadow at the bottom of the door casing. The woman's eyes grow wider, tears forming. She holds her breath. The man Lon shot and stunned has regained his bearings as he was wearing a bulletproof vest, padding and impeding the impact of the revolver round.

"Lawyer lady," he taunts. "Come out, come out, wherever you are." He jerks the door open to the closet, holstering his handgun, walking the full length of the lavish walk-in rectangle.

"You find her?" his partner yells from the bedroom where he has bound and gagged Lon's lifeless body to a chair, purposely positioned at the foot of the large California King bed.

"I think I'm getting warmer," he jeers, hearing the labored breathing of both the woman and the boy.

She lunges at him from the corner, an iron clothes bar in her hand. She misjudges her target in the dark, the bar misses his face, falling into the bulkiness of hanging clothes. He deflects the bar from her grasp, twisting her wrist until she has no other option but to let go. The man wields the bar crushingly down onto her back, dropping her to her knees. The boy surges from the corner, coming to his mother's aid.

"Leave her alone!" he screams, banging his fists against the man's legs.

The man, in all black from head to toe, with only the whites of his eyes visible, laughs, winding up his right leg heavy with a steel-toe boot. He releases into the boys stomach, catapulting him into the air until his back hits with a staggering thud against the wall behind him.

"No!" The woman screams, on her hands and knees, reaching for her child. His body limp, the air fully knocked from his lungs.

The man kicks her in the stomach, knocking her over onto her side in the fetal position, then allows all of his weight to fall onto his knee which he buries into the side of her face. She cries out.

"What the hell's taking so long?" his partner calls, accompanying him in the closet.

"The bitch is noncompliant." He laughs, grabbing her by the hair and dragging her to the bedroom. She kicks her legs trying to get them underneath her body, only to have him jerk her down every time, handfuls of hair scattering about.

"Jesus Christ. I didn't say kill the kid. Not yet, anyway," his partner sputters, picking the boy up off the closet floor by the back of his neck.

"He's not dead. Just stunned," the man chimes, dragging the woman up on top of the bed.

"Lon! Lon!" she screams, seeing him sitting in a chair at the foot of the bed. His head, face and chest are covered in blood.

"Bria..." he gurgles, attempting to call her name, Brianna. His head hangs to his shoulder, as he has been beaten so intensely the strength to hold it upright has escaped him. He fumbles deliriously with the rope holding his arms behind his back.

She swings and kicks at the man straddling her. He remains unaffected, wrapping his hand around her neck and bearing down. She grabs at him, searching for some place to bury her fingernails. There is no flesh to be found as he is effectively covered. With swift thought, she jabs her fingers into the whites of his eyes.

"Fuckin' bitch!" he stammers, covering his eyes with his palms.

His partner busily ties the little boy, who is slowly coming to, in a chair beside his father. "Am I gonna have to handle your business too, bro?"

"Tie her goddamned hands down, man. Fuckin' whore's trying to scratch my eyes out," he confirms, still astraddle her waist.

"Daddy?" the boy whispers, regaining consciousness. He pulls against the ropes tying his feet and hands down to the chair.

The man's partner accompanies him on the bed.

"Braydon," his father calls, blood trickling out of his mouth, unable to hold his head up to search the direction of the voice.

The partner hastily grabs the woman's wrists, binding them with rope, he stretches each one out to its respective corner at the top of the four-poster bed. She writhes against him the entire time, inciting him to jerk and pull against the rope, making it burn and cut into her flesh. "Lawyer lady. Lawyer lady." He touches his tongue to the roof of his mouth, *tut tut tut* goes the sound. "This is one case you're not gonna win. You might as well quit fighting."

The man sitting on top of her finally quits seeing stars, removing his hands from his eyes, he pummels her across the face.

"Mama!" Braydon screams. "What are they doing to her, daddy? Why?" He cries.

"It's okay, baby," she soothes. "It's going to be okay. Just close your eyes, Braydon. Close them so tight. Like when you and mommy pray. Close your eyes and pray, baby."

"Shut your fuckin' mouth!" the guy straddling her orders, ripping her satin nightie from her body, while his partner secures her ankles to the bottom of the bed.

"Please. Don't do this," she whimpers, pulling and kicking against the restraints.

"Now you're not so tough, are ya, lawyer lady?" the man's partner taunts, moving from the foot of the bed to her husband. He grabs Lon's head by his hair, jerking it up from his shoulder, physically having to hold it in an upright position after the beating his neck and face took from the shotgun. He puts his mouth right beside Lon's ear. "We're gonna take turns with your wife. Look at your spread-eagled little slut. Legs wide open. She's begging for it. And the best part, you're gonna watch." He turns to Braydon, whose eyes are closed. He slaps the kid upside the head. "You too. Open your eyes."

Braydon cries, bearing down, keeping his eyes closed.

"You sorry mother-fucker," Lon attempts to raise his voice, only audible as a gurgled whisper.

"Braydon, baby, keep your eyes closed," the woman coaxes, tears falling from hers as she watches helplessly the man astraddle her naked body loosen his belt, pushing his pants down around his thighs.

"What's that?" the man exaggerates, putting his ear to Lon's mouth. "Speak up, pretty boy. You're probably used to being quiet. Lawyer lady does enough talking for the both of ya. Isn't that right lawyer lady?"

The man straddling her on the bed shoves himself inside her.

She cries out, a combination of pain and disgust. "Talked us into a ten-year sentence," he grunts, thrusting in and out of her. She closes her eyes, turning her head away from him, attempting to imagine herself anywhere but there. Pausing momentarily, he licks the side of her face, his mouth coming to rest over her ear. "But we're such good little boys, we got released early." She moans, mournfully. "Oh yeah, you like that, baby?" Her body convulses with each tearful, guttural wail released from her lungs.

The man standing behind Lon laughs. "She likes it, pretty boy. Hear your dirty little whore moan?"

With one last fit of strength, Lon throws himself and the chair backward into the man, causing him to fall back against the wall, the chair pinning him underneath. The man heaves and kicks at the chair until it tips over sideways, Lon still tied to it.

"Ha, ha, ha," the man raping Brianna laughs, his sweaty flesh grinding against her.

"Shut up!" his partner yells, getting to his feet. He positions himself in front of Lon, kicking him over and over again, until he is panting from the exertion.

"You pray, Braydon," the woman cries to her son. "Close your eyes, baby."

"'Yea, tho I walk through the valley of the shadow of death,'" he begins, his eyelids tightly pressed together, pausing to catch his breath between sobs. "'I will fear no evil...'"

"You about done?" the partner huffs, walking to the bed, pushing his pants down around his ankles and stroking himself. "I'm gonna roll her over. Fuck her like the bitch she is."

"Almost," he pants, followed by a series of grunts, releasing himself inside her. His bodyweight collapsing onto his arms, he leans over her face. "Open your eyes, lawyer lady. I got something to show ya." She turns her face toward him, a stoic calmness displayed. As she opens her eyes, he pulls the ski mask from his neck, revealing a spider web tattoo. Shedding the black fabric, his long greasy hair falls around his shabby facial scruff, maintaining his anonymity. He smiles a menacing, toothy grin, causing Brianna's recollection to surface. She is numb, silent. "What's the matter, cat got your tongue?" he says, a wicked laugh escaping his disturbed soul.

TONY IS STARTLED from his sleep by a rattling of the shackles holding Gina down to the bed. She writhes and cries with great strength, her eyes shut. Tony jumps up, bolting to her side as the monitors flash and ding signifying her vital signs have increased. Her heart rate pounding, her blood pressure surging, her chest rises and falls at a rapid pace. Nervously, Tony eyes the pins in the shackles, as if they may miraculously break with her power. He wants to touch her, wake her, console her...something, but he's not sure who he'll be addressing, Gina or Vigilare?

Now you're as paranoid as Dr. Godfrey, he scolds, reaching out to her. He gently places his hand to her forehead stroking it through her hair. "DeLuca," he speaks quietly. "Gina," he says, louder this time.

She opens her eyes, desperately searching. Much to his relief, they are not sparkling emerald green, they are dark green, the eyes of his entrusted partner.

"Oh, thank God," he sighs, grabbing her hand.

She fixates on his voice, his image before her. "Tony?"

"Yeah, baby." He smiles, pleased at her deduction. "It's Tony."

A nurse walks briskly into the room, assessing the monitors, and Gina.

"What's going on?" Gina looks to him. "What happened? Where's the little boy? Where the hell am I?" She pulls against the restraints, causing the shackles to start clinking.

"Ms. DeLuca," the nurse leans over her. "You're in the hospital. You were shot in the shoulder." She resets the monitors, quelling their incessant beeping. "Can you tell me your birthday?" the nurse asks, assessing a baseline memory.

"7, 7, 77," she rattles off.

Judy eyes the identification band around Gina's wrist, verifying her answer. "Maybe you'd like to buy my lotto tickets. Doesn't get much luckier than that," she says, smiling. "I'm Judy, your nurse. How many fingers am I holding up?" She holds up her index finger and her middle finger.

"Two," Gina states flatly. "Where's the little boy?" She looks to Tony.

"What little boy?"

"I couldn't get to him." Her eyes fill with tears.

"You were having a dream, Gina. It's not real," he consoles.

"Ms. DeLuca, are you having any pain?" Judy interjects, busily documenting her assessment.

"Yes," she says sharply.

"Where?"

She pulls against the padded restraints secured inside the shackles. "These things. They're a pain in my ass. Will you please untie me?"

Tony chuckles at her response, happy to see she hasn't lost her spunk.

Judy smiles with an understanding nod. "I'm afraid I can't do that. They're for your own safety. So you don't accidentally pull out your IV lines."

"Yeah," Gina says, dismissively.

"I'm going to report to your medical team. I'm sure they'll want to do a thorough examination now that you're awake." Judy excuses herself from the room.

Tony continues leaning over the side rail of her bed, looking her over as if he's never laid eyes on her before.

"What's really going on here, Gronkowski?" She grimaces, the pain in her shoulder building. "And why are you looking at me like that?"

He is taken aback. "You really don't know. You don't remember."

"Remember what? The last thing I remember is falling asleep on my couch after I showered. After I met with Aubrey Raines. A strange duck, that one. Nice enough, but she kept looking at me like she could see right through me. Like she knew something I didn't."

"You don't remember last night? Randall Barnes' apartment."

"Ooh, did we take him in?" she hopes. "Did he shoot me in the shoulder? That son of a..."

"Gina," Tony interrupts. "You're the Vigilare...or whatever," he blurts out.

She smiles, starting to laugh, only to quickly stifle herself due to the pain the otherwise pleasurable action causes in her shoulder. "So, I guess that makes you my sidekick." She rolls her eyes. "Batman and Robin. The Green Hornet and Kato. What kind of a sidekick does Vigilare have?" She ponders. "Just for the record, if I was her, that... whatever...I would have a much cooler name than Vigilare. What kind of name is Vi-gi-lare?" she stretches it out, fully enunciating the word.

Tony smiles with a shrug. "I think it's kind of sexy." He pauses. "Except for that eye thing you do. That's kind of spooky."

"You're freaking me out. Alright, seriously, stop kidding around, Gronkowski. What the hell's going on? And, what's that?" She looks to the crucifix dangling from the side rail of her bed, the same crucifix the woman in her dream wore. "How'd that get here?" Her mind spinning, attempting to make sense of the entire chaotic scenario.

Tony looks to the crucifix. "Dr. Godfrey hung it there." He shrugs his shoulders. "As for what's going on, I don't know where to begin. It's going to sound crazy, Gina." He paces beside her, running his hands through his hair, coming to rest on the back of his neck. "I was there, and I still don't believe it."

Nurse Judy returns with the medical team. A stream of white coats with clipboards march into the room, lining up around Gina's bed. Dr. Godfrey meanders in at the end of the line. "Mr. Gronkowski, would you care to accompany me to the waiting room?" Judy offers kindly.

He looks to Gina who shakes her head, her eyes wild and nervous at the commotion in the room.

"No. Thank you. I'm not leaving her." Gina opens her hand. Tony fills the void, placing his inside hers.

"Only for a little while," Judy coaxes. "The team needs to fully evaluate her now that she's conscious."

He stays put.

"Ms. DeLuca," a white coat addresses her. "Could you please state your given birth name?"

Another white coat shines a penlight into her eyes, peering down into them, as his cohort begins connecting electrodes to her scalp to conduct an EEG (electroencephalograph) in order to measure brain activity. They crowd around her as if she is some sort of exhibit they have come to see.

"What the hell's going on here?" Tony demands.

"Get off me," Gina says, feeling claustrophobic, her body surges with adrenaline.

"Orderlies," a white coat calls through the wall intercom.

"Orderlies?" Tony challenges. "Get your hands off her!" He starts pulling and pushing white coats away from Gina's bed.

Gina is writhing and pulling against her restraints.

Two large orderlies who conceivably could have played professional football as offensive linemen enter the room. The white coat who called them points to Tony. The men grab him, each one mashing against the sides of his neck, bearing down on the muscle, causing him a paralyzing amount of pain. As they escort him from the room, Dr. Godfrey smiles and winks at him reassuringly.

Amidst the commotion and chatter in the room, Dr. Godfrey maintains his stature, shuffling calmly to the head of Gina's bed. She continues to fight, her vital signs soaring off the charts. Her strength gaining by leaps and bounds, the pins holding the shackles together start to give way. Her head feels as though it is about to explode from the blood pulsing through it, steady and rhythmic like a drum.

"Close your eyes, my dear," he instructs, noticing her incision site holding together the gunshot wound to her shoulder is starting to tear. Blood trickles out. Something soothing and familiar about his voice causes her to obey. She closes her eyes, shielding the ever-pressing emerald green light.

Dr. Godfrey pulls a syringe from his pocket, loaded with an amnesic and sedating cocktail. He stealthily pushes the potion through her IV, quickly disposing of the evidence. "There, there," he soothes, running his thumb over Gina's forehead at the juncture of her eyes. Within seconds, her heart rate decelerates back to normal, her respiratory rate slows, her body sinks into the bed, weightless. She sleeps.

Outside in the hallway, near the nurses' station, the orderlies shove Tony off to Chief Burns before taking their position across from the door to Gina's room. They stand at attention shoulder-to-shoulder, arms to their sides, hands clasped behind their backs.

Tony rubs at his shoulders, wincing. "Who hired the Guidos?"

"The Feds," Chief Burns replies. "The white coats. They're all Feds. Got their own unit for these types of occurrences."

"You mean like Sector 5?"

Chief nods. "How is she?"

"Goddamn sci-fi shit." He shakes his head. "She was a hell of a lot better before they showed up."

The two local officers with Vanguard PD confront a woman who is requesting entry to the hallway and into Gina's room. She shows them the proper credentials and they let her pass. As she rounds the corner, Tony spots her.

"What's she doing here?" he asks Chief. "Does she have clearance?" he questions the officers. Dr. Patricia Ryan smiles at him daringly, waving her federally issued identification card as she passes him by, carrying with her a small stainless steel case.

"Psychological evaluation," Chief answers.

"She's not federal." Tony slaps his hand down on the counter. "I'm telling ya Chief, that woman is up to something. I know it! Besides Gina can't stand her ass. She's not going to get anywhere with DeLuca."

"Remember that fake, made-up blood? Forensics thought it was planted...tampered with because it wasn't natural?" Chief asks.

Tony nods.

"Gina's a match. The only match, Gronkowski." Chief scratches the side of his head. "And the skin flakes from Aubrey Raines' apartment, two matches, the dead guy and Gina. You're going to have to accept the facts, Tony. Gina isn't who you think she is."

Tony paces, biting his bottom lip, a tough truth to swallow. "Maybe. But she's not some freak show either. Some ancient astronaut...alien...crossbreed hybrid," he spews, his mind spinning with Dr. Godfrey's theories.

"Alien?" Chief asks confused. "Nobody thinks she's an alien. You alright, Gronkowski?"

"They've got her tied down in there. With iron shackles. Like she's some kind of animal."

"She's killed fifteen men, Gronkowski. That we know of. She's not exactly a law abiding citizen."

"Rapists and pedophiles, Chief. It's not like she's going out here targeting innocent people." Tony continues to pace. "Besides, she doesn't even remember doing those things. When she's the *thing*... Vigilare," Tony says, scornfully. "She doesn't have any recollection of the things she does. She didn't even know she was in Randall Barnes' apartment last night. She really doesn't remember."

Chief pauses momentarily before spitting it out. "Temporary insanity is a very common claim. Sometimes it's easier to say you don't remember, or that you weren't yourself when you did something you know isn't right."

Tony eyes Chief, shaking his head with contempt. "If Gina says she doesn't remember, she doesn't remember. End of story." Tony's mind in overdrive searches through all the acute data. "Maybe there's something, the blood thing, that makes her flip a switch, turns her into someone or something else."

"You know how ridiculous that sounds, Gronkowski? Now you sound like them. Vigilares and aliens."

"I know. But Jesus, something's not right. That wild ass sparkling emerald green light Aubrey Raines reported. That's not something she made up, Chief." Tony hovers close to him, his voice almost at a whisper. "I saw it last night. Gina's eyes. I know it sounds crazy, but as soon as that gun went off and she got shot. It was like the freaking Incredible Hulk." His voice rises as he returns to pacing. "She had power, man. Like nothing else. Held me down on the floor. In a choke hold." He smiles. "She could've killed me. I couldn't match her strength. It was unreal, Chief. And when she looked at me and her eyes were ablaze, I couldn't look away. It was like some kind of force. I swear she looked right through me, inside me, something."

Chief pats him on the back. "I think you need some rest. Go home, get some grub, a shower, some sleep."

"Barnes. He saw it. You won't take my word, ask him," Tony says flippantly. "And I'm fine. I'm not leaving her."

Chief sighs. "I didn't say I don't believe you. It's just that maybe you got caught up in the moment. Incidences have a way of exaggerating themselves. Becoming larger than what they really are. That's all. And you're not getting back in that room for hours. Could be tomorrow before they're done. They'll leave no pebble unturned. She's their property until they say otherwise. Go home."

Tony lets Chief's *pebble* ride rather than correcting him, his mind not quite as playful as usual. "She could've killed me, Chief. She didn't."

"Of course she didn't kill you. She knows you." Chief grabs him by the arm of his coat, pulling him toward the exit door. "At least let me buy you a coffee, something to eat." Tony resists. "For crying out loud, I'll bring you right back here." Tony gives in, falling in step with him.

He smiles at Chief. "You finally got one right."

"What?"

"For crying out loud," Tony exaggerates, "you finally got one right."

Chief slaps a Vanguard PD baseball cap over Tony's hair, pulling it tightly down over his forehead. "You're beginning to give me a complex here." Chief puts his thumbs inside the waist of his pants, giving them a swift hoist. "Reminds me of my third grade English teacher." He shudders with the thought. "Used to whack me on the knuckles with her ruler. English wasn't my best subject. She was a big ol' broad. Wore a girdle to iron out her figure. Made me sit in the front row right across from her desk. I just knew someday that girdle would give out and I would go home shy of an eye."

Tony chuckles. "What's with the cap?"

"Ah, got a feeling you might need it."

Tony shrugs, joking vainly, "The M.O. of a local hero."

Chief raises his eyebrows doubtfully, pushing the door open to the outside world.

"There he is!" a mob of journalists and television news reporters chime.

"Detective," a reporter approaches, shoving a microphone in Tony's face. "Is it true you brought down Vigilare?"

"Our sources say the Vigilare is female. Is this true, Detective?" a journalist inquires. "One of your own? A Vanguard PD Detective?"

Tony pulls his cap down further over his face, shoving the reporters' hands away, declining to answer.

"Viva Vigilare! Viva Vigilare!" a crowd of protestors chant.

"You should be ashamed, turning in one of your own," a woman shouts from the crowd. *Splat!* the sound resonates off Tony's back.

He turns to see her holding a carton of eggs. Instinctively he takes off in her direction.

Chief grabs him, pulling him toward the squad car. "Choose your battles, Gronkowski...Police 101."

"Oh, you want to arrest me too, big bad detective?" She picks another egg from the carton. "Always gunning for the women, huh? She was your partner. You ingrate." She wings the egg. It goes flying by his shoulder splatting onto the squad car.

"You gonna let her get away with that, Chief?" Tony quips.

"Sure am," he says slipping into the driver's seat.

"That's it. You run away little boy," the woman jeers, sticking her thumb in her mouth. "Mama's titty baby!"

Tony's eyes light up, his temper aching for release. Chief imagines the steam blowing out both sides of his ears, if only emotion were visible. "Gronkowski, get in the car. That's an order."

Tony slaps the top of the roof before ducking in and closing the passenger side door. "Freaking bra burners," he scoffs.

Another egg catapults into the air, landing directly atop the windshield, *Splat!* Chief pushes the lock button, peeling out from the street, shaking his head as Tony furiously jerks on the door handle.

CHAPTER 10

Vanguard Courthouse. Tony sits in the back of the room, unsettled, leaning forward, his elbows resting on his knees, his hands clasped together tightly. His right knee bounces up and down, a combination of an inability to sit still for long periods of time and his nerves. He hears the chatter around him as the room continues to fill up. Opening statements have been delivered, followed by a short recess, and now witness testimony and cross-examination begin. Vanguard PD guards the door to his right, culling citizens and the media, turning folks away as the room has quickly grown to capacity. Everybody in town wants in on this trial.

Tony looks around the room identifying a few familiar faces. Bonnie, Chief's secretary, sits on the bench directly behind the defendant's chair. Tony smiles at her protective, nurturing stance. A few rows up from his vantage point, he spots William Truly and his daughter, Emily, sitting shoulder-to-shoulder among the packed house. On the other side of the room, Dr. Godfrey sits, fully contented, the fascination of the case completely vibrant in his facial expression. His bench filled with white coats, inflexible in their form and expression. Hard, swift footsteps, followed by the clicking of high-heels reverberate off the vaulted ceiling. Tony turns his attention toward the sound to find the prosecutor, accompanied by Dr. Patricia Ryan, exchanging pleasantries. Tony pulls his eyes from them, looking down at the floor, for fear he may end up in contempt of court if he acts on his initial instinct.

Dr. Ryan takes a seat at the front of the room, turning around, she addresses the white coats. The prosecutor confidently flops down into his chair, his Brooks Brothers suit perfectly tailored to his long, lean frame. He leans back, crossing one leg over the other, casually resting his elbow on the table. Fluffing his thick, wavy dirty blonde hair, he acutely assesses the jury as the bailiff escorts them in.

The chatter in the courtroom rises, Tony senses her presence. His gaze shifts from the floor to Gina. She is chaperoned through the side door by Aubrey Raines. Aubrey wears a smart, stylish navy blue pencil skirt, accompanied by a tailored white silk blouse and red Jimmy Choo's. She holds a legal binder nervously to her chest.

"DeLuca," Tony mutters under his breath, displeased at her choice of legal representation.

His jaw clenches, his expression less than enthused, seeing her in standard issue prison garb. He shakes his head, disturbed at the iron cuffs formed to her wrists and ankles, joined together by one long chain running from her waistline to her feet. A string of numbers imprinted on her jumpsuit over the left side of her chest, no longer representing an honorable identification to protect and serve as her Vanguard PD badge once exemplified. Now, just a number, in a long line of numbers, identifying her as dishonorable, a criminal, attached to her permanent record for life. All the work she had done to save lives, put criminals behind bars, to serve and protect. That slate wiped clean, its relevance vanished, as she had become one of those she swore to eliminate.

Reading the dissatisfaction on Tony's face, she gives him a quick smile, returning her attention to Aubrey Raines, following her to their table in front of the judge's bench. Tony watches her, his pity quickly turning to admiration. Her long, wavy auburn hair pulled back loosely into a ponytail, a few wisps lazily cascading around her face. Her green eyes, wide and attentive, free of fear. Her shoulders squared, even the right one cradled by a sling, held high and proud, her chin up. He grins, acknowledging her position. If anyone could make shackles and a dingy blue jumpsuit look regal and distinguished, DeLuca could. She takes a seat beside Aubrey, who instructs her to remain emotionless, look straight ahead, and avoid eye contact with the jurors.

Bonnie reaches forward in her seat, tapping Gina on the shoulder, causing her to smile with recognition. Aubrey attempts to quell Gina's expression and shoo Bonnie away. The women do not oblige her intrusion. Bonnie holds up a makeup bag as an offering, to which Gina quickly nods. Bonnie makes her way through the knee-high swinging gate separating the observers from the observees. She plops her makeup bag down on the table, and kneels in front of Gina, giving her a quick embrace and a warm smile before she diligently applies a nice base powder to Gina's face. She works quickly, as she knows her time is limited. The clock on the wall sounds, *tick tock,* as the seconds slip away, seemingly much faster in this moment. 12:58pm—the proceedings set to start at 1:00pm.

"Ah, that feels so good," Gina encourages, the delicate brush gently stroking her face. Her skin devoid of and aching for anything soft and remotely feminine as of her incarceration weeks ago.

Bonnie smiles. "Are they treating you okay?" she asks intently, referencing Gina's holding cell at County.

"As best they can," she says, acknowledging their efforts to respect the fact she once was a cop, a detective, however having to reconcile that with the fact that she is now the primary suspect in a *killing spree.*

"Close your eyes," Bonnie instructs, lightly dusting them with a modest shadow, making them pop by accentuating her eyelashes with mascara.

Dr. Ryan looks on at the two women, purely disapproving. She nudges the prosecutor. He waves her off, dismissing the importance of bringing attention to them or requesting a reprimand. She sits back, purposely refusing to give them any more of her attention.

"Chief wanted to be here," Bonnie sympathizes. "Okay, open your eyes." Gina does as instructed, her eyes now luminous and calling for attention. Bonnie smiles at her work, pulling from her bag a smooth peach blush and applying it to the apples of Gina's cheeks.

"I understand," Gina says, referencing Chief's position, knowing he cannot very well show up in court in support of her, constituting a definitive conflict of interest. The local news would eat him up.

"Detective Gronkowski's here though." Bonnie lights up with insinuation.

Gina glances in his direction. His line of sight unwavering as he watches her and Bonnie intently, his mind somewhere between the dire seriousness of Gina's predicament and imagining himself inserted into the current scenario being played out by the two women. "You know you're giving him quite the show," Gina says, with a curt smile.

"That's the plan," Bonnie affirms. "A show for one, a show for all." She motions nonchalantly toward the jury. "Show them you're just like them."

The bailiff takes his place in front of the judge's entryway.

Bonnie grabs a tube of lipstick, quickly, skillfully applying its naturally appealing hue to Gina's full lips as she continues, "A woman. Soft, competent, and warm. Show them you're human."

"Am I?" Gina asks.

"All rise," the bailiff orders. "The Honorable Judge Maybelline Carter."

Bonnie smiles at Gina, gently squeezing her hand before swiftly gathering her makeup bag and returning to her seat.

"Please be seated," Judge Carter addresses the courtroom upon taking her place at the front of the room. Pulling from her pocket a pair of glasses, she situates them comfortably across the bridge of her nose to read from the docket placed on her desk, reviewing the case.

Gina situates herself into her chair, slightly off balance due to the heavy irons, causing the links in the chains surrounding her frame to clink and clank, pulling Judge Carter's attention. Gina gives her a respectful, slightly embarrassed, apologetic nod. The judge shakes her head.

"Bailiff," she requests. He comes to the front of her bench. "I know we can find a way to avoid such racket." Reading between the lines, he immediately maneuvers to Gina, keys in hand, diligently removing cuffs and shackles. "Ms. Raines," Judge Carter reads her name from her file, unfamiliar with her presence in the courthouse.

"Yes, Your Honor," she answers, her voice breaking, giving in slightly to her nerves.

"Is this how you advocate for your client?" She motions her arm in Gina's direction. "Allow her to walk into a courtroom with chains and shackles hanging off of her? You might as well stamp 'guilty' on her forehead. Either image is one in the same."

Aubrey clears her throat, looking to Gina. Gina nods her head supportively. "If you hadn't requested they be removed, I...I would have, Your Honor," she replies, thinking quickly on her feet.

"Judge Carter," the prosecutor, Mr. McVain addresses.

"Yes, Counselor," she turns her attention to him.

"If you will read through the charges, you may reconsider un-cuffing the defendant, Your Honor. She has murdered fifteen men... that we know of. In quite gruesome fashion."

"Mr. McVain, you'll have plenty of opportunities to make your case. And might I advise you busy yourself with your responsibility, I will tend to mine." She smiles coyly. "I need not reconsider uncuff-ing the defendant. I *have* read through the charges."

"I would not insinuate otherwise, Your Honor," he says.

Judge Carter shakes her head, motioning to him, "Your first wit-ness, Counselor."

"Defense calls Gina DeLuca to the stand," Aubrey says boldly, standing to attention.

A low rumble is heard among the room. Judge Carter is caught off guard. Gina looks to Aubrey as if to say, *It's not your turn.* Mr. McVain chuckles, confidently.

Judge Carter softly bangs her gavel, causing the buzz in the courtroom to cease. Crossing her hands into one another, she leans forward across her desk, her expression a mixture of contempt and pity. "Ms. Raines, if you'll follow up on your criminal court procedures, you'll find the prosecution usually kicks off this process." She points to Mr. McVain. "He prosecutes, you defend. Understood?"

Aubrey nods her head, dropping her chin, the blush of embarrassment fully visible on her face.

"Your first witness, Counselor," Judge Carter repeats to Mr. McVain.

He smiles, remaining seated. "Ladies first," he says in his most chivalrous tone. "That is, of course, if you don't mind, Madam Judge."

Tony rolls his eyes, fatigued by this guy already.

Judge Carter grants him a quick, less than enthused smile. She is well aware of the prowess of Counselor E. Blaine McVain, his last name superbly fitting. Handsome, keen and slick as a snake, he has all the makings for an extremely successful lawyer. His record flaunts a perfect win, to this point. "Go ahead, Ms. Raines."

Aubrey clears her throat, standing cautiously. "Defense calls Gina DeLuca," she says quietly, her confidence wounded.

Tony runs his hands through his hair, pressing his back against his seat, folding his arms rigidly across his chest. His leg resumes its incessant bouncing, his mouth dry as cotton as Gina approaches the bench. She takes her oath and settles into the elevated swivel chair beside Judge Maybelline Carter.

"Ms. DeLuca, please state your occupation," Aubrey directs, standing before the witness rail. Gina eyes Aubrey, her shoulders slouched, she timidly hugs her legal file to her chest. Mindfully, Gina exaggerates her own posture, her back straight and solid as a board, her chin leveled, her ears resting anatomically correct over her shoulders. As she does so, Aubrey begins to mirror her physical presence with her own. Gina smiles at her reassuringly.

"I'm a detective with Vanguard Police Department."

"Objection," Mr. McVain interjects, pleased at getting one in this early in the process.

"Was," Gina quickly corrects herself, her eyes darting in his direction, annoyed. "I was a detective with Vanguard Police Department."

"Not just any detective," Aubrey points out, turning to face the jury. "The most highly-decorated female detective at Vanguard PD. Ms. DeLuca was Valedictorian of her police academy. And she is the current Vanguard PD Detective of the Year, as voted by her cohorts."

Mr. McVain smiles effectively, appropriately, a good showing as he takes notes at his desk.

Aubrey opens a file, laying it in front of Gina. "Do you recognize any of these men, Detective DeLuca?" The file contains photos of the fifteen slain men.

"Objection," Mr. McVain bites. "Her detective status has been suspended."

"Sustained," Judge Carter says.

Aubrey nods.

"Yes, I recognize all of them."

"How is that, *Ms.* DeLuca?"

"My partner and I were assigned to the case."

"The Vigilare case," she leads.

Gina shrugs. "If you want to call it that."

"Let me clarify. You are being accused of killing these men. Men whom you were assigned to find justice for." Aubrey moves away from the bench, placing herself between Gina and the jury. "Have you ever killed anyone, Detective DeLuca?"

"Objection." Mr. McVain flippantly slaps his hand down on his desk.

"Sustained," Judge Carter says, growing annoyed. "Ms. Raines, don't let it happen again."

Aubrey nods. "Let me rephrase. Have you ever killed anyone, *Ms.* DeLuca?"

"Yes," she answers. The courtroom stirs to an audible buzz.

"In the line of duty?"

"Yes."

"In defense of your life or the life of another?" Aubrey clarifies.

"Yes."

She holds her index finger up in the air, accompanied by a dramatic pause. "Now, have you ever murdered anyone, Ms. DeLuca, in cold blood?"

"No," she says. "Not to my knowledge."

"*Ob*-jection," Mr. McVain accentuates, holding out the syllable. "You haven't murdered anyone, *to your knowledge.* One would think simple yes or no answers would be a breeze for such a decorated detective."

"A simple yes or no answer will suffice," Judge Carter directs Gina. Her attention immediately returning to Mr. McVain, "And, I'll thank you to keep the sarcasm limited to the water cooler."

"No, I have not murdered anyone, in cold blood," Gina clarifies. Unable to rein in her tongue, she continues, "And one would think the inclusion of simple commentary would be a breeze for a Harvard-educated lawyer."

The courtroom is a mixture of disgruntled mumbles and pleased chuckles, as Mr. McVain and Gina now communicate with their eyes, assisted by the most powerful communicator, their body language. Her response stirs Tony up, causing him to smile. Judge Carter launches a reprimanding glance at Gina and Mr. McVain.

"Do you believe in superheroes, Ms. DeLuca?" Aubrey quickly quells the atmosphere before Judge Carter takes the liberty.

"I guess I do," she ponders. "Yes, I believe in superheroes," she states, cleaning up her answer before Mr. McVain objects again. "Everyday, ordinary people. They're superheroes."

"Police Officers, Teachers, Firefighters, Soldiers? Ordinary people, pulling off the extraordinary," Aubrey leads.

"Yes."

"What about superhuman superheroes? Vigilares? Do you believe in Vigilare?"

"I have a tendency to believe what I see. I've never seen Vigilare." She looks to Mr. McVain purposely, simply waiting for him to object to her circular answer. He does not.

"I believe in Vigilare," Aubrey says. "I've never seen Vigilare either, but I felt her presence."

Mr. McVain tosses his pencil down on his desk. "And I'm Superman," he scoffs.

"Is that an objection, Mr. McVain?" Judge Carter questions.

"No, Your Honor. I am, however, curious as to when we are going to get beyond speculation to the facts." He flips his hands through his hair ruffling the blonde locks, simultaneously swiveling in his chair addressing the jury and the courtroom at large. "I understand Ms. Raines is fresh out of law school. That's why I granted her the privilege of going first. But, come now, I'm ready for substantiation. Some concrete evidence."

He receives a few nods from the jury and the crowd.

"I would appreciate it if you would address me when spoken to, Mr. McVain," Judge Carter recalls his attention. "And, Ms. Raines, I'll thank you to think about where you're going with your current line of questioning. Proceed."

"There have been reports. Documented reports that you are the Vigilare. Are you Vigilare, Ms. DeLuca," Aubrey asks, with an almost starry-eyed gleam.

Gina shuffles her bodyweight from one hip to the other in her chair. "If I am Vigilare, I have no recollection of it."

"The fifteen men who were murdered, most likely in self-defense, as all CSI reports reflect a struggle of some sort, were convicted rapists and pedophiles. Do you believe those men deserved to die, Ms. DeLuca?"

"No. I believe they should be tried in a court of law and sentenced in accordance with the severity of their crimes. If I believed in vigilante justice, I certainly wouldn't waste my time jumping through all the legal hoops as a detective."

"Let the record show, my client has no memory of being Vigilare and she empathizes with the fifteen victims, believing they should have had a right to fair and just treatment in accordance with the law," Aubrey concludes. "Thank you, Detective...Ms. DeLuca," she quickly corrects, taking her place at the defense table.

Mr. McVain, in exaggerated fashion, pushes himself up from his chair. He removes his suit jacket, laying it nonchalantly across his desk. As if that gesture wasn't enough to say *the gloves are off,* he continues, rolling up the sleeves of his neatly pressed, white button-down shirt, purposefully drawing out his approach to the witness chair.

Gina intuitively sinks back into her chair, propping herself against it, rather than remaining attentive. Her arms fold across her chest, displaying closed and completely disinterested body language.

"Ms. DeLuca," he begins. "You were a detective for several years. A highly-decorated detective, as we have learned." He extends an arm to Aubrey Raines. "What are the chances a person murders fifteen men, on fifteen different occasions, all in self-defense, without premeditation of some sort, or without intent?"

"Slim to none."

"Is it possible the reflection of a struggle reported by CSI in each incident was not initiated by the victim? Could it be indicative of each man defending himself against the perpetrator?"

"Anything's possible."

"Ms. Raines made a point to acknowledge the fact that you do not recall being the *Vigilare,* who at this time is considered the primary suspect in this string of murders." He shakes his head at the very premise of a Vigilare. "Am I correct in assuming your counsel may be headed toward a temporary insanity plea."

"You know what they say about assuming, Mr. McVain."

He smiles. "Yes I do, Ms. DeLuca." Walking back to his desk, he pulls two evidence bags attached to files from his briefcase. "Therefore, I shall rely on concrete evidence." He holds the bags up to Aubrey Raines as he passes by her desk, making a beeline for the jury, sure to drive home the point of substantiation. "So far, we've heard only speculation. I give you evidence. Fact." He holds up the bag in his left hand. "Blood. A very rare and distinct blood type, matching only that of the defendant. Found at eight of the fifteen murder scenes." His left hand returns to his side as he hoists the bag in his right hand. "Skin. A perfect match to Ms. DeLuca. Found at one of the fifteen murder scenes. Two different types of DNA on one rope used to strangle the victim to death. The skin of the victim, and the skin of one Gina Marie DeLuca." He walks to Judge Carter, handing her the evidence bags. "Ms. De-Luca is a fan of circular answers," he says, eyeing her. "Making two relative statements, garnishing a proposed outcome. What would you make of such evidence, Ms. DeLuca?"

She leans forward in her chair, resting her forearms on the rail-ing separating her from Mr. McVain. "I would say, if it walks like a duck, talks like a duck, and looks like a duck...it must be a duck, Mr. McVain."

He props himself against the railing, catty-corner to Gina. She does not flinch with his closeness, simply maintains eye contact. "You're quite indifferent to this whole process aren't you, Ms. De-Luca? Are we boring you?" He gestures to the jury and the court-room at large. "Do you have something more important to do with your time?"

"Objection," Aubrey Raines intercedes.

"Slay another human being, perhaps?" he asks.

"Sustained," Judge Carter confirms.

"Who will it be this time? A rapist? A pedophile?" Mr. McVain continues, walking away from the witness chair, his hands shifting up and down alternatively symbolizing a scale, his voice on the rise and projecting to the back of the courtroom.

"Objection!" Aubrey stands.

"Sustained," Judge Carter warns again.

"Maybe an ordinary Joe? Your brother?" He points to a juror. "Your son?" He extends his hand, making eye contact with a woman midway back in the courtroom. The place erupts at a low rumble. Tony watches, both legs nearly clearing air as they bounce feverishly off the bench beneath him, his system surging with pent-up adrenaline.

Judge Carter beats her gavel. "Counselor, one more leading statement, and I'll have you in my chambers."

He holds his hands up at shoulder level, a sign of retreat, returning to the space in front of the witness bench. "Ms. DeLuca, do you remember the first person you ever killed? In the line of duty?"

"Yes."

"Do you remember the second?"

She sits back in her chair, reasoning his line of questioning. "It's not like smoking your first cigarette, or saying your first cussword. It doesn't get any easier. Even if they are criminals."

"A regular martyr," he sputters. "Ms. DeLuca, do you have any children?"

"No, I do not."

"Any sisters?"

"No."

"Female friends?"

"Not many."

"Have you ever been the victim of rape or sexual assault, Ms. DeLuca?"

"No." Growing agitated, she continues, "If you're trying to establish a motive, you're wasting your time, Mr. McVain. I have no personal experience with rape or pedophilia. I have no reason, nothing harbored in the recesses of my being to justify taking an active stance in killing men convicted of such crimes." She leans forward in her chair. "Now, if you want to know, am I capable of killing a rapist...a pedophile? I think we all are. If a man assaulted my body without my consent or the body of someone I loved, especially an innocent child, then yes, I'm sure I would be capable of murder. Why don't you just ask me what you really want to ask me? Did I murder those men?" She props her hands up on the railing, one crossed into the other. "The truth is, I don't know."

"Here we go again," he scoffs. "That's not an answer Ms. De-Luca. That's why I have to beat around the bush, finding questions and ways to ask them to find out the truth, because you seem to have reverted back to childhood. 'Jenny, did you break the lamp?'" he mocks in a fatherly tone, speaking to a young child. "'I don't know,'" he replies in a childlike manner. "Once again, either you did or you didn't. Yes or no, Ms. DeLuca." He slaps his hand down on the railing in front of her.

She slaps her hand down harder, drawing a berated reaction from Judge Carter.

Gina nods, toning it down, her vocal cadence controlled, but still biting. "I have no recollection of killing those men. I have no recollection of being some Vigilare. Check the polygraph report. It will verify my answers to be true. Unless of course, you think I *beat* the lie detector."

"Are you saying the evidence was planted? You were framed?" he challenges. "The report given by your fellow officers, Sam Marks and Tony Gronkowski, finding you at the scene of the attempted murder of Randall Barnes, in full *Vigilare-mode,* dressed in black from head to toe...that was a lie?" He turns toward the courtroom, pointing out Tony and Officer Marks. Both of them, displaying sympathy mixed with contempt on their faces. "When Officer Gronkowski..."

"Detective," Gina corrects him. "Detective Gronkowski."

Mr. McVain shakes his head agitatedly. "When *Detective* Gronkowski pulled the black ski mask from *Vigilare's* face—your face—that was a lie? Somebody was impersonating you?"

"Don't put words in my mouth," she warns quietly through nearly gritting teeth. "If Officer Marks and Detective Gronkowski say that was me under the ski mask, then it was me. I don't deny that. What I am saying is, I have no recollection of that moment, nor any other moment involving myself as some Vigilare, killing rapists and child molesters. No matter how many times you ask me, or how many different ways you rephrase the question, you're going to get the same answer—I have no recollection. *I...don't...know.*"

"You seem to have all the answers, Ms. DeLuca. At least when it suits your point. So, just exactly how do you propose I continue?" he beams sarcastically.

"Objection," Aubrey Raines speaks up.

Judge Carter, annoyed yet strangely amused, responds, "Sustained."

"I *propose* you do your job, Counselor. Is that too much to ask?" she beams back sarcastically. "Instead of strutting around here, flipping your golden locks, putting on a show, why don't you try talking less and showing more. Hell, you've got my blood and my skin, what more do you need? Let the evidence speak for itself."

"Language, Ms. DeLuca," Judge Carter scolds routinely.

Mr. McVain approaches the witness chair, smiling, running his fingers through his *golden locks*, clearly pleased that she mentioned them. "I guess that's what I'll have to do. Let the evidence speak for itself, because conveniently, you have no recollection, and cooperation from your Vanguard PD counterparts seems relatively akin to pulling teeth. Mums the word." He places his arm across the railing in front of her, leaning in curiously with his body. "So tell me, just exactly how did you get Detective Gronkowski wrapped around your pretty little finger?" he asks with full insinuation of a sexual relationship.

Gina smiles charmingly, leaning in toward him with her body in kind. "You think I'm pretty?"

Her response causes quiet laughter to surface through the courtroom, with a few exceptions. Dr. Patricia Ryan sits stiff-armed, unimpressed at the interplay between the two, as does Tony.

"My courtroom is not an appropriate arena for foreplay," Judge Maybelline Carter curbs any further repartee. She thumps her gavel with authority, sending a ripple of silence through the room. "Bring it back around, Counselor, and Ms. DeLuca."

Mr. McVain smiles at her cunningly. She nestles gracefully back against her chair. "A *Vigilare* in sheep's clothing," he says, pulling away from her. "Femme fatale or sly fox?" he builds an image for the jury.

"I assure you, I'm not that complicated," Gina replies.

"How would you know? You claim you don't even know if you're the said *Vigilare*." His mannerisms have softened, no longer interested in sparring, he seeks the truth.

A moment of ingenuousness passes between the two. "Follow the evidence." Addressing the jury, she continues, "Trust your instinct. Somewhere between evidence and instinct, therein lies the truth." She focuses her attention back to Mr. McVain and the courtroom at large. "Two weeks ago I thought I knew who I was, Gina DeLuca, Detective, Vanguard PD. Now, I'm not so sure. I woke up in a hospital bed surrounded by a bunch of strange faces." She gestures to the white coats. "Poking and prodding me, testing this and testing that. As if I am some kind of *thing*, inhuman." With the words, the emotion hits her. She looks down at her lap, refocusing her mind before making eye contact again. "You think I want to run around killing people in the middle of the night? As a cop, I took an oath to serve and protect. If I am the...*Vigilare*," the word barely audible, as if it hurts to say. "If I have murdered fifteen men, in cold blood, then find me guilty and punish me to the fullest extent of the law."

The courtroom is silent.

Mr. McVain could easily clap dramatically, sarcastically, and comment on what a *noble* declaration she makes. He does not. He simply unrolls his shirt sleeves, attaching the buttons at his wrists as he walks back to the prosecution desk. "No further questions, Your Honor."

CHAPTER 11

"You may step down, Ms. DeLuca," Judge Carter dismisses her. "Your next witness, Counselor."

Aubrey Raines looks to the judge, a humble grin on her face, showing understanding that she is referring to the prosecution. Gina takes her seat next to Aubrey.

"The prosecution calls Dr. Patricia Ryan."

Dr. Ryan makes her way hastily to the witness stand, as if she has something to say that can barely wait to be heard. If attractive and precise were ever to mesh into one definition, she would be that word in the dictionary.

"Please clarify where you work, and in what position," Mr. McVain directs.

"Vanguard Police Department. Doctor of Psychology."

"What is your relationship to the fifteen victims?"

"They were all in my care at some point in time for the city's rehabilitation program. Three years ago, the city mandated any man or woman, convicted of rape or sexual assault of a child or an adult, must undergo psychological rehabilitative counseling for the duration of their probation, quite possibly even longer."

"What is the purpose of such a program?"

"To prepare them to be better citizens once they return to society."

An audible huff is heard from William Truly, garnering a disciplinary glance from Judge Carter, her head cocked, hand positioned over her gavel should he feel the need to continue. His daughter pats his arm, quieting him.

"In your opinion, does the program work?" Mr. McVain continues.

"For some," she keeps it short, without elaborating, refusing to make eye contact with William Truly. She can feel his eyes burning through her.

Mr. McVain holds up several notable psychological journals. "You're quite the celebrity in your field, Dr. Ryan."

She neither confirms nor denies the statement, allowing her work to speak for itself.

Mr. McVain addresses the jury, "If anyone has doubts as to the qualifications of Dr. Patricia Ryan, her numerous studies and innovations within the professional psychological realm speak for themselves. She's quite the trailblazer, especially in the topic of rehabilitation, as it pertains to sexual misconduct among criminal populations." He stacks the journals neatly on top of many other journals, providing a visual tower of Dr. Ryan's work. "We're not here to talk about your involvement with the deceased, however." He runs his hand across the railing in front of the witness stand, making a circle until he stands between Dr. Ryan and Gina. "What is your relationship to Ms. DeLuca?"

"As a psychologist for Vanguard PD, I was asked to monitor her case and mental well-being after the discovery that she fancies herself the *Vigilare.*"

Gina nudges Aubrey. "Objection," Aubrey blurts out. "My client has never *fancied* herself the Vigilare."

"Sustained," Judge Carter advises.

"Is it accurate to assume you worked with Ms. DeLuca and her partner, Detective Gronkowski, in their assignment to the case?"

"Yes. I had the pleasure of meeting and collaborating with them both."

Gina and Tony roll their eyes at the same time, both of them crossing their arms over their chest and sitting back, unimpressed.

"What is your personal opinion of Ms. DeLuca?"

She crosses her hands, one over the other, her expression and her body language softening. She looks to Gina and smiles. "I find Ms. DeLuca to be a fine individual and a top-rate detective."

Gina does not soften her position, remaining sunk back in her chair, arms closed across her torso, simply waiting for the venomous shrew to strike.

"A little misguided, though," Dr. Ryan finishes, a deeply concerned expression settling across her face.

"Misguided?" Mr. McVain asks.

"Impulsive, eager. Quite possibly positive traits, if directed in the appropriate manner. However, borderline dangerous if mixed with desperation. Creating an outlaw of sorts. On the few occasions I interacted with Detective...Ms. DeLuca, her intensity was exasperating."

"She was nervous? Antsy?"

Dr. Ryan nods. "She would say things. Alarming things about the victims. Asking me if I believe they reap what they sow. And very protective of her files regarding the case."

Gina slaps her hand down on the witness table in frustration, earning another reprimanding glance from Judge Carter. She hastily scribbles notes onto Aubrey's legal pad.

Dr. Ryan looks down at her hands lying in her lap momentarily, purposefully as if Gina's actions scared her.

Mr. McVain plays to her, "What is it, Dr. Ryan?"

"The rope burn. I saw Ms. DeLuca the morning after the incident with Aubrey Raines, her current legal representation, which, might I add, I believe to be a conflict of interest. Ms. Raines was nearly raped, in her bedroom while studying for the Bar exam. The alleged rapist ended up strangled to death in the corner of her bedroom. The rope used to strangle the alleged rapist is the one you speak of, Mr. McVain, the one that carried two types of DNA, the skin of the alleged rapist and the skin of Gina DeLuca." She pauses.

"I saw Ms. DeLuca the day thereafter, and she had a visible rope burn on her neck."

"Visible rope burn? And you're the only one who saw this pivotal evidence?"

"No," she says defiantly. "Her partner, Detective Gronkowski." She points to him in the back of the courtroom. "He saw it too."

Mr. McVain circles the floor, shaking his head and clicking his tongue off the roof of his mouth, much like a mother would admonish a child who has done something inappropriate. "Why would Detective Gronkowski keep such evidence a secret? Evidence that was obviously pertinent to his case."

"Therein lies the issue," Dr. Ryan confirms. "It is my opinion, after careful psychological evaluation, that Gina DeLuca is of astute sound mind. She is not insane, nor was she temporarily insane at the time of the murders, even though she testifies she has no recollection." Dr. Ryan's speech becomes more direct, confident and biting. "Ms. DeLuca's IQ is off the charts. We're looking at a highly intelligent, competent woman, equipped with the appropriate goods in the form of beauty and a *bangin' body,*" Dr. Ryan resorts to slang to make her point. "There is a perfectly good reason Detective Gronkowksi would keep such pivotal evidence a secret. The wiles of female seduction. It's not a new concept," she retorts.

"Objection," Aubrey defends. "Speculation, Your Honor."

"Sustained." Judge Carter's perturbed tone spurs Mr. McVain to get to his point.

He fluffs his hair, approaching closer to Dr. Ryan. "Under your evaluation, does Ms. DeLuca have any pressing psychological issues that would result in temporary insanity—multiple personality, or any other condition thereof that would cause her to *turn into* a Vigilare or alter-ego, calling for the death of fifteen men?"

"No," she states very matter-of-factly. "After thorough psychological evaluation, Gina DeLuca is of sound mind, perfectly sane. If you reference her medical file, you will find my conclusion is doubly backed by two federally employed psychologists." She points to the white coats. "Who spent nearly a week at her bedside, thoroughly evaluating and documenting her every move and thought."

"Thank you, Dr. Ryan." Mr. McVain takes a seat, victoriously.

"Your witness," Judge Carter addresses Aubrey Raines.

Aubrey approaches Dr. Ryan, her inner and outer selves at odds. Externally, she appears calm and confident, her body language proud. While on the inside, she feels as if her stomach turns somersaults, its contents sure to be regurgitated.

Dr. Ryan inherently, and at this point subconsciously, intimidates with her arrogant posture and pretentious glare.

Aubrey swallows hard. "Dr. Ryan, you say your rehabilitation program helps 'some.' Exactly how many is 'some?'"

Dr. Ryan looks at Aubrey as if the question certainly does not require an answer.

Aubrey takes another step closer to the witness stand. "Isn't it true that rehabilitation rates of sexual offenders are quite slim?"

"Ms. Raines..." Dr. Ryan begins.

"So slim, in fact," Aubrey cuts her off, predicting a pompous, indirect answer, "that on a national scale, only three percent of sexual offenders are fully rehabilitated. The remaining ninety-seven percent will continue to offend, or turn to other illegal activities. Isn't that correct, Dr. Ryan?"

"Not exactly."

Aubrey waits for her to elaborate. She does not. "What is the success rate of your patients? How many repeat offenders do you treat?"

"The national scale is based on statistics. Statistics of standardization, variances, select groups. There are people who defy statistics every day."

"The tests you gave Ms. DeLuca to verify her sanity...aren't they standardized, variant? Are you discrediting statistics?"

Dr. Ryan's chin slowly settles from its arrogant position until it is leveled, her eyes narrowed, her head cocked slightly to the side. She has Aubrey Raines in the center of her crosshairs. "What I am saying, Ms. Raines, is that rehabilitation is subjective. What may be a simple step for one, may be a leap for another. The national scale is correct, give a percentage or two. However, it does not take into consideration, the varying degrees of rehabilitation. It's very linear in it's outcome."

"What is the success rate of your patients, Dr. Ryan?" Aubrey continues, her focus unwavering.

"Higher than the national average."

"The number, Dr. Ryan. What is the actual number, in terms of percentage?" Aubrey further jabs.

"I don't know the exact percentage." Dr. Ryan grins provokingly. "That answer should sound familiar to you," she says, referring to Gina's previous answers regarding her status as the Vigilare.

Aubrey grins back, her confidence growing. "Isn't it true that all fifteen of those men in your care were repeat offenders?"

Dr. Ryan does not answer.

Aubrey picks up a journal, Dr. Ryan's subpoenaed journal, and begins to read from its entry. "'Thomas Sinclair, 32 years of age. Two prior counts of rape. Served a total of 18 months for both offenses. Released six months ago. Remains resistant to rehabilitation. Continues to attempt manipulation and blame tactics. Closed to acceptance and positive coping strategies. I fear he may repeat-offend.'" Aubrey turns the page. "I can continue, Dr. Ryan."

"Yes," she says. "They were repeat offenders." She crosses one leg over the other. "That proves nothing. All addicts fall off the wagon occasionally."

"Addicts? Now there's a disease for sex offenders? How convenient." Aubrey turns to the courtroom at large, extending her arm and index finger. "Can you identify that man?"

"Yes."

Aubrey waits quietly, as if to say, *Well then, go ahead.*

"Randall Barnes," Dr. Ryan clarifies.

"Mr. Barnes is in your care as well?"

"Yes."

Aubrey flips through the journal, searching for his name.

"Two previous counts of sexual misconduct," Dr. Ryan offers.

"With a child," Aubrey adds. "One, a 15 year old boy, the other, a 12 year old boy. And currently, he is being tried for the attempted rape of a 15 year old girl." The courtroom lights up, a-buzz with protest. Randall is protected by two police officers, one to the right of him, the other to the left.

"Objection," Mr. McVain asserts. "Randall Barnes is not on trial here."

"Sustained," Judge Carter concurs.

Aubrey slaps the journal down on the defense table. The sharpness of the journal against the wood regains the attention of the room. "Sounds like rehabilitation is working great for him."

"Ms. Raines," Judge Carter further addresses her, "your novice status in the courtroom has garnered you a few exceptions. However, it does not excuse you from the obligation of conducting yourself appropriately."

Aubrey nods, her attention pulled back to Dr. Ryan.

"Just exactly what do you propose we do, Ms. Raines? Unleash a lynch mob and promote vigilante justice? It's an ignorant society that thinks it can bring about change through the employ of fear and force."

Aubrey approaches nearer the witness chair. "You seem to have great sympathy for these men. Have you forgotten they rape women and children?"

"Most of these men were victims of sexual abuse, as well as other forms of abuse. Where do you think they learned such behavior?" Dr. Ryan reasons.

"Victims?" Aubrey questions, disbelieving. "When exactly did the predator become the victim?"

"You tell me," Dr. Ryan responds, her touché aimed directly at Gina.

Aubrey moves on. "Isn't it true Detective Gronkowski, the same detective you so willingly dragged through the mud in your earlier testimony, saved you from becoming a victim? Randall Barnes' victim?"

"That's a bit of a stretch, Ms. Raines," Dr. Ryan responds, a haughty chuckle emerging.

"You're denying Detective Gronkowski walked into your office when Randall Barnes had you pinned in a vulnerable position, holding you by force?"

"I had full control of that situation," Dr. Ryan snaps. "Detective Gronkowski broke in like some macho male chauvinist, eager to save the damsel in distress." She leans forward, her hands resting across the railing of the witness chair. "I assure you, I am no damsel."

"I am well aware of that fact," Aubrey scoffs. "In fact, at one time you were considered a suspect in the murders."

Dr. Ryan chuckles. "Sure I was. Detective Gronkowski needed someone to take the fall for his gal pal."

"Who better to be involved in the alleged murders than the psychologist who has access to pertinent information concerning the men—their cases, previous arrests, current addresses, everything."

"Objection," Mr. McVain calls.

"Sustained," Judge Carter repeats. "Dr. Ryan is not on trial here, Counselor."

Aubrey affirms. "You stated earlier that Detectives Gronkowksi and DeLuca were protective of their files and lacked empathy for the deceased. You were describing yourself, weren't you, Dr. Ryan?"

"I have to be protective of my files. Patient confidentiality is key in my line of work," she responds, unshaken.

"Did you tell Ms. DeLuca you believed the department had its priorities screwed up, focusing on the deaths of convicted rapists and pedophiles, when they could be helping innocent people?"

"Not in so many words."

"Okay," Aubrey circles the area in front of the witness stand. "I have a question that requires only one word, yes or no." She faces Dr. Ryan, her eye contact intense. "Do you believe any of the fifteen deceased men were capable of rehabilitation?"

Dr. Ryan meets her eye contact with equal intensity. "No."

"In your professional opinion, would they have repeated past behaviors of rape and sexual assault?"

"Yes."

"Do you believe those men deserved to die?"

"*Deserved* to die? No. Better off dead? Yes," Dr. Ryan clarifies. The questions and answers fly off one another, surprising Gina and Tony, and nearly offending Mr. McVain.

"Do you believe the murders may have been in self-defense? Is it possible the men were, in fact, repeating old patterns, and Vigilare came to the rescue?"

"Yes. And yes, except for the Vigilare reference. I do not believe in such nonsense," Dr. Ryan clarifies.

"I know it to be true. The Vigilare. She saved me."

"Objection. Testifying. She's an attorney, not a witness," Mr. McVain spouts, his tone completely disinterested as if he can no longer bear Aubrey's lack of experience.

"Sustained." Judge Carter follows her ruling with an exasperated glance toward Mr. McVain.

Aubrey regroups. "Others believe in the Vigilare, as evident by the rally held at City Hall." She looks around the room, a few heads nod affirmatively. Her attention returning to Dr. Ryan, she continues, "Why do you believe the men are better off dead?"

"Maybe they can finally be at peace," she says very matter-of-factly.

"And maybe their victims can, too," Aubrey adds.

Dr. Ryan nods.

"To clarify, you believe the defendant, Gina DeLuca to be clinically sane?"

"Yes."

"And, you believe the murders, of all fifteen previously convicted rapists and child molesters, could have been committed in self-defense?"

"Yes."

"No further questions, Your Honor." Aubrey takes a seat beside Gina at the defense table.

Dr. Ryan shares an unexpected respectful glance with Gina as she passes her after being released from the witness stand. Tony remains confused, albeit pleasantly so, by her seemingly purposeful contradictory testimony, unclear as to her angle.

CHAPTER 12

J udge Carter eyes the clock. "Your next witness, Counselor."
"Prosecution calls Dr. Bernard Shaw." Mr. McVain remains seated until Dr. Ryan makes her way back out into the courtroom and
Dr. Shaw, of the white coats, is sworn in and takes his seat in the
witness chair.

"Please state your occupation," Mr. McVain directs his witness.

"I am Chief Medical Director for the U.S. Government, ETNA
Division," a surprisingly quiet, high-pitched voice emerges from a
tall, robust frame.

"What exactly is the ETNA Division?"

"We deal in the supernatural. Anything that may be out of the
ordinary."

"Unidentified Flying Objects? Aliens? Things of the like?" Mr.
McVain questions, with a disbelieving smile.

"Something like that." Dr. Shaw smiles back. "You may be surprised at what we find, Mr. McVain."

"I'm sure I would be." He drags his hands through the length of
his hair. "Vigilares...you ever heard of such a thing?"

"Not until this case."

"You were brought in to test Ms. DeLuca. Is that correct?"

Dr. Shaw smiles again. "I wouldn't exactly refer to it as a *test*." He
shifts his weight, propping himself onto his elbow in order to better
face the jury. "We observed Ms. DeLuca. Our job, to find anything
extraordinary."

"Did you? Find anything extraordinary?"

"Yes. Ms. DeLuca has a very rare blood type." Dr. Shaw looks to Gina, pride in his inflection. She rolls her eyes, unimpressed, as her memory of the white coats poking and prodding her for days was anything but extraordinary. "The only one in the world, that we know of, to exhibit such a blood type."

"What is the significance of this blood type?" Mr. McVain leads.

"At this point, the only significance is that Ms. DeLuca is truly unique. One of a kind." Again, he smiles at her, beaming, further annoying her.

"I wish he'd quit looking at me like some kind of lab rat," Gina mutters to Aubrey, swiftly turning her attention from him.

"We may not know the significance, if any, for some time," Dr. Shaw continues, causing Gina's ears to perk up.

"Other than the blood, did you find anything extraordinary about Ms. DeLuca that would lead you to believe she could be superhuman...a *Vigilare?*"

"For some time?" Gina questions aloud, causing Mr. McVain to turn in her direction.

"Shh," Aubrey directs.

"Oh, I'm sorry. Ms. DeLuca, would you like to question the witness?" Mr. McVain says sarcastically.

"Are you hoarding my blood?" Gina ignores Mr. McVain, her question directed at Dr. Shaw.

"First, you try to tell me how to do my job. Then, you try to do it for me," Mr. McVain needles.

"Order," Judge Carter demands, banging her gavel. "Ms. De-Luca, your Counsel will have plenty of time to ask questions during cross-examination."

Dr. Shaw says nothing, a grin surfacing on his lips.

"You son of a bitch," Gina snarls, leaning offensively across the defense table.

Mr. McVain grabs at his chest dramatically at her outburst.

Aubrey gently takes hold of Gina, coaxing her back down into her chair.

"Order!" Judge Carter bangs her gavel incessantly until the courtroom quells. "Ms. DeLuca," she continues, wielding her gavel in Gina's direction. "One more outburst and I'll hold you in contempt of court." Gina leans back in her chair, her arms folded defiantly over her chest, her eyes fixed on Dr. Shaw. Judge Carter shakes her head, momentarily tidying herself and her desk. "Proceed, Mr. McVain."

"My apologies Madam Judge," he says. "We'll attempt to maintain some semblance of civility." He looks at Gina accusingly. His efforts wasted, as she refuses to draw her stare from Dr. Shaw.

Unimpressed with his aggravating attempt at chivalry, Judge Carter remains mum, her lips pressed firmly together. She hastily motions toward the witness, urging Mr. McVain to carry on.

He does so expeditiously. "Did you find anything substantial that would lead you to believe Ms. DeLuca is the Vigilare? Superhuman strength? *Sparkling emerald green eyes?*" he reads disbelieving, from the compiled reports.

"Unfortunately, we did not," Dr. Shaw replies.

"Unfortunately?" Mr. McVain asks.

"The possibility is exciting." Dr. Shaw's eyes widen with wonder. "Reading through the reports, we expected to find something... someone truly extraordinary. We don't get much satisfaction in the ETNA Division. A lot of potential. Some promise, every now and then." His manner growing flat and disappointed. "But, most of the time the things and people we investigate are just exactly that, things and people. Maybe once every fifty years, we truly find that diamond in the rough. That one connection to life outside of Earth."

"Is Ms. DeLuca that diamond in the rough?"

"Unfortunately, no, she is not. We monitored her for a full week, twenty-four-seven, round-the-clock. We never witnessed the sparkling emerald green eyes, nor the superhuman strength." Dr. Shaw meets Gina's glare. "We did, however, witness a strong character with much resolve, unwavering in her attitude," he says, putting his hand up to the side of his mouth, his lips visible to the jury-side and continues, "which could use some adjusting at times." He smiles. "She can be very accommodating or extremely noncompliant."

"How so?"

"She would pull and push and kick against the restraints, swearing like a sailor, during standard procedure testing," he embellishes. "Nothing painful, simple psychological and physical evaluations. Sometimes to the point of convulsing and knocking herself out, completely unconscious. We tried several times to witness Ms. De-Luca in the state of the Vigilare. Each time unsuccessfully."

"It is my understanding her temper was such that you actually lost a few team members, because they refused to work under such conditions."

"Oh yes," Dr. Shaw confirms. "Very retaliatory. We were testing bone density and strength...for super bones, super strength, which we did not find, of course. However, she managed to finagle the device away from the tester and used it on him...mashing down, nearly breaking his radius...his forearm bone." Tony, still seated in the back of the room, can't help but chuckle with the image.

"Dr. Patricia Ryan testified that Ms. DeLuca is of sound mind. Would you and your team agree?"

"Oh yes."

Mr. McVain nods. "Thank you, Dr. Shaw." He proceeds to the prosecution table.

Judge Carter signals to Aubrey. She stands, shimmying her pencil skirt down a smidge until the hem settles mid-kneeline. Making her way around the table, she holds a pen in her hand, subconsciously working it between her forefinger and her thumb, continuously pulling the cap off and pushing it back on.

"I witnessed the sparkling emerald green light," Aubrey begins before catching herself, stopping abruptly in hopes of deterring Mr.

McVain's objection at her testimony. She glances at him. He smiles boastfully and winks at her, letting this one slide. She quickly regroups, spotting Tony and Randall Barnes in the courtroom. "Two individuals have reported seeing the sparkling emerald green light. What do you say to that, Dr. Shaw?"

He ponders momentarily. "I am inclined to believe there are those individuals who want to see something so desperately, they may eventually see it, even though it wasn't physically present."

"So, we imagined the sparkling emerald green light?"

"It's not that you imagined it. You wanted to see it so badly, your mind may actually be convinced you did. It's the same premise as the kid who watches the movie E.T. and wants so badly to have the same experience, that every passing plane with a light becomes E.T. Or, better yet, Santa Claus. Every parent wants their kid to experience Santa Claus. At Christmastime, any pleasantly plump individual with white hair and a white beard to match may fit the bill." He shifts in his chair. "The world is full of wonder, and it's natural to want to be a part of that, to believe and experience things that may be possible but not quite tangible. It's the mystery that makes it magical. That's why this city is in an uproar right now. You've got citizens who want something to believe in, so desperately need something to believe in, that they too have latched onto the possibility of a Vigilare."

"I assure you, Dr. Shaw, what I witnessed was not a figment of my imagination."

"Objection." Mr. Vain does not let this one slide.

"Sustained."

Aubrey nods, simply pleased that her statement reached the jury's ears regardless. "What I'm getting at, Dr. Shaw," she begins, "there are those who have witnessed Gina DeLuca as Vigilare. Do you propose we discount those records simply because you did not witness such? And we are to assume anyone who believes in Vigilare does so because they need something to believe in? You may consider giving my fellow Vanguardians a little more credit, Dr. Shaw."

A few muffled cheers are heard from the courtroom, quickly quieted by one repressing glance from Judge Maybelline Carter.

Aubrey continues, "What are the skills required to effectively observe a Vigilare? Do you have the appropriate skills to do so? Is it possible that Ms. DeLuca is exactly that diamond in the rough you are looking for, but that you simply do not know how to tap into her?"

"The skills?" he questions, offended.

"Yes. Instead of restraining and tying Ms. DeLuca down like some vile, dangerous thing, poking and prodding her for hours on end, did the thought to observe her in her natural environment ever occur to you?"

"Oh, I don't know why that thought never occurred to me," he begins sarcastically. "Could it be the fact that the reported Vigilare murdered fifteen men and was also reported to have superhuman strength? Yes, let me volunteer to watch her...*it*...in its natural environment. Do you hear yourself, Ms. Raines?"

"Has the fact escaped your mind that the only people Vigilare retaliates against are evildoers? In self-defense, or in the defense of others."

"Objection," Mr. McVain interrupts. "Speculation."

"She did not kill me. She did not kill Detective Gronkowski," Aubrey continues.

"Sustained..." Judge Carter begins.

"She almost killed me," Randall Barnes yells out from the back of the courtroom.

Aubrey flings her arm out in his direction, her index finger accusing in its position. "A credit to my point," she scoffs.

The courtroom erupts with a rumbling of voices and quick glances.

"Order!" Judge Carter reprimands, her trusty gavel finding its way to the wood block repetitively until the crowd idles. She aims the end of her gavel in Randall's direction. "I've read your file, Mr. Barnes," she says with full contempt. "You, sir, are treading on thin ice. Consider this your first and last warning. Open your mouth again, when your derriere is not in the witness chair, and I'll see that it's shut for you." She returns her attention to Aubrey assertively. "Wrap it up, Ms. Raines."

"Roswell, New Mexico, Area 51...ring any bells, Dr. Shaw?" Aubrey asks.

By his facial expression, he identifies what she is referring to. "Those files are top secret," he states, bewildered at her knowledge of them.

"A light force found in the sand. After ETNA Division's inspection, under your direction, deemed to be a child's toy of some sort. Russia's SPLUNKIN Division, similar to your ETNA, inspected the same site, and took the light force home with them. The same light force that won them the prestigious International Metaphysical Science Award, for its possible link to the ancient astronauts. And here you are discounting another supernatural wonder."

"We tested that light force for days," he defends.

"The same way you tested Ms. DeLuca for days," Aubrey cleverly derives. "No further questions, Your Honor."

CHAPTER 13

"Dr. Shaw," Judge Carter addresses him. "You may step down." She waits until he leaves the bench, returning to the courtroom. "Mr. McVain, how many witnesses do you have left this afternoon?" she asks as she eyes the clock.

"Two, Madam Judge."

"Just as well. Proceed, Counselor."

"The prosecution calls Randall Barnes to the witness stand," Mr. McVain states, once again rolling up his sleeves and fluffing his abnormally abundant locks. Gina watches him, partly intrigued, mainly annoyed. She chuckles to herself, barely audible, and looks away.

Randall Barnes walks apprehensively to the bench, his eyes shifty and darting, his hands visibly shaking, his voice almost a whisper as he is sworn in.

"Mr. Barnes, do you need a moment," Mr. McVain asks him out of earshot of the jury.

Randall's knee jitters against the witness railing as he bounces it up and down. Placing his hand over his knee, the nervous tick ceases. His face is as white as a ghost, beads of sweat surface on his forehead.

He shakes his head. "Let's just get this over with."

"We'll keep it short," Mr. McVain assures, assuming his position between Randall and the jury. Clearing his throat, he speaks up into a leading statement, "Mr. Barnes, you seem nervous. Scared. You're safe here."

Randall wipes his brow with his forearm. "No, I'm not. No one's safe with her around." He points at Gina, looking away quickly, unable to maintain eye contact. "She stalked me. Trapped me in an elevator. Almost let me fall to my death. Then, she hunted me down, like a predator hunts down its prey, and tried to strangle me," his voice on the rise, becomes more confident. "She would've killed me if he hadn't stopped her." He points to Tony. Tony's jaw clenches, disappointment surfacing as he curses himself, a fact he is not in the least proud of.

"You were with Ms. DeLuca and Detective Gronkowski in your girlfriend's apartment the night of the attempted murder on your life, correct?"

"Yes."

"Briefly describe the scene for me, for us?"

"She broke into the apartment, carrying on with her wicked banter about how she was going to kill me and I was going to pay. Reap what I sowed. For such a fan of the Bible, I swore I was in the company of the devil." Randall grins, amused at his play on words.

"Continue," Mr. McVain leads him, quickly.

"Then, that guy comes barging in." He identifies Tony again. "They get into a fisticuff, go rolling around on the floor, and before I know it she has him pinned on the floor, strangling him. I thought she was going to kill him. So, I grab his gun...the gun she took from him earlier. I aimed it at her and pulled the trigger."

Gasps are heard throughout the courtroom.

"I had to do something," Randall rebukes. "Don't let her fool you. She is not some superhero Vigilare. She's ruthless and evil. A cold-blooded murderer."

"Objection," Aubrey calls.

"Sustained," Judge Carter agrees. "Please refrain from elaboration and personal opinion, Mr. Barnes. Stick with the facts."

Mr. McVain jumps in, assisting him back to his point, "You pull the trigger, and then what happens?"

Randall shakes his head, still in disbelief as he replays the scene over again. "She got up and came after me. Really! The bullet went through her shoulder when she was choking that man. And, I'll be damned if she didn't get up and come after me. I'm telling ya, she's one determined freak."

Mr. McVain motions with his hand to Randall, a calming gesture, simply waiting for Judge Carter to reprimand Randall for his cursing and name-calling. She let's this one slide. "When she came after you, what did she do?"

"She choked the shit out of me, that's what she did," Randall answers, adrenaline continuing to run through his system.

"Mr. Barnes," Judge Carter speaks his name. "I know you're nervous. Testifying is no easy task, but you must refrain from using profanity in my courtroom."

Mr. McVain gives her an assuring nod. "One more point, Judge."

"When Ms. DeLuca was strangling you, was she facing your direction?"

"Yes. She was looking right at me."

"Her eyes were open?"

"Yes."

"Were they emitting a sparkling emerald green light?"

"What?" Randall acts as though he's never heard or seen such a thing.

"The sparkling emerald green light Ms. Raines speaks of, constituting Ms. DeLuca as the Vigilare...of something out of this world. Did you witness such a light?"

Randall huffs. "No. All I witnessed was a crazed lunatic trying to choke the life out of me."

"You're a lying piece of shit, Barnes," Tony pipes up from the back of the room. "You saw the same thing I did. You said so in the police report."

Randall looks to Mr. McVain, who nods his head reassuringly, giving Randall a mimed *shush* with his lips.

"Detective," Judge Carter advises.

"Lying piece of..." Tony sputters, trailing off his words before further instigating Judge Carter.

She gives Mr. McVain the go ahead to continue questioning. He turns back to Randall. "You asked for help from Vanguard PD when you were being stalked, is that correct?"

"Yes."

"Who did you report to at the police department?"

Randall points to Tony, quickly shifting his eyes away from him.

"Detective Gronkowski," Mr. McVain clarifies. "Did he help you?"

"No," Randall says flatly. "He took my statement, then turned me away. Told me he didn't have to do a 'goddamned' thing for me." He looks to Judge Carter. "Sorry Judge, that's what he said." He returns his attention to Mr. McVain. "Said he hoped she got to me before he did."

Tony nods in agreement, with total disregard for pretense. Gina smirks, as her mind allows her to imagine Tony saying those exact sentiments in his own endearing manner.

Mr. McVain parades toward the prosecution table, disgust and a total lack of reverence exuding from his expression and body language, as if he simply cannot tolerate any further testimony on the subject. "No further questions, Madam Judge."

"Ms. Raines," Judge Carter signals to Aubrey.

Gina notices how Randall smiles, ogling Aubrey as she stands to approach the witness chair. She calms her urge to say something, reminding herself not to distract from Aubrey's line of questioning.

"Looks like he got to you before she did," Aubrey clarifies snarkily, reciting *unfortunately* to herself. "You're awful eager to bury the guy who saved your life."

Randall's smile dissipates, replaced with subtle anger.

"Let's see if you're as forthcoming with your own truths," Aubrey challenges.

"Objection," Mr. McVain charges. "Counsel's interrogating the witness."

"Sustained. Simple Q & A will suffice, Ms. Raines."

"What were you doing in your girlfriend's apartment that evening, Mr. Barnes?" Aubrey asks.

"Babysitting," he says, shortly.

"Babysitting whom?"

"My girlfriend's daughter."

"Tessa?"

"Yeah," he says, his demeanor cocky as he leans back in his chair, casually flopping his arm upon the bench, eyeing Aubrey up and down.

Gina clenches a pencil in her hand, snapping it in two attempting to curb her desire to reprimand him. Mr. McVain clears his throat, begging Randall's attention.

Judge Carter takes him in with her eyes, her brow furrowed intensely, less than impressed at his arm disrespectfully resting in her personal space. "Sit up," she commands bluntly.

Randall sits upright. Although his posture has been adjusted, his attitude and body language scream defiance.

"Tessa," Aubrey quickly circles back around. "I spoke with Tessa and her mother this morning. They inform me the proceedings for their sexual assault case against you are going quite well."

"Objection," Mr. McVain states. "The witness is not on trial here."

"No, he is not," Aubrey agrees. "However, it is imperative to this case to clarify just exactly what he was doing prior to his run-in with Vigilare. It establishes a motive of self-defense. And, it establishes a pattern, one where Vigilare is rescuing victims, much like a hero, rather than a cold-blooded villain."

"Overruled," Judge Carter interjects. "You may continue, Ms.

Raines. Do so carefully."

"On the night in question, did you follow Tessa into her bedroom, hover over her bed, touch her inappropriately, asking if she'd ever made it with a boy, and would she like to?"

"No," Randall huffs and puffs. "She's fifteen. She's going to say anything to get attention,"

"Tessa and her mother testify Vigilare is a hero. If she hadn't arrived, they believe you would have raped Tessa. Would you? Have raped her, Randall?"

"No." His eyes darting about. "I was tucking her in, that's all. She must've misunderstood."

"Like Rudy Sangino and Tiffany Darcy? I'm sure they misunderstood your intentions, too. That's why your DNA was found on the body of, and inside Tiffany Darcy, and surely why Rudy Sangino was able to describe, in great detail, your anatomy and what you made him do to it."

Randall's face reddens. He grows angry.

"Oh, excuse me. Am I offending you, Mr. Barnes?" Aubrey bites. "Is that cause for you to make threats about pinning me against the wall and pulling my skirt up over my head, like you did in your rehab session with Dr. Ryan?"

"Objection," Mr. McVain jumps in.

"Sustained," Judge Carter backs him. "You've made your point, Ms. Raines. Move on."

"'The freak lunged at me. Threw its hands around my neck and squeezed. Its eyes. I couldn't look away from them, and they shined like a ray of green light, burning mine,'" Aubrey quotes. "Does that statement sound familiar, Randall?"

He looks at her, without answering. His expression still laced with contempt, fully retaliatory and pissed off.

"That's the statement you gave to Vanguard Police Department hours after the incident at your apartment with Vigilare." She walks closer to him, forcing him to look at her.

He does not answer, only continues to boil.

She presses on, "You do realize you're under oath, right? It's so rare and off the wall...'a ray of green light.' Why would you even mention such a thing to Vanguard PD, if you never really saw it, as you stated here, earlier?"

His lip quivers, his jaw clenching, attempting to hold back venomous words, unsuccessfully. "Why would you wear a tight blouse hugging every curve of your tits if you didn't want it. You stand there and chastise me," he stands from his chair, pointing his finger in Aubrey's direction. "You're asking for it!"

"Mr. Barnes," Judge Carter begins.

A loud clatter is heard from the defense table. Gina flips the entire table onto its surface in her effort to get to Randall.

"And I'm gonna give it to you. You little slut, bitch..."

The words from Randall's mouth are muted by Gina's hands grasping around his neck as she leaps up onto the witness stand, pummeling into Randall. The force knocks him back into his chair.

"Order!" Judge Carter shouts. The courtroom explodes. Dr. Ryan looks to Mr. McVain, who stays seated at the prosecution table. He returns her glance, shrugging his shoulders and throwing his hands up in the air.

Tony stands in the back of the room, making swift progress toward the front. The bailiff heads him off as two guards grab hold of Gina, pulling her from Randall. Aubrey goes to her side, as the guards hold her at bay, perched in front of the witness stand.

"Order!" Judge Carter adamantly bangs her gavel.

Tony watches Aubrey talk quietly to Gina, stroking her arm. The guards continue to hold her, one on each side. Aubrey feels moisture on her hand at the same time Tony notices a trickle of red running down Gina's forearm.

Shit! Aubrey and Tony choke simultaneously to themselves. Tony motions across the courtroom to Dr. Godfrey, who watches the scene with a gentle smile. He too notices the blood, the smile quickly vanishing from his expression. Dr. Ryan now catching sight of the sticky red substance running down Gina's arm, eyes Dr. Godfrey, a concerned expression overriding her usual dicey demeanor. He reaches in his pocket, for his ever-trusty syringe, pulling himself to a standing position.

Judge Carter shakes her head at the entire scene and continues to bang her gavel, waiting momentarily for the commotion to pass.

Randall wipes his hand across his face, blowing air out of his puffed cheeks, symbolizing a close call. His fingernails exhibiting traces of Gina's skin, accompanied by a red tint. He sits back in his chair, his heart pounding fast and furious as Gina's picks up its own rhythm. Feeling brave with her containment, "What's the matter, cat got your tongue?" he says, smirking, the question sticking in his mind from his run-in with her in the elevator.

The question rings through her head, echoing. An image of herself behind the prosecution table flashes through her mind. She shakes her head, but the snapshots keep coming. Randall is replaced by the guy with the spider web tattoo on his neck. She is questioning him. Gina closes her eyes trying to focus, unable to as the steady thud of her internal pulse begins to race, keeping time in her head, once again as strong and audible as a drum.

"That's it, close your eyes, Gina," Aubrey coaches as she busily tears the sleeve off her blouse, wrapping it around Gina's arm, attempting to fully cover the exposed flesh and blood. "Just breathe."

Gina obeys, inhaling, a task that seems to take forever, filling her lungs. The expansion of her ribcage nearly causing her pain, the surging of her muscle fibers begins with each extra oxygen molecule delivered to them via her air and blood exchange. The images continue to flood her memory. She is crawling from a bed, the sheets and her body covered in blood. She feels limp and lifeless. It takes every ounce of her strength to get to the foot of the bed, where she plummets off onto the floor weeping at the sight of a man and a little boy.

"You can't come back here," Judge Carter's directions to Dr. Godfrey sound hollow and detached as Gina hears them ripple through the air, temporarily interrupting her memory. Dr. Godfrey is met by the bailiff at the gate to the prosecution table, leaving Tony unaccompanied. "Detective," Judge Carter turns her attention to him as he slips through the gate on the defense end. Judge Carter bangs her gavel repetitively, as the courtroom chatter rises once again. "Detective, take your seat."

"DeLuca," Tony speaks her name gently, approaching her. The guards to each side of her brace themselves, tightening their grip around her shoulders as her resistance grows with each *lub dub* of her heart. "Stay with me," Tony coaxes, his hands firm and familiar, placed on each side of her hips.

With the touch of his hand, the snapshots begin again. The man and little boy lay on the floor of the bedroom, heads side by side, their feet at opposite ends. The boy's hand lies still, firmly tucked inside his father's. The blood from their bodies pools around them, forming an all-encompassing circle.

Aubrey stands in front of Gina, having fully covered the blood from her arm. Gina opens her eyes, attempting to stop the images of the man and the little boy. Her eyes instinctively dart around Aubrey, swiftly falling on Randall. Once she zeroes in on him, the outer silhouette of her iris begins to sparkle emerald green.

"Gina," Aubrey beckons. "Detective," she calls to Tony, readily bracing herself in front of Gina.

"DeLuca," Tony keeps his voice soothing and low. "Not here." He steps even closer to her until his firm, perpetually swollen chest rests against her back. Gina's eyelids settle, as lash meets lash with his closeness. One more image of the man and the little boy is delivered as she sees herself, her head nestled beside theirs, her hand under the boy's, cupping it tightly against his father's. Her final tears shed into the mixture of blood cascading over the wooden floor.

She opens her eyes, empty and hollow now. Solitary tears, one from each eye, mimic those of her memory, trailing down the side of her face. Aubrey quickly and gently extinguishes them. The tiny sparkle on the outer rim of Gina's large, almond-shaped green eyes flickers, much like a light bulb dimming out.

"Court dismissed," Judge Carter sputters, fully perturbed and exhausted. "Show's over. Everybody out. I should hold the lot of you in contempt."

"Good enough," Mr. McVain agrees, packing up his briefcase, leading the white coats and Dr. Ryan out of the room.

"Guards," Judge Carter addresses the men continuing to hold Gina. "Take her back to County."

"My client's sincerest apologies, Your Honor," Aubrey offers.

Judge Carter nods her head dismissively, simply ready to be free of the chaotic courtroom. "Detective," she calls to Tony.

Oh great, he mutters to himself. *Here we go.*

"Can I trust you to take Mr. Barnes to the station?" she asks. Tony looks at her perplexed. "I want him booked to the fullest extent for assault of an attorney and disruption of a court of law."

"Yes, Ma'am," Tony happily confirms, making a beeline for Randall.

The guards finish re-shackling Gina, escorting her to the side door.

"Viva Vigilare! Viva Vigilare!" chants erupt sporadically throughout the courtroom.

Judge Carter smacks her gavel, finally cracking the handle. "Get out of my courtroom." She throws her hands up in the air, motioning for the bailiff. He helps her down from her podium and accompanies her through the exit.

CHAPTER 14

She, who knows not of her power, purpose nor her gift,
Unaccepting of such burden,
Surely awaits the spell to lift.

Visions, confusion, her flesh bleeds of crimson red,
Eyes sparkle emerald green,
Voices, heartbeats, sounds of raging thunder in her head.

Involuntary of her body, instinct leads the way,
Akin to the lone wolf,
Trudging bravely into evil, is she predator or prey?

If all things happen for a reason, the sunshine, rain and snow,
If the ones she loved lie dead,
When will it, too, be her time to go?

A mission left unfinished, two wrongs for a right?
The chosen one emerges,
A Vigilare, the keeper of the night.

Midnight. Vanguard County Jail. Gina lies on her back on the dingy mattress free of a sheet, her eyes focused on the ceiling. Her dinner, from six hours earlier, remains fully intact on its tray in front of the sliding barred door. Footsteps saunter down the hallway, stopping in front of her cell.

"Didn't care for dinner?" The voice certainly not the one she expected.

A slight grin immediately forms on her lips. "How'd you get in here? Wait," she quiets his reply. "Let me guess...your charm," she says, playfully rolling her eyes as she sits up on the edge of the bed. "Ah man," she chirps, her taste buds poked and watering.

"From Aniello's," Tony says, carrying a pizza under one arm, a six-pack of lager under the other. "Pizza Margaret," he famously fumbles the name with a wide smile. "Your favorite."

"Margherita," she snickers. "Pizza Margherita, Gronkowski." His last name rolling off her tongue, something routine and familiar, provides her with comfort. "Just exactly how do you propose we do this?" she asks, walking to the cell door, assuming he will have to sit outside the door as she sits on the inside.

Dangling a key in front of her, he grins, shrugging his shoulders. "Night guard at the front, she and I were in the same academy. We used to..."

Gina holds up her hand. "I don't care to know what you used to do."

"Jealous?" he inquires playfully.

"What if I am?" she spars back.

He shakes his head, chuckling. The turn of the key offers up a *cha-chink* as the lock is released. Internally, Gina feels quite excited by both the prospect of the pizza as well as human interaction, especially with Tony. Externally, she maintains, controlling the urge to throw her arms around his neck as he slides the door back and steps over the threshold. Tony is thankful his arms are full of pizza and beer, or he may not have the willpower to refrain from throwing them around her. She sits on the concrete in front of the bed, crossing her legs, one into the other. Tony does the same, setting the large, flat cardboard box down between them. For the moment, neither one speaks, exchanging glances and preparing for a much-needed meal, simply enjoying the comfort of being together again, even if not as partners. Tony flips the box open, divvying out two slices of pizza while Gina pops the tops of two beers.

"Hmm," she sounds as the first bite of pizza hits her palate, her eyes open momentarily. "Spit it out," she says, identifying the urgency in Tony's face.

He wipes his hands in his napkin, washing a bite of pizza down with some lager. "The elevator. Randall Barnes," he speaks in clues first. "Your DNA was never found at that scene, right?"

"Right. But it wasn't found at a few of the other scenes either. Apparently, when, and if I'm Vigilare, I'm pretty crafty." She smiles weakly.

"Dr. Ryan. Her DNA was found on a strand of hair from the elevator."

"What?"

"Yep. I turned her in to CSI then as a suspect. It's public record. No favors." He grins.

"Her hair could've been on Randall, from the incident in her office," Gina defends.

"Could've," Tony agrees. "But, maybe not."

Gina starts on her second piece of pizza, finally finding some comfort in food after being exposed to three-squares of *slop* while incarcerated. "You still think she's involved somehow." Gina shakes her head. "You were in the courtroom today. There's one major suspect in this case, and you're looking at her. Hell, you're one of the only people to witness me in *Vigilare-mode* and live to tell about it." Guilt and shame audible in her confession. She looks around the cell, and at Tony. "Aren't you scared? Of me?"

He chuckles. "No, DeLuca, I'm not scared of you. If you were a threat, you would've taken me out that night at Randall's. You didn't. Aubrey, Tessa, me...you or Vigilare," he shrugs his shoulders, continuing, "knows the difference between good and evil, somehow. I think it's that eye thing you do." He throws his napkin into the cardboard box, a sign of bowing out of the eating arena, opening one more bottle of lager, his dessert. "Besides, there has to be a logical explanation for this Vigilare thing. And she...you...it...whatever." He shakes his head. "Has to be a direct extension of you. And I know that's good and just. You have to trust yourself, Gina."

"But, if I'm *Vigilare,*" she says, still half disbelieving, "and I killed all those people, don't you think I deserve to be punished?" She pushes her food away, instantly devoid of an appetite.

He gently tugs at the collar of her standard issue, navy blue prison top. "I think you have done the city a favor. Look at all the people at City Hall, and this afternoon in the courtroom. 'Viva Vigilare, Viva Vigilare,'" he whispers the catch phrase, a grin forming at the corners of his mouth. "They need someone to believe in. And quit saying *if.* There are no *ifs,* DeLuca, you're Vigilare."

"Now you sound like Dr. Godfrey," she dismisses, pulling away from him.

"Where's your sling, anyway?" he asks, noticing the arm sling has been removed from her right shoulder.

"I've been healed up for days. Aubrey thought it would look good in court. Empathy," she says with a slight roll of her eyes.

"Healed?"

She nods her head. "Wouldn't believe it, if I didn't see if for myself. Barely even a scar left."

"Speaking of, Aubrey. What in hell caused you to choose her as your counsel? Can I see?" He positions his hands over her shoulder, anxiously.

She turns her head to the side as he slides the rather loose shirt collar down over her right shoulder. "She asked if she could represent me. A favor, she said. I didn't have a whole lot of options. Who else is going to represent me, with my DNA at eight of the fifteen homicides?" She shrugs her shoulders. "I like her. A little inexperienced, but her heart's in the right place."

"I guess," he agrees. "Just wish you had someone a little more accomplished. Ruthless," he adds.

"Like Mr. McVain," she huffs, disapprovingly.

"Pompous ass. But he's good at what he does," Tony grudgingly acknowledges. "You upping your workout?" he asks, the sensuous swell in her arms and chest quite prominent.

"What else do I have to do in here?" She swallows the urge to emit a pleasurable sound effect as Tony traces his hand lightly over her shoulder, searching for evidence of the gunshot wound. "Lower," she directs. "Besides, if I have to be a *superhero,* I need to be up for the job, right?" She chuckles.

"Good to hear you laugh," he says, tracing the small exit wound scar before turning her slightly to check out the entry sight.

She pulls her hair out of his way, wisping it over her left shoulder, exposing the right side of her neck and back. He studies her seriously, his closeness a bit unnerving.

"I think I might wake up sick, on my death bed tomorrow morning," he says.

"You can't get out of it, Gronkowski."

"I know. I just don't think I'm going to help your case any. No matter what I say, McVain is going to twist it to his favor."

"Let him twist it. All you have to do is tell the truth," she says, her voice low and relaxed, trailing off her words. Her head ducks to her chin, eyes closed as Tony inspects her flesh. The heat from his hands, his cool expiration causes her skin to tingle, displaying goosebumps along her spine and up her neck.

"This is amazing," he says, his fingers tracing the even smaller entry wound over her shoulder. "Nobody heals this fast. Let me guess, Vigilares do."

"So says Dr. Godfrey. Something with the blood," she mumbles, distracted by his touch.

He encircles his arms around her waist, pulling her back into his chest. "Are you scared?" he asks, referencing her feelings on the trial, possible conviction and sentencing. He trails the curve of her neck with his lips, unable to resist the urge any longer.

"A little," she whispers, leaning into his frame. "Okay, maybe a lot." He pulls her closer, his chin now gently resting on her shoulder. "On three different levels," she adds.

"Scared of going to prison?" he guesses.

"Uh-huh. That's the lowest level. Least of my worries. If it happens, it happens. Nothing I can do about it, only adapt," she says very matter-of-factly.

"The *Can-Do* kid, huh," he chuckles, lacing his hands in hers around the front of her waist, squeezing gently. "What's next?"

"This Vigilare thing. If that's who I am, or what I am...some of the time, why can't I recall? It's like I'm one of those people who sleep walks or wanders away from home and has no recollection of how they got there or who they are. Maybe it's like Alzheimer's or something."

"Ah, you're reaching, DeLuca," he confirms what she already knows. "You may just have to embrace it. Ya know, the more you accept it, maybe the more control you'll have over it?"

"What changed your mind? About the Vigilare thing. I thought you were calling all kinds of bullshit on the idea."

"I don't know. Maybe the lore, the edginess. Maybe the kid in me. Maybe the fact it's you." He chuckles. "Or maybe some unrequited sexual fantasy."

"Gronkowski," she elbows him.

"Uh," he groans with the jab. "Seriously, you were sexy as hell, that night...all black-oped out, sparring with me, rolling around on the floor...hmm."

"Whatever." She giggles, pushing away from him unsuccessfully, as he pulls her back against him, tighter still.

"So, what's the last level? The thing that scares you most?" he prods.

His heart beats prominently through his chest, *lub dub...lub dub...lub dub,* against her back, calling her attention to the fact that a handsome, warm-blooded, fully functional, capable man is holding her. If she goes to prison, or is some Vigilare freak of nature, will she ever be able to experience a man again? She exhales slowly, inhaling sharply, preparing to speak, but the words won't come.

"This?" he fills the silence.

She nods sharply, finally pulling away from him. She stands, taking several safe steps in the opposite direction before turning around to face him. Her eyes a mixture of apprehension and desire, send a surge of initiative right through Tony's core. He picks up the pizza box and the six-pack holder, replacing the open slots with empties upon standing.

"Give me a day to make something happen, and we'll remedy that fear," he says with full intent, dismissing himself from her cell, leaving the door wide open.

She watches him walk away, pushing her weight into the sliding door until the ominous lock sounds, *Clink.*

CHAPTER 15

Vanguard Courthouse. Next day. The proceedings are well underway for the final witnesses. The courtroom hosts the same crowd as the day before, with a few minor exceptions. Judge Carter happily eyes her new gavel, a gift from Detective Gronkowski, a peace offering for the late afternoon events of yesterday, causing her to crack her mallet while re-establishing order. A keen, yet brave attempt at wooing the unwooable Judge Maybelline Carter, the gavel elicits a distasteful response from Mr. McVain, compelling Gina to smile, shaking her head, wondering when Gronkowski would advance to politics, seeing as how he had schmoozing down to a science.

Mr. McVain circles the witness bench in front of Tony, well into his line of tedious and repetitive questioning. "Could you summarize your relationship with Ms. DeLuca?"

"We're partners," Tony responds, yet another short answer, further irritating Mr. McVain.

"Were partners," Mr. McVain corrects.

"You ever worked in law enforcement?"

"No. And I'll thank you to allow me to ask the questions, Detective."

"You entrust your life to someone, your partner, there is no past tense. Of course, that's a matter of honor and pride." Tony grins. "Something I wouldn't expect you to know anything about."

"Could we skip the insults and stay on track." Mr. McVain loosens his tie, unbuttoning the stifling top button of his perfectly pressed suit shirt, the tensed interplay between him and Tony causing his blood to warm. "Are you denying any relationship outside of work with Ms. DeLuca?" he presses.

"You mean, are we an item? Do we get hot and heavy under the sheets?" He wets his lips, running his fingers through his hair. "God, I wish!" His frank answer evokes a few blushed faces and quiet chuckles throughout the courtroom.

Mr. McVain bites at the inside of his lip, approaches the railing separating him and Tony, props his arm upon it, taking a casual position. "Okay, *hotshot,* let's talk about the night you found out your partner, at the time, Detective Gina DeLuca, was the *Vigilare.*"

"Okay, *boss,*" Tony fires back in the same tone delivered to him, leaning onto the railing himself, leveling his intense focus on Mr. McVain's. "Fire away."

"You were camped out in front of Randall Barnes' apartment complex, using him as bait. Correct?"

"Yes," Tony confirms quickly. "It's called a stakeout. We don't *campout,* Mr. McVain. That's the Boy Scouts." He grins.

"Waiting for your murderer?" he continues, bypassing Tony's add-ons. "Willing to risk Randall's life and the life of a fifteen-year old girl to crack your case?"

"I assure you, his life nor Tessa's was in danger, evident by the fact she escaped with her innocence intact, and Randall wasn't taken out in a body bag."

"What triggered you to follow Randall Barnes?"

"That's a loaded question." He scratches his handsome five o'clock shadow, assembling the various answers. "His complaint, earlier that day at the station. His behavior with Dr. Ryan during his session. Dr. Ryan was a suspect at that time, and her records indicated some animosity toward..."

"Are you insinuating..." Mr. McVain butts in.

"I'm not insinuating anything," Tony cuts him off. "And if you interrupt me before I finish answering your question, I'm going to have to assume that's your way of fishing for a different answer. Or you're one rude, arrogant prick who thinks he already has all the answers. Which is it?"

Oohs and shifting of bodies become audible throughout the courtroom. Mr. McVain pushes himself off the railing, creating a relative distance from Tony.

"Detective," Judge Carter warns. "And do allow ample time for questions to be answered," she checks Mr. McVain as well.

"To sum it up," Tony jumps in, after an apologetic nod to Judge Carter. "I was following Randall Barnes because I had a hunch he was up to no good. And the way the case was going, he was next on the chopping block. As for insinuating," he continues, cutting Mr. McVain off from interjecting, again. "I did not *insinuate* anything about Dr. Ryan. She was a suspect in the murders, based on the evidence at the time."

"Evidence?" Mr. McVain questions. "You don't consider rope burns on your partner's neck evidentiary?"

"She trained that morning with the department Krav Maga instructor. Check the roster if you'd like to confirm. You'll find her name, with witnesses attesting that she attended class, which focused on choke holds, to include ropes."

"How convenient," Mr. McVain huffs.

"Was that supposed to be a question?" Tony mocks.

Mr. McVain nods and grins, as if to acknowledge Tony's *move*, and counteracts with his own. "You believe in Vigilares, Detective?"

"If you would've asked me that question a month ago, I would have said 'no.' Excuse me Judge Carter," he prefaces, "but 'hell no.'"

"So you do believe in Vigilares?" Mr. McVain probes, his expression pleased at Tony's admission, believing it will surely aid in discrediting his testimony.

"I believe in *a* Vigilare," he clarifies. "I saw her," he nods in Gina's direction, playing into the whole superhero theory as it seems to be the only saving grace for her at this point.

"Of course you did." Mr. McVain smiles.

"Jealous?" Tony fires back.

He shakes his head pretentiously accompanied by a smirk. "No, Detective, I am not jealous. Simply concerned."

"My mental and psychological aptitudes are available for your viewing, if that's what you're bringing into question here."

"It's not your *mental* nor *psychological* aptitude I am concerned with, Detective," Mr. McVain coyly prances around his point, rather than addressing it directly.

Tony grins mischievously, his animated eyes fueling the flame. "I assure you, my *physical* aptitude is above average. Well above average." Yet again, he draws a few more quiet chuckles from the courtroom

"Wrap it up, Mr. McVain," Judge Carter orders, growing further annoyed with their banter.

He nods, finally getting to his point. "When you stormed into Randall Barnes' apartment, who did you find there besides Randall?"

"An unidentified individual, in black from head to toe."

"Man or woman?"

"From the voice and build, a woman."

"Is it true this individual...woman...was attempting to murder Randall?"

"She was attempting to save Tessa from Randall. Defending one's self or the life of another hardly constitutes murder," Tony clarifies.

"Who did you find when you removed the ski mask?"

Tony pauses, looking to Gina. She nods, knowing he has to tell the truth. "My partner. Detective DeLuca."

"Did anyone else see Ms. DeLuca?"

"My accompanying officer. Officer Sam Marks."

"The blood collected and taken from the scene matches that of

Detective...Ms. DeLuca?" Mr. McVain inquires, quickly correcting himself in reference to her title.

"Yes."

"And the same blood, Ms. DeLuca's, matches that found at eight of the other murders in this case. Correct?"

"According to our CSI lab."

"No further questions, Your Honor." Mr. McVain returns to the prosecution table confident, yet partly annoyed.

Aubrey Raines makes her way to the witness bench, smiling, quite smitten with Detective Gronkowski. Of course, he smiles back. "Detective, how long have you worked for our fine city?"

"Going on twelve years now. Born and raised in Vanguard."

"I checked your background, interviewed a few of your superiors, as well as men and women who've trained under you. Very impressive. Straight into the academy out of high school, Detective, Sergeant, four Medals of Valor, among many other accolades."

"Happy to do it, Ms. Raines," he humbly ducks his head, oddly enough.

"How long have you known Ms. DeLuca?"

"About a year. Since she hired on with VPD."

"I understand you were hesitant to be partnered up with her," Aubrey says, a friendly smile surfacing.

He grins, shifting in his chair. "You ever try and put two alpha dogs together, Ms. Raines?"

She shakes her head enthusiastically, encouraging him to continue.

"There's a reason everyone isn't a born leader. Betas partner best with alphas. When you put two alphas together, it's like a tug-of-war, they dig in with all they've got, but rarely get anywhere because both want to lead. Occasionally," he says, his focus shifting to and remaining on Gina, "you put two alphas together, and instead of pulling, they push one another...to be better."

"So your hesitancy had nothing to do with her qualifications as

[182]

an officer?"

"If you've talked to my counterparts, then you know I have one of the most hardcore reputations when it comes to standards, worthiness. It's a pride thing. I expect the best, of myself, and anyone who's assigned to my unit. If I had my choice of partners, I'd pick Gina DeLuca every day of the week. Hands down."

Mr. McVain rolls his eyes dismissively, wondering when the love fest will end and the real questioning will begin.

"On the night in question, at Randall Barnes' apartment, when you walked in on Gina...Vigilare and Randall. Can you describe the scene?"

"Gina...Vigilare had chased Randall from Tessa's bedroom into the living room. She had plenty of time to run. Save herself from getting caught, but she didn't. She couldn't leave Tessa."

Aubrey circles in front of the witness stand, her eyes searching from Tony to the jury, attempting to read their interpretation of his testimony. "So she was there, in the apartment when you broke through the door?"

"Yes."

"Was Randall harmed in any way, at that point?"

"Not physically, no. Scared out of his mind, maybe, for getting caught with his pants down," Tony scoffs.

"Objection," Mr. McVain states.

"Objection, my ass! Hell, I think the city ought to hire her." He motions to Gina.

"Detective," Judge Carter warns, "clean it up."

"Yes Ma'am," he quickly acknowledges. "That's what these guys need. Imagine, every time someone in the city thought about raping a kid or a woman, and they get a little visit from a kick-butt female vigilante," his voice on the rise simply by the excitement of such a premise. "Bet we'd have a lot fewer predators lurking around the streets."

Aubrey nods affirmatively, redirecting him, "Once you entered the apartment, did she come at you in a threatening manner?"

"No," he answers quickly. "I hemmed her up in the kitchen. Fight or flight kicked in, and she chose to fight. Fair and skilled, I might add."

Mr. McVain tosses his pencil into the air, allowing it to plummet down onto the prosecution table, completely annoyed at Tony's continuous defense of Gina's actions.

"How long did this go on? The two of you squaring off?"

"Long enough for her to tell me about Tessa, in the bedroom, and what Randall had attempted to do to her."

"She had the opportunity to run, escape, but opted not to for the safety of a young girl. And even amidst a sparring match with you, endangering her life as well as her identity, her main concern was to inform you about Tessa?"

Tony nods. "Sounds real dangerous, doesn't she?" he dismisses sarcastically.

"How did you get away from her?" Aubrey leads.

"I didn't," he exclaims, a smile forming. "She had me in a choke hold. Told me all about it. How I would feel a little pressure and then I would be out, just for a few seconds, and she would be gone when I woke. Felt like I was talking to the anesthesiologist right before going under for surgery," he jokes, receiving yet another scattered round of chuckles from the courtroom.

"Objection," Mr. McVain intervenes. "You can't compare a murderer to a Doctor of Medicine."

"Sustained," Judge Carter upholds. "This is not Comedy Central, Detective. Please refrain from ad-libs."

Tony nods, answering directly, "Randall shot her, in the back. That's how I got away from her."

"She went down?"

"No. The gunshot stunned her, momentarily, but within seconds she had this power, like nothing else," Tony testifies with wonderment as if he still can't believe it.

"Power?" Aubrey inquires.

"Yeah. It was like the gunshot made her stronger. And her eyes sparkled, luminescent emerald green. I know it sounds crazy," Tony addresses the jury. "I wouldn't have believed it if I didn't see it with my own eyes."

"It's amazing, isn't it?" She smiles.

"Mesmerizing," he confirms. "Literally. I couldn't look away. I tried, but when she locked her eyes on mine, it was like she was getting a read on me."

"Where was Randall when all of this was taking place?"

"Watching, from a distance."

"So he saw her eyes, the light? You can't miss it if you're in the same room," Aubrey reasons knowingly.

"Oh yeah. She's the one who pulled her eyes from me to him. She could've killed me, but she didn't. She went after Randall. That's why I'm convinced she is no cold-blooded murderer. She delivers retribution. An eye for an eye, so to speak. Evil for evil."

"Objection," Mr. McVain spews. "Speculation."

"Overruled. Continue," Judge Carter allows curiously.

Aubrey beckons Tony to carry on.

"She looked up from me, kind of like she didn't find what she expected to find. And as soon as she locked eyes on Randall, she lunged at him. From me to you," he addresses the jury, pointing out the distance. "Her mark, spot on. She had him up against the wall, her eyes locked on his. He couldn't close his eyes or pull them away from her. I surely couldn't get her off of him. Whatever she was looking for, she found it in Randall. In his eyes."

"The window to the soul, so they say," Aubrey concludes.

Tony nods his head. "Must be the blood loss from her shoulder wound was too much to sustain the energy she was exerting, because she fainted. Fell to the floor, her hold on Randall released."

"And when you took the mask off, she was unconscious?"

"Yes."

"And when you brought up the episode, during her recovery at the hospital, what was her reaction?"

"No recollection," he confirms. "Total confusion and disbelief."

Aubrey digresses, "She's been your partner on the case, correct?"

"Yes."

"Eight of the fifteen homicide scenes have resulted in evidence of her DNA?"

"Yes."

"What about the remaining seven scenes?"

"Still unclarified."

"There's been a lot of press around this case. Public outcries and support of Vigilare. Is it possible to have a copy cat, of sorts?"

"Certainly. That's always a possibility." Tony leans forward, his forearms resting on his knees, his time in the witness chair beginning to wear on him. "Civilians getting fed up, waiting for the system to deliver. Those looking for their fifteen minutes of fame. Opportunists, hopeful someone else in the spotlight will take the fall for their actions. We see all kinds."

"How will we know?"

"There are no guarantees. I guess, you have to ask yourself, do you feel safer as a community with Gina DeLuca locked up, or not?"

"A woman, who in the midst of ridding the city of rapists and child molesters, saved my life, and recognized you as an *off-mark*, a good guy. A vigilante with a conscience," Aubrey reasons.

Tony nods affirmatively. "Just imagine, if Vanguard had its very own Batman...woman," he says with a smile. The idea processing and registering in a few hopeful faces of the jury and courtroom at large.

"Jesus," Mr. McVain mutters, pushing himself back into his chair, kicking his legs up onto the table as if he is removing himself from the scenario, simply unable to tolerate anymore garble.

"That will be all, Detective. Thank you," Aubrey dismisses him. She looks to Judge Carter, who gives her a nod while multi-tasking a cautionary gesture to Mr. McVain causing him to quickly pull his legs from the table, sitting upright. "Defense calls Dr. Gerald Godfrey to the stand."

CHAPTER 16

Dr. Godfrey's steps are short and casual, his round face happy, the white lab coat swallowing his small, slightly stooped frame. Upon nestling into the witness chair, he scrunches up his nose assisting his glasses to the appropriate eye level.

"Dr. Godfrey, could you summarize your specialty for the jury?" Aubrey asks, her voice kind and gentle, reciprocating the face looking back at her.

"I'm a hematologist. A blood doctor, basically. I study the blood...its components, both healthy and diseased."

"Do you work for the federal government, the ETNA division?"

"No. I'm what we in the business call a 'freelance vampire,'" he chuckles with the blood reference. "I'm an independent contractor, Ms. Raines. Anybody can hire me."

"Not just *any* independent contractor," she notes. "The best, according to the latest poll in the Journal of Hematology."

"Ah, they simply needed a new name to top the list this year," he excuses. "I do tend to hire out to rather high profile cases. Those are the most interesting, I find."

"ETNA hired you?" Aubrey clarifies.

"Yes."

"Do you agree with Dr. Shaw's evaluation of Ms. DeLuca?"

"In terms of the psychological evaluation, I'm afraid I have no authority in that jurisdiction." He smiles. "However, as a hematologist, I can say blood constitutes seven percent of the human body.

[188]

And if it is abnormal, it most certainly could affect every other aspect of bodily functions to include the psyche."

"You concur, Ms. DeLuca's blood is unique?"

"The most peculiar I've witnessed thus far in my career."

"Without getting into too many specifics, could you help us understand the significance of her blood type and how it may lend itself to her Vigilare persona?"

"After intense study, I would theorize that Ms. DeLuca's blood, when exposed to external oxygen, morphs into something catastrophic to her entire system. It changes her DNA, her strength, her abilities, everything, to which she is fully unaware."

"As Ms. DeLuca testified, do you believe she does not recall when she transforms from her current self," Aubrey pauses, motioning in her direction, "into Vigilare?"

"Would bet my life on it," he says astutely.

"Could you elaborate?" Aubrey leads.

"While in my care, Ms. DeLuca had several amnesic episodes and flashbacks. My theory is that she is experiencing a mixture of severe post-traumatic stress, accompanied with dissociation when her sympathetic nervous system is fully engaged. The sympathetic nervous system jolts the body, propelling it to fight or flight—enhanced heart rate, respiratory rate, strength and keenness of senses." Dr. Godfrey begins to talk with his hands now, the subject quite exciting to him. His animation pulls in the jury, as well as the rest of the courtroom. "When Gina transitions to Vigilare-mode, all of these things increase tenfold, brought on by the exposure of her infinitely unique blood to the external air. The severe change in her physical self, combined with the dissociation to her mental self, most likely brought on by a past traumatic experience, results in inability to recall herself as Vigilare. A blackout, so to speak. "

"Can she learn to identify and control the transformations?"

"Essentially," he says, a poised index finger appearing to further explain. "She will have breakthroughs, as anyone experiences with any trait, talent."

"Objection," Mr. McVain calls. "Since when did a mental disorder become a talent?"

"Overruled, Counselor," Judge Carter quiets his challenge, respectful of Dr. Godfrey's perspective.

Aubrey spurs him along.

"My point," he continues. "An olympic athlete does not simply become an olympic athlete. They train, prepare, identify, acknowledge, rally and regroup, until they figure out the winning combination. Ms. DeLuca has a lot of work ahead of her. Her power, her gift is untapped. Would be a shame to see such potential go to waste in a jail cell."

Mr. McVain rolls his eyes.

"Were you able to witness her transformation into Vigilare during your evaluation?" Aubrey follows up.

"Unfortunately, no. The medications administered to maintain life often counteract natural trends in the body. It would be inhumane to force her to transform simply for our observation." He gives Dr. Shaw of the white coats a reprimanding glance.

Aubrey pats the railing between her and Dr. Godfrey. "Thank you," she says before returning to the defense table beside Gina.

"Mr. McVain," Judge Carter beckons, sitting back in her chair, reviewing the witness list, pleased only one name remains.

Mr. McVain smirks, making his way to the witness stand while fingering his perfectly fluffy locks. "Inhumane," he says. "Did you not observe Ms. DeLuca in a controlled environment, Dr. Godfrey?"

"Yes, the environment was controlled."

"Then, why not a simple cut...a paper cut, if you will, to witness her *transformation?*"

Dr. Godfrey crosses one leg over the other, shifting in his chair. "It's not that *simple,* Mr. McVain."

Mr. McVain appears purposely and condescendingly perplexed,

looking back and forth from Dr. Godfrey to the jury. "You said the key to Ms. DeLuca's transformation was the exposure of her blood to external oxygen. A paper cut on one's finger would expose the blood to external oxygen. Would it not?"

Dr. Godfrey leans onto his elbow against the armrest. The usual easygoing soul, slightly stirred by Mr. McVain's arrogant presence. He forces a smile, attempting to feel the gesture. "Gina's blood is not solely responsible for the transformation. Something inherently worthy of such a response has to trigger the transformation, in addition to the exposure of blood to oxygen."

"Inherently worthy?" Mr. McVain prods.

"Something that causes the sympathetic nervous system to engage. Fear, anger, competition, intense exercise."

Mr. McVain chuckles. "Sex," he says astutely, causing Tony's ears to perk up in the back of the courtroom. "Biologically, sexual intercourse engages both the sympathetic and parasympathetic nervous systems. Are you proposing, exposure to Ms. DeLuca's blood to external oxygen during sexual intercourse would also cause her to transform into this *Vigilare?*"

"Objection," Aubrey calls.

"Whew, I feel sorry for that guy. He won't know what hit him!" Mr. McVain causes a few giggles among the courtroom.

"Order," Judge Carter lightly taps her gavel, muffling the crowd. "Sustained. Move along, Counselor."

"Seriously," Mr. McVain quips, eyeing Dr. Godfrey. "Do you hear yourself?"

Dr. Godfrey nods. "It's a new concept. There will be difficulty understanding it. Full comprehension may take years."

"Either it is, or it isn't, Dr. Godfrey. You sound as though you've been taking lessons from Ms. DeLuca." He throws an arm out in her direction. "She doesn't know. She cannot recall. Now, you're backpedaling, theorizing, speculating." He taps his hand down on the witness railing. "Do you believe murder is inhumane, Dr. Godfrey?"

"Murder is inhumane, yes. Self-defense," he begins to explain.

Mr. McVain cuts him off, "But to test Ms. DeLuca, to force her transformation from dutiful detective to murderous Vigilare would be inhumane?"

"There was no reason to force," Dr. Godfrey begins again.

"Or is it possible there is, in fact, nothing to transform?" Mr. McVain interrupts. "All of your theories and speculations are just that. No proof." He circles the floor in front of the witness stand. "If I were a Vigilare, I would do whatever I had to do to prove I was such. Ms. DeLuca has failed to do so. You and your team of doctors failed to do so. You say her *talent* will be wasted in jail. If it's so unique, so extraordinary, why not show it off, display it for all to see? If she is such a hero, why are you so afraid of what she may do when transformed." He stops circling, the perfected condescending look making its way across his face. "If this were a game of cards, I would be calling 'bullshit.'"

"Objection," Aubrey advocates.

"Sustained. Take care with your language, Mr. McVain," Judge Carter directs.

Mr. McVain nods, tightening his tie. Even though stricken from the record, his point has been made.

"Are you a Christian, Mr. McVain?" Dr. Godfrey asks.

Mr. McVain smiles. "Yes, even though I cannot see Jesus, I still believe in him," he answers, plowing through Dr. Godfrey's suggestion before heading right back on track with his own agenda. "There's another loophole in your testimony, *Doctor.* What occurs before the attacks, before Ms. DeLuca's blood is exposed to external oxygen? How does she just so happen to be in the same vicinity as these men? If she becomes the Vigilare only when her blood is exposed, and," he chuckles, continuing, "the appropriate stimuli for engagement of the sympathetic nervous system is present...and the clock strikes one...and the moon is three-quarters full. How does she find these men, in such precarious circumstances?"

"Why don't you tell me, Mr. McVain," Dr. Godfrey replies, his usually happy round face has grown taught and pressing. He peers down over the tops of his bifocals, authoritatively. "You seem to have all the answers, and are quick to ridicule any given to you with which you disagree."

Mr. McVain says nothing, his arms folded over his chest.

"I realize all the pieces don't quite fit...yet. There are many unanswered questions." Dr. Godfrey leans forward, his arm perched upon the witness railing. "The way to find out such answers is to work with her in a controlled setting, facilitating her memory and abilities, not locking her up in some jail cell."

Mr. McVain taps his chin with his index finger, contemplating. "If she's so capable, a true Vigilare, how could a jail cell contain her?"

"Lock her up, and I guess we'll find out," Dr. Godfrey replies, his attention shifting to the jury.

"You know a little something about being locked up, don't you?" Mr. McVain quips.

Dr. Godfrey sits back in his chair, preparing for what's to come.

"1968. Your freshman year of college was the first time. Wasn't it?"

"Yes," Dr. Godfrey answers solemnly.

"Delusional. Paranoid Schizophrenia. Electroconvulsive Therapy. Psychiatric Ward. Ring any bells, Dr. Godfrey?" Mr. McVain reads from a medical record.

"Objection," Aubrey calls. "My witness' medical record is not pertinent to this case."

"Your Honor, I am not attempting to defame Dr. Godfrey, simply establishing a questionable pattern," Mr. McVain pleads.

"Overruled," Judge Carter decides. "Tread lightly, Mr. McVain."

He nods, turning back to Dr. Godfrey. "And again, in your graduate studies. Once, early in your career. And, just five-years ago, another episode. Correct?"

"Relapses are common," Dr. Godfrey says.

"I understand," Mr. McVain makes an attempt with empathy. "However, you see where it may be difficult to take your testimony to heart, considering your past with paranoia and delusional episodes? Particularly of the supernatural kind." He flips through the medical records. "You once thought you witnessed an alien attempting to take your blood. On another account, you reported a descendant of the ancient astronauts attempted to implant a chip into your person. And again..."

"You've made your point," Dr. Godfrey interrupts. "The difference between those episodes and my testimony is that I am not currently relapsing, nor have I in five years. At the time, due to my paranoia and delusion, I believed those things to be true. However, once in my healthy frame of mind, I could identify those things as untruths...delusions." He scrunches up his nose, pulling his glasses further to its bridge, looking through them. "Why don't you pull my current medical records. You will find my illness has been successfully micromanaged by my own initiative in collaboration with my doctors. Therefore, your point is invalid, unless you are saying mental illness indefinitely makes one incompetent."

"I would never insinuate such," Mr. McVain grabs at his chest, as if he is fully apologetic.

"Some of the greatest minds of our time fought mental illness. Einstein, Newton, Nash. If directed appropriately, mental illness has been shown to exude creativity, genius." Dr. Godfrey smiles. "Something you'll never have to worry yourself with, Mr. McVain."

"No further questions, Your Honor," Mr. McVain dismisses, returning to his seat at the prosecution table.

"Your last witness, Ms. Raines," Judge Carter requests, with a happy gleam in her eye.

CHAPTER 17

"Defense calls Emily Truly to the stand."

Emily Truly, the daughter of ex-Navy Seal, William Truly, makes her way to the stand. Slightly above average height, she displays an exotic beauty, dark hair and skin, accompanied by Elizabeth Taylor-esque violet eyes. She carries herself with a quiet confidence. Her facial expression is unwavering, hard and intent.

Aubrey extends to her a soft smile. Emily does not return the gesture. "Miss Truly, could you tell the court what you do for a living?"

"I'm a martial arts instructor. I specialize in self-defense for women."

"How long have you done so?"

"Three years."

"What piqued your interest in martial arts?" Aubrey leads.

"My own experience with rape."

Aubrey waits patiently, her hands folded and hanging at hip level.

Emily Truly sits tall and proud, her posture immaculate, her chin jutting out, the action somewhere between confidence and defiance. "I got tired of feeling like a victim. Action, anger, empowerment... all more comfortable to me than weakness and vulnerability." She looks down at her lap momentarily, returning her fierce gaze to the back wall of the courtroom. "I was raped in an alleyway three years ago. I was a kid, nineteen. Sophomore year of college. I was fulfilling credits for my Humanities curriculum. Neighborhood cleanup project. MLK was my assigned area. It was Sunday evening, my last day. There was this guy...man, from the neighborhood. He seemed like a decent guy. He helped me the day before, carry my oversized trash bags to the dumpster. He didn't hurt me then. So, when he came out Sunday to help me carry the bags to the dumpster, I assumed it wouldn't hurt to let him help me." She pauses, wetting her palate with the glass of water provided to the side of the witness stand, her eyes returning to the back wall of the courtroom, uninterrupted. "We started down the alleyway with hands full of trash bags. It's quite dark at this point. The sun almost set. He walked behind me. I looked back at him and something felt wrong. In the pit of my stomach. The way he looked at me in that moment. It wasn't right, and I knew it instinctively. But I buried the feeling, pushing the thought from my mind, afraid I was simply being paranoid. I smiled at him to ease my own anxiety." She shakes her head, her mouth turning into a condemning smile. "I was so naive. Stupid."

Her eyes fall to her father, William Truly. He looks at her with love and understanding. She gives him a genuine smile before gathering herself to continue. Her eyes refocused on the imaginary X at the back of the room. "With the last bag of trash loaded into the dumpster, he tried to kiss me. When I pushed him away, that *decent guy,*" she chokes out, disdainfully, "grabbed me by my hair and repeatedly slammed my face into the side of the dumpster until I couldn't even stand up on my own. He dragged me to the back side of the green metal box, threw me down on the concrete, covered in garbage and sludge. Symbolism that I was no better than yesterday's leftovers, trash. He had a knife. He cut my shirt open, along with my bra, which he so cleverly used to tie my hands behind my back," she spews with a smirk. "It was then that I knew he had done this before. He went through the motions as if it was as common to him as his day job. Every time I would attempt to yell out or fight back, he would kick me into the dumpster. The impact robbing me of my strength, my breath. Until he had me on my stomach on the ground, my face bleeding and mashed into the concrete, my arms behind my back, my pants down around my ankles, my knees painfully bent underneath me." Her jaw clenches as she holds back hurt and rage. "If all of that wasn't enough, he held a knife to my throat, the sharp edge cutting into my flesh with every thrust of his body." She pulls her hair back from the right side of her neck, displaying a light, white scar indicative of such injury. "My pleas, my tears, my pain meant nothing to him. Surely a monster." Her eyes meet Mr. McVain's. "And you defend them? Call them victims? Insist someone should pay for taking their lives?"

He quickly diverts his gaze from hers.

"I lay there in that alleyway, behind the dumpster, reeking of stench, and all I could think was, *please don't let my father find me like this.*" Tears fall from her eyes as she quickly wipes them away. William Truly's reaction mimics hers. "I wanted to die. It would've been easier if he would have killed me. Instead, I was forced to live with the memory every day." She slams her hand down onto the railing, causing already tensed bodies within the courtroom to react, startled and jumpy. "Sick fucks!"

"Ms. Truly," Judge Carter calls to her, quietly but firmly.

Emily eyes her defiantly, wondering if she would be so reprimanding if the same happened to her daughter. Aubrey interjects, attempting to pull her back on subject, "You find martial arts helpful in your healing?"

"Before my soul was ravaged from my body, my heart shattered into a million little pieces, I was a good girl. Kind, sweet, believing in humanity. I actually thought people were good and decent." She chuckles at herself, reprimandingly. "After I was raped, I became weepy, needy, a shell of my former self, scared and damaged. I didn't leave my home for months. My father had to retire to stay with me, take care of me. I locked myself up in my bedroom for days at a time, while I sat in the corner shaking and crying, wondering what I had done to deserve to be raped, my body mutilated. I didn't go back to college. Even the locks on my doors couldn't keep out the night-mares, the constant movie in my head, replaying my raping, over and over and over again. These pigs get tried and sent away for one offense, the single act of rape. My attacker didn't rape me only once. He raped me at least a thousand times in my mind and in my soul." She shifts her weight in the chair, still maintaining strict posture, a rock. Lifting her arms simultaneously, she shows the interior of her wrists to the jury. Both wrists displaying scars from one side to the other. "I hated myself...for allowing him to rape me, for being so pathetic, for being so scared. I hated myself for the way my father looked at me. The pain and the pity in his eyes almost too much to bear. I hated myself because I did not have the courage to tes-tify against my attacker. He got a lighter sentence because I was too scared to look him in the eye and testify about what he had done to me. I was a coward. I did not want to live." She pulls her arms down into her lap, looking at her scars. "It felt so good mashing the blades into my wrists, bearing down and pulling them from one side to the other. I felt deserving of such pain."

The courtroom silence is deafening.

Her mind taking her back to that point in time, she stares blank-ly at the interior of her arms at their juncture with her hands. "My dad saved me," she says, looking up at him, tears welling in her eyes. She clears her throat, continuing, "He got me the help I needed. I was in therapy for months, attended support groups with other sur-vivors of sexual assault and rape, then came martial arts." She smiles, genuinely this time. "Finally, something that made sense to me. I could kick, punch and slap an object, or a sparring partner, to relieve my frustrations. I became very well acquainted with anger. Learned how to express it, ultimately gaining control of it. I did not like be-ing a victim, and I didn't have to be anymore. And in light of that, I could help other women prepare for their own defense. It's going to happen, rape. The numbers are staggering. One in seven women will be raped in her lifetime. One in ten men will be raped in his lifetime.

Look around this courtroom. Do the math."

Heads of the jurors and observers in the courtroom swivel, each individual calculating their odds.

"Your rapist was murdered in the same alleyway in which he raped you, his neck slit from ear to ear," Aubrey begins. "He's one of the men Ms. DeLuca is accused of murdering, although no evidence of her DNA nor presence at the scene has been proven."

Emily nods. "Death is too good for him. Too easy. One thing's for certain though, whoever or *whatever,*" she pauses, a deliberate address to Gina's Vigilare, "killed him, you can rest assured he deserved it, provoked it somehow."

"Self-defense?" Aubrey leads.

"Without a doubt." Emily's gaze instinctively meets Mr. McVain's, who appears as though he may object. "Save yourself the time," she says. "I am neither impressed nor swayed by the defense to speculate anything. I assure you, I am no fan of Vanguard PD. And, I'm unclear as to whether I am willing to believe in a so-called Vigilare. I am on no one's side, except my own. Frankly, I think the whole system sucks." She looks to Judge Carter expecting a reprimand, which does not come. She shrugs, continuing, "All I know, someone's finally delivering some justice in this town, be it vigilante or avenger style. I don't care who it is, or their motivation. I say keep up the good work. In one month's time, this person or group of people has done more for this city than the police department and the justice department combined. Hell, I might as well start paying taxes to them."

"Are you through, Ms. Truly?" Judge Carter finally speaks, her tone laced with disapproval.

"It wasn't my idea to testify," Emily pipes, defensively.

"No further questions, Your Honor," Aubrey quickly interjects.

"Mr. McVain," Judge Carter calls to him.

Mr. McVain looks to Dr. Ryan, sitting behind him. She shakes her head, her eyes trailing down. "Prosecution has no questions for this witness, Madam Judge," he reports, disappointedly.

"Great," Judge Carter replies. "Now for closing statements. Counselors, please bear in mind it has been a long few days. Say what you need to say, however, keep it relevant and concise." She looks to Mr. McVain, his cue to begin.

Mr. McVain stands, pulling his suit coat off, laying it on the table. He pulls at his tie, loosening it a bit around his neck, going for a more casual, less intimidating look in his interaction with the jury. Fluffing his lavish hair yet again, he makes his way to the railing, acknowledging the twelve faces looking back at him. A mixture of men and women, some faces friendly, some ardently serious. Mr. McVain smiles at them graciously. "Thank you for your time and patience, and your incredibly important service to your community. You have been exposed to vast amounts of information over the past two days, some logical and proven, some speculative and unsupported. After we leave this courtroom today, it's up to you to determine how you will process such information, and what conclusions you will draw."

He paces from one end of the jury to the other, making sure to share eye contact with each and every member at some point in his delivery. "Regardless of whether you are inclined to believe in superhero theory, or only in those things which can be verified, one thing is for certain. The defendant, Gina DeLuca's DNA, in the form of blood or skin was found at eight of the fifteen homicide scenes. The defense would have you focus on the remaining seven homicides where her DNA was not found. Are eight lives not enough? Would it be more agreeable to convict her for murdering fifteen men, rather than eight? The number is arbitrary. What needs to be heard, remembered, is that lives were taken. The lives of men who meant something to someone. Fathers, brothers, husbands, friends, neighbors...men. The defense would have you believe the lives of these men are expendable because of their character flaws, their mental illnesses. So, what? They deserved to die? What if one of those men was your brother?" he asks, eyeing a male juror in the front row. "Your son?" he continues, asking a female juror in the back. "Would you be so willing to believe their lives were worth nothing?"

He pauses for affect, standing still as he shifts his gaze from the courtroom at large, back to the jury, eyeing what emotional response, if any, he is successful in conjuring up. "The defense would also have you believe Ms. DeLuca murdered these men in self-defense. Plausible? Yes, one murder may happen in self-defense. Two murders, that's pushing it. Eight murders, that's absolutely ludicrous. Who, other than a soldier in combat, finds himself in the precarious position of having to kill numerous human beings in self-defense?" He throws his hands up in the air, letting them fall heavily against his thighs. "Even in giving her a huge benefit of a doubt, theorizing all eight murders, possibly fifteen were committed in self-defense. She went looking for these men, sought them out. Knew their patterns, exposed herself to them in order to provoke an action to which she already knew her reaction. That's pre-meditation folks. Most murders in self-defense do not end in the victim strangling the attacker. Defendees do not go looking for a fight, they find themselves in one, and choose the quickest way out. Do you know how long it takes to strangle another human to death? Most experts report anywhere from three to seven minutes. That's a lot of time to consider one's actions. When does that action go from self-defense to intent to kill?"

Mr. McVain points to Gina sitting at the defendant table. "Superhero or not. Intent to murder or murder in self-defense, Gina DeLuca is responsible for the deaths of eight men, possibly fifteen. Will you let her go unpunished? A woman who believes she is above the law, above the average citizen, such as you or I. A woman who obviously believes in delivering justice on her own terms, an eye for an eye." He drops his arm from her direction, turns toward the jury, dramatically delivering his final words. "She should be held accountable for her actions with the same ferocity she holds others accountable." He quotes the Bible, Matthew 7:2, cleverly as a large percentage of the remaining jury members checked the box labeled *Christian* during their preliminary screenings for duty. "'For in the same way you judge others, you will be judged, and with the measure you use, it will be measured to you.'"

He saunters back to the prosecution table, flashing a flirtatious grin at Gina as he passes by. She nods, the corners of her mouth softening, acknowledging his well-played delivery.

Aubrey Raines stands, her nerves surfacing, doubt rearing its ugly head. Her inexperience, Mr. McVain's eloquent closing, combined with the dreadful feeling that Gina's fate now rests in her words, causes her to sit back down momentarily. Gina puts her hand over Aubrey's and gives it a reassuring squeeze.

"It's going to be alright," Gina whispers, encouragingly, letting go of her hand and nodding her head in the jury's direction.

Aubrey smiles vaguely as she stands from her chair, making her way to the railing separating the bench from the jury. "That was quite a moving delivery by Mr. McVain. May I point out, the biblical scripture he quoted about judgment is in reference to hypocrites, not the righteous. When we know the truth, we are commanded to judge in order to help others see the truth, have a clearer vision of right and wrong. Ms. DeLuca is no hypocrite. She has asked for no special treatment. In her testimony, she urged you to go with the evidence, go with your instinct. She has told the truth as she knows it to be true. Now, it is up to you to use your judgment, based on the information you obtained during the trial, to determine whether her actions were right or wrong, just or unjust."

Aubrey walks the length of the railing, trailing her hand over the polished wood as she continues, making eye contact with the jurors, each and every one. "That's the bottom line folks, right or wrong. Is it right to try and convict my client, Gina DeLuca, for murders she may have committed, in self-defense, as Vigilare? Mr. McVain wants to hammer home evidence, proof, fact. Ms. DeLuca passed a polygraph examination, not guilty of each and every homicide about which she was questioned. That's proof, fact, evidence. If we could turn her into Vigilare and contain her for questioning," Aubrey reasons, an alarmed grin surfacing, "maybe the polygraph results would differ. We're so inclined to believe only what we can see. Superheroes don't exist, so we are told since our childhood. It is clear to me, as it should be to you, this woman is a superhero of sorts, even though she may not know it yet."

Aubrey looks to Tony in the back of the courtroom. "Detective Gronkowski witnessed her in action. What would he gain by making up such a story? If anything, he has probably sacrificed his own credibility in telling the truth. Mr. McVain would have you believe there is no way she killed eight men in self-defense. How do you kill eight different people, in eight different circumstances in self-defense, he asks. There's your proof." She extends her arm to Tony. "Detective Gronkowski testified Vigilare could've killed him, easily. She did not. The only men she is alleged to have killed were those with rap sheets of rape, pedophilia, other crimes. Patterns of some sort. Mr. McVain wants to portray Gina DeLuca as the predator, victimizing men with significant histories of destroying the lives of numerous women and children. When, exactly, did the predators become the victims? Not a single innocent individual was harmed in any of these instances. In fact, my life, my body, my sanity was saved by Vigilare, as was Tessa Ortiz's." She pauses, turning to the jury with intent. "Obviously, there is something in her that can sense just and unjust, right and wrong. The same as all of you in this very situation. You know what is right and what is wrong. Even though you may not know exactly what to make of Gina DeLuca...Vigilare, it's relatively simple. Ask yourselves, do you feel safer with her guarding your streets, or locked behind bars where her gift would be wasted? If you were a victim of an attempted rape, would you want Vigilare to come to your rescue, or would you rather suffer at the hands of a true predator?"

Aubrey nods her head, her hands meeting in prayer fashion at the center of her chest, a gesture of thanks to the jury before returning to her chair beside Gina.

Judge Carter assesses both the prosecution and defense before turning her attention to the jury. "Jurors, it is your duty to make your decision based only on the facts presented and not on how you feel." She turns back to the court at large, with a gentle tap of her gavel. "Court is now adjourned. We'll return when a verdict has been reached." Idle chatter rings through the large room with high ceilings, providing ample acoustic affect. Judge Carter motions for the guards to reclaim custody of Gina and for her bailiff to assist her to her chambers. Tony eyes the judge intently, and slips out the back of the courtroom.

Chapter 18

Early Evening. Vanguard County Jail. Unable to rest or lay still as her fate now rests in the judgment of the jury, Gina hangs from the top bunk in her cell. Her knees locked over the frame, her torso dangles toward the floor as she pulls herself up and down, repetitively working her abdominals. She alternates between sit-ups and push-ups, attempting to wear herself out physically, in hopes of dually inspiring mental exhaustion. Working hard to block out the accompanying sounds of the jail, her senses focus inward until the voices, clinks and clanks of doors, and the clatter of booking equipment become distant. The only thing prevalent at this time is the sound of her heart beating, her lungs forcefully grabbing at air, her pulse driving blood through her veins, the creaking of the metal frame on the bed with each flexion and extension of her body. She is in the zone. So much so, she is unaware of the visitor at her cell door.

"Shouldn't you be resting for your big day tomorrow?" Dr. Ryan's voice carries through the cell bars.

Gina flips herself backward from the top bunk, a perfect landing to the floor beneath as she stands upright in the corner of her cell, now facing Dr. Ryan.

Dr. Ryan claps quietly, a smirk forming on her lips. Gina remains silent, assessing the situation. Emily Truly stands to the right and slightly behind the psychologist, her expression less than enthused.

"You must be curious as to my visit," Dr. Ryan prods.

"I have far more pressing issues to prick my curiosity," Gina dismisses, taking a seat on the dingy mattress. She rests her elbows on her knees, leaning forward in recuperation from her exertion.

Dr. Ryan chuckles. "Such animosity, when you should be thanking me."

Gina looks up at Dr. Ryan skeptically, her curiosity beyond *pricked*. Emily Truly remains at her side, her arms folded insolently across her chest, eyeing Gina.

"I petitioned Judge Carter to release you into psychiatric care rather than incarceration," Dr. Ryan continues, self-righteously.

Gina shrugs her shoulders. "I didn't ask you to do that."

"Maybe you should consider dropping your arrogant attitude and replace it with humility," Emily accuses.

Gina stands, approaching the bars separating her from them. Her eyes meet Emily's with reciprocal disdain. "The same could be said to you. What happened to that wounded, gracious young woman? In the alleyway of MLK?" Gina asks suspiciously, referencing the scene of Emily's murdered rapist, when Emily took solace in her embrace.

Emily smiles haughtily. "I was such a good little victim, wasn't I?" Her smirk dissipating, she wraps her hands around the bars, briskly shaking them, her teeth painfully gritting together. "I owe you nothing. You took from me what was mine."

"Ladies," Dr. Ryan interjects, gently coercing Emily's fists from the cold steel. "We all could stand a little gratitude in our presentation."

"Gratitude," Gina scoffs, maintaining a searing glance toward Emily. "You can rest assured, whatever Dr. Ryan has done for me will ultimately benefit her. You may consider that fact, if you choose to keep such company." Gina's eyes are called to Emily's neck, where a crucifix rests, bearing a striking resemblance to the crucifix in one of her visions. The same crucifix that dangled from the rail of her bed in the hospital.

Emily smirks shrewdly, watching Gina search, attempting to put it all together. "Your arrogance saddens me," Emily speaks, her tone icy, her hands once again winding around the bars. "Sparkling emerald green eyes, superhuman strength, a regular *Vigilare*. You know nothing of the power you possess." The bars begin to sound as the pressure exerted on them forces their strict steel frame to bow.

"Emily," Dr. Ryan warns.

"You're no better than a punk. An ingrate, undeserving of the gift that encompasses you," Emily continues, her hands now at rest on the crescented bars that once were straight and parallel. "Vigilare," Emily huffs. "Good luck with those visions, know-it-all," she dismisses as she walks away.

Gina scans the two bars, a perfect circle large enough to pass a large ball between. "What the hell was that?"

Dr. Ryan winks, smiling. "She's a very powerful girl." She tucks her briefcase under her arm. "Goodnight, Ms. DeLuca. Or do you prefer Vigilare?"

"How does she know about the visions?" Gina's mind races.

Dr. Ryan shrugs her shoulders. "Either way, goodnight." She pivots militaristically, exiting the cellblock.

Gina wants to call after her, something her pride will not allow. "What the...?" her words fade into an internal whisper.

SEVERAL HOURS LATER, Gina rests on her bed, her eyes and mind searching for understanding. She hears footsteps echoing down the corridor. Jumping from her supine position, she stands erect, her expression grows disappointed.

Tony stands in front of her cell. "Not who you were expecting?" he quizzes, his feelings hurt. Gina was hoping for Emily Truly's return. "Should I leave?" he continues.

Gina shakes her head and smiles.

"What the hell happened here?" Tony inspects the bowed bars on her cell door, looking to her concerned. "Did it happen again?

Did you turn?"

"No." She thinks for a moment. "Not to my knowledge." She grabs her hair, tousling it through her fingers. "Do you know how frustrating it is to not know who you are, or what you are?" Her question utterly rhetorical. Her hands rest on the back of her neck, bearing down firmly. "At least I know I didn't do that." She directs to the bent steel.

Tony waits for her explanation.

"I was so fortunate to have a visit from Dr. Ryan." She rolls her eyes. "Strutted up in here bragging about how she petitioned the judge to send me to a psych facility. So kind of her."

"I saw her coming out of Judge Carter's chambers this afternoon, before my meeting. I knew she was up to something. Why would she do that?" Tony's wheels spin.

Gina shrugs. "Power. Bragging rights. Control. If she has me locked up on the tenth floor, tied down to some electric table, like some Frankenstein project, promise me you'll come for me," she teases, a bit of worry in her inflection.

"Dr. Ryan pried those bars apart?" he asks, disbelieving.

"Emily Truly," she answers.

"What? Dr. Ryan *and* Emily Truly came to see you? What did Emily want?" Tony scratches his head, pacing. "I tell ya Gina, this whole thing is getting weird. Something's going on. What the hell is going on?" His thoughts jumbled, he continues intermittently, "Emily pried those bars apart? With what? For what?"

"With her hands. Because I made her mad."

"Gina, come on." He knocks his knuckles against the bars. "These things are made of iron. You expect me to believe some woman, well other than you, when you're her...Vigilare, pried these things apart with her bare hands."

"Believe what you want. I stood right here and watched her do it. And I saw the look in Dr. Ryan's eyes. She wasn't the least bit surprised." Gina circles the concrete floor. "And she knew about my visions, Emily."

"Visions? You think Emily's superhuman too? Aw shit, Gina, don't tell me there's two of you." Tony shakes his head, the pieces coming together.

"Yeah, visions. I have them sometimes. Don't know what they mean though." Gina talks, her mouth unable to keep up with her mind. "Two of us? *Vigilares?*" she exaggerates the plural. "Ya think?"

"I don't know what to think." Tony inspects the hole between the bars, mesmerized. "No five-foot-eight, one-hundred and thirty-five-pound female of human origin did this."

"She's a martial artist. They do that stuff all the time. Breaking boards with their hands, concrete with their heads. Probably some trick thing she learned." Gina attempts to convince herself, while working on convincing Tony.

"There are seven homicide scenes unaccounted for, Gina. We better put a call in to the CSI lab. Throw her name in the hat as a possible suspect." Tony unlocks the door between them. "Maybe that's the missing link. Why would they show up here together? Why was Dr. Ryan at the rally at City Hall led by the Truly's? You thinking what I'm thinking?"

"Not unless, you're wondering why you came empty handed? No pizza tonight?" she asks.

"You're impossible, DeLuca." He grins, shaking his head, taking hold of her hand. "We're on the brink of a breakthrough here and you're worried about dinner." He pulls at her arm.

She pulls back against him. "Did you forget where I am? I can't just walk out of here, Gronkowski."

"Oh, yeah. That's why I'm here," he recalls amongst all the incoming news and commotion. "I posted your bail. Judge Carter released you into my custody. Just for tonight." He smiles, pulling her in his direction.

"You can't be serious," she inquires, stalling his momentum.

"Come with me and find out," he coaxes, his smile growing larger. "We've got work to do, DeLuca."

She pulls back against him, one more time, a gleam in her eye. "If I have one night...one night before I spend the rest of my life behind bars, I'm not spending it working, Gronkowski."

"Hmm," he growls, clutching at his chest, music to his ears. Quickly, he leads her down the corridor to the exit.

Chapter 19

Late evening. Detective Gronkowski's home. After a long, lavish bubble bath, Gina saunters down the hallway, her hair wound on top of her head in a plush white bath towel, a matching robe snuggled around her frame.

"Ah man, it's the little things," she says contentedly, joining Tony in the dining room.

He smiles at her, his phone tucked under his ear. "I gotta run. Let me know if you hear anything," he says into the phone before ending the call.

"Would you relax?" Gina requests.

"Gina, what if the jury comes back tomorrow with their verdict? We don't have much time to figure out if Dr. Ryan and that Truly lady are involved in this." He scans his contacts list. "I'm calling in every favor I have." He starts dialing.

Gina gently places her hand over his phone, taking it from him without protest. She powers it off, laying it on the table. "I see what you're trying to do, and I appreciate it. Really, I do." She pulls the towel from her head, letting her hair down, running her fingers through it from root to tip.

Tony's expression softens with the image. "How can you be so calm about this, Gina?" he asks tentatively.

"I don't know that I'm calm, necessarily. I'm at peace, with whatever decision the jury makes. If I did what the evidence says I did, Vigilare or not, then I deserve whatever punishment I'm dealt. It's that simple. We uphold the law every day, or at least, I used to." Her eyebrows furrow as she processes that statement. "We arrest people when the evidence leads us to believe they're guilty. Those people are tried before a court of law, and most times receive due justice." She shrugs. "Now it's my turn." She smiles. "Besides, there's nothing more I can do for myself than you're already doing for me. Speaking of, just exactly what did you do, or promise Judge Carter for tonight," she teases.

Tony nods, sucking air through his teeth. "That one's gonna cost me."

Gina giggles, ducking her chin to her chest.

"You scared?"

She looks up at him, her smile disappearing. "Yeah." She circles the table slowly, her hand grazing its surface. "Scared of being locked up for the rest of my life. That could drive a person crazy, I think. Scared of who I am. What if I turn into her, it...that Vigilare thing in prison? If she has an inclination toward evil, can you even begin to imagine the slaughter if I'm surrounded by a bunch of criminals." She stops, holding her hand up in the air in testimony. "Amongst whom, I am no better."

"You don't have to go," Tony suggests keenly. "We could get you out of here, out of the country, tonight."

Gina smiles at him, pleased, trailing her hand over his rugged jawline. "And get you fired and thrown in the clink for aiding and abetting. Or worse yet, a lashing with a rather large wet noodle from Judge Carter for breaking her confidence." She drops her hand from his face, continuing to mindlessly circle the table. "It'll all come out in the wash, Gronkowski. I think maybe my mother, or someone in my life, I don't know, it all seems so foggy, told me 'everything happens for a reason.' You believe that?" She stops, across the table from him.

He shakes his head, accompanied by a sigh. "I think we all have to believe that. What's the alternative?" He shrugs. "Shit happens?"

Gina chuckles. "That's what I like about you. Your delicate way with words and your eloquent delivery."

Tony laughs, briefly.

"You know what scares me more than going to prison?"

Tony waits for her to answer.

"Going to sleep at night."

He tilts his head as if to say, *Huh?*

She begins circling the table again. "Those visions. The ones Emily Truly knows about," she adds, skeptically. "They keep coming. Stronger. Over and over. I don't know what the hell they mean, but I feel like I should." Her hands flail in time with her words. "I don't ever get the whole story. Just pieces, parts, clips. Like a freaking movie trailer. And Dr. Godfrey said my *condition* may be due to dissociation and traumatic experiences, and yada yada yada." She stops, eyeing Tony intently. "You think those visions, was that me? My life? My past traumatic experience? If so, why can't I recall? Why does it seem so foreign? Is my life, my past, really not what I think it is or know it to be at all?" She slaps her hand down on the table. "And this Vigilare thing. Why can't I remember any of that? I hear people talking about it. You, and Aubrey. The things you saw, the things you say I did...as Vigilare. I feel like a freaking video game character. Like Ms. Pac-Man. Like someone takes over with a joystick, and apparently I go through the motions. It's ludicrous, Tony. The whole damn thing. It's crazy!" Unexpected tears form in her eyes, a combination of frustration, anger and hurt.

Tony, experiencing his own frustration, wanting so desperately to help her, make it all better, taps his hand on the table, the wheels of his mind in motion. Apprehensively, he pulls his utility tool from its casing attached to his belt. Opening it up, he searches for the thinnest, shiny piece of steel in the set—a razor blade. "You trust me?" he asks aloud, the words surfacing in his own conscience.

Gina looks at him, subconsciously biting the inside of her lip and shaking her head. "I don't like where you're going with this."

"You trust me?" he insists.

"Yes," she replies, frustrated. "I trust you. You're not the problem."

"You are?"

Nodding, she elaborates, "I don't trust me, and if you do, you're crazier than I thought. We're not doing this." She wraps her hands around the cinch on the waist of her housecoat, jerking at both ends, squeezing adamantly against her middle. "Absolutely not. No freaking way, Jose."

"Dr.Godfrey said you can learn to control this thing. I've already seen it, Gina."

"Dr. Godfrey also said it's not just about bleeding. It's about the environment. I have to be amped up somehow, or something like that. I'm too relaxed right now. It won't work," she dismisses. "It?" she sputters as an afterthought. "Did you refer to me as *it?*"

"You," Tony quickly corrects. "You...as it...ah, shit...you as Vigilare," he continues fumbling over his words. "You know what I mean. I've already seen you, like that. What's it...you," he interjects, wincing uncomfortably. "What are *you* going to do? Scare me? Shit, Gina, if you didn't give me a heart attack that night at Randall's, I'm sure I'll be fine tonight. At least I'll be expecting it." He runs his hands through his hair, his eyes wild with excitement.

"You must be a masochist," Gina scoffs, miming his body language, running her fingers through her own hair.

"Maybe." He winks, followed up with a grin.

Gina shakes her head, waving her finger, a nervous giggle escaping her vocal chords. "I know what you're doing here, Gronkowski, and it's not working. Save that signature bullshit for someone who's buying." She plants her hands firmly on the table across from him, leaning her weight onto her arms, leveling her eyes with his. "Just because you smile and wink doesn't make everything light and carefree. It's not cute." She smiles, briefly. "Okay, well maybe just a little bit. You're a little cute." She slaps her hand down on the table, snapping herself out of it. "But it's not cute. Not in this context. Save the charm. You're not getting your way. Not with this." She turns, walking away from him.

He grabs her by the arm, pulling her into him. Their bodies pressed together, their mouths inches apart, her eyes frantically search his. "Trust me?" he asks, his breath warm and intoxicating.

"Yes," she whispers, unable to refuse him.

He lifts her hand, inspecting its palm.

She pulls her hand from him, using it to push the robe down over her right shoulder, exposing a small scar from the gunshot wound. "No need for a new scar, is there?" she asks timidly, her skin instantly cool with the thought, sends a shiver through her.

Tony traces the scar with the tips of his fingers before laying his hand out flat, stroking it across her skin. Gina moans faintly with his touch, warm and soothing, causing her eyes to close and her lips to part.

"Still can't believe how small this scar is," Tony admits, his voice low and sensual, somewhere between fear and desire. Her mouth, the fullness of it and the moisture collecting on her bottom lip, almost unbearable.

"Faster healing," she reinforces, slowly opening her eyes. "One of the perks, I guess." She smiles faintly.

Tony narrows his glance, asking for permission. She nods, her breathing becoming more pronounced, suddenly matching his. Tony raises the blade to her shoulder, steadying his hand under the labored rise and fall of her chest. Her eyes watch his focusing on her flesh, preparing to bear down with the thin, shiny piece of metal. He readjusts it in his hands several times, attempting to find the least painful position. He looks up at her, her eyes fixed on his. She nods, holding her breath, an attempt to hold still for him. He prepares holding the skin around the scar taut with one hand, while he makes contact with the tip of the scar, the razor blade in the other. Gina closes her eyes, waiting for the sensation, only to be interrupted by a *Whisht!*

"I can't do it," he says, the blade tucked tightly back into the armor of the utility tool. He drops it to the floor, disappointment in his expression.

"It's okay," Gina insists, her eyes darting back and forth between his. "I didn't want you to do it. Must be pretty freaky, huh?" Shame replaces the wonder in her eyes.

Tony cups her face in his unsteady hands, looking at her intently. "Farthest thing from it. It's amazing, DeLuca. Fucking beautiful." His hand slides down to her chest, covering the scar. "Just can't tear your flesh open. I don't want to hurt you."

"Is that all?" she inquires coyly, placing her hand over his. "You really wanna do this?"

His forehead now resting against hers, his hand trailing from her face to the back of her neck. He gives her an affirmative squeeze, nodding his head. His eyes completely salacious, his mouth grows wet being so close to hers, just to taste her.

"You trust me?" The tide's now turned.

"Yes," he half whispers, half groans.

"Kiss me," she says, somewhere between a plea and a command.

With the fervor inside him successfully knotted into a full-blown frenzy, his mouth crushes down on hers. She returns his momentum, stride for stride. Her hands wound in the collar of his shirt, his in the strands of her hair, their melding is equally craved, raw and satisfying. Breathing, sporadic and inconvenient at this point, each shows the other every trick they've got. Tony groans, resonant and prideful, from the depths of his chest, causing Gina to purr deep and low, in the back of her throat. His bottom lip between hers, she bears down, drawing blood, causing him to do the same to her in kind. She quickly follows up with a sweetly apologetic lick and suck.

A different kind of groan escapes Tony this time, one of both pleasure and pain. His mouth curves into a smile. "Clever, baby."

"One of the richest blood supplies. The mouth." She smiles back, the taste of the viscous substance finding its way to her taste buds. "Now what?"

He shrugs. "Guess we'll have to wait and see." He inspects her, specifically her eyes, waiting for the transformation. "You feel anything?"

She ponders. "Aroused."

He grabs her up in his arms, carrying her to the bedroom.

"What are you doing?"

"We gotta get you worked up, right? Dr. Godfrey's orders." He grins. "Get the blood flowing, your heart pumping."

She giggles, throwing her head back. "If I turn into that thing and don't remember this, I'm going to be pissed."

"And if it results in death for me, all I have to say is, what a way to go." He playfully throws her onto his bed, rapidly peeling his clothes off.

She meets his enthusiasm, coming up onto her knees, hastily removing her robe. "Modest much?" she inquires, looking around at the walls and the ceiling nearly covered with mirrors.

"One of the earliest sex toys known to man," he confirms, kneeling as she is on the bed. She takes him in with open arms, he takes her mouth in his, their blood meshing and mingling with each caress of their lips. Her breathing and her heartbeat escalating, her body aches.

"Tony," she calls his name, clutching his body next to hers. "Something's happening here. Oh, God." The pulse in her head starts its incessant throbbing. "Can we skip the foreplay? Just get to it," she requests adamantly through ragged breaths, praying she can remain cognizant, and that Tony will remain intact.

"You gotta let me get you warmed up," he contests.

She takes his hand and strokes it between her thighs. "Warm enough for ya?"

"Aw baby," he growls with the contact of her hot, moist flesh.

Her chest heaves up and down, she closes her eyes, grabbing her head between her hands, surely to explode. "Please, please, please... Tony," she begs.

He obliges, entering her slowly, studying her face. She moans, appeased with the release, stifling her body motionless. "Gina," he coaxes.

"I'm afraid to move," she whispers.

He grins, understanding her apprehension. "Open your eyes."

He strokes her deeper this time, causing her to gasp, flitting her eyes open. In between the fear and doubt, a dim sparkling emerald green cast exudes from her stare. Tony smiles, triumphantly. She darts her eyes away from him, the luminous green glow ricochets from mirror to mirror. She squeezes her eyes shut, hiding her head in his chest.

"What the hell was that?" she pants.

Tony chuckles, coaxing her head up. "Amazing, huh?"

"Alarming," she corrects, her eyes remain closed.

"Gina, baby...you gotta see yourself." He trails kisses up her neck. She nuzzles into him, moving against him rhythmically. "Relax, baby. I gotcha." She meets his lips with her own, a little more powerful than she realizes, drawing blood again. Tony groans, pulling away slightly.

"Shit!" she scolds. "Sorry. Let me see." She inspects with her eyes, finally unaware of their appearance. Every action she makes is efficient and fast with great fluidity and finesse. Tony watches her, intrigued. "This isn't going to work," she sighs, wiping the blood from his lip, running her tongue across the metallic-tasting substance on her own. "I'm too scared of what I might do to enjoy it."

"Nothing bad is going to happen," he pacifies, laying her down flat on the bed.

Her body grows uncomfortable, her mind working through snapshots, visions. She closes her eyes, shaking her head, attempting to drive them out. Tony bends down to her, his voice soothing, coaxing her to open her eyes. As she does, her central focus is his neck, displaying a spider web tattoo.

"Gina," he says her name, only a distant murmur to her as the intense ringing inside her head fills her auditory sensors. *Ga-gung...ga-gung...ga-gung,* her heart surges. She breathes deeply, forcefully, providing every nerve and muscle fiber within her body with adequate oxygenation. She snarls, grabbing Tony by the neck with one hand, wrapping the other around his back.

"Oh shit!" he stammers, knowing he has no defense, only to hold on.

Her eyes dart to the mirror above, the concentrated power they exude to the reflective surface causes it to shatter all over them and the bed below.

"Close your eyes!" Tony advises.

With great momentum, she swings up from her supine position, taking Tony with her, directing her body forward. Tony pushes against her, causing her to release even more exertion. She lurches from the bed to the back wall, completely airborne. His back crushes against the mirror lining the wall, crumbling it into sharp, jagged pieces.

"Ugh!" he gasps, the air knocked from his lungs with the impact. He does what comes naturally to him, sweeping her leg and taking the tussle to the ground. The sparkling emerald green light fills the room, as they spin body over body, end over end, across the floor, grappling. "Goddammit, DeLuca, snap out of it, would ya? You're giving me a hell of a rug burn," he grunts between hold maneuvers.

"Quit fighting me," she says, annoyed, as if he should know that.

"You're in there? Gina?" he pants.

"I think. Somewhere." She finally gets him pinned onto his back, sitting upright astraddle of him.

He puts his arms over his head, a gesture of defeat. His chest moves up and down erratically, his body glistening with moisture from exertion, certain his heart will leap out of his chest at any moment. She sits atop him, firm and calm, as if she exerted the bare minimum.

"I have an overwhelming urge to choke you right now," she says, looking down at him, her head cocked to the side curiously, her eyes studying him with intent.

He grins. "How come you're so calm?" he puffs between breaths.

"I was just getting warmed up," she says matter-of-factly with a straight face. Her hands remain at her side as she scans him egregiously. "I feel like I'm supposed to do something to you. But what?"

He sits up underneath her. She leans back, defensively. He puts his hands up, palms out, shoulder level.

"Maybe I should close my eyes," she suggests.

"Unh-uh," he quickly nixes that idea, shaking his head. "We're getting somewhere, De Luca...Gina...Vigilare." He smiles, shrugging his shoulders. "Keep 'em open. God, your beautiful," he exclaims, studying her, his hand aching for contact with her flesh. "Can I touch you?"

"I might touch you back," she warns, miming his hand positioning as if she is prepared to deliver whatever he does.

He steadily moves his hand in her direction, letting it contact her skin. At first, only the fingertips, then the fingers, and finally the palm. He firmly but gently strokes her neck, her shoulders, her arms.

"That feels nice," she affirms, shuddering against his hands, feeling as though her nerve endings might explode, everything amplified tenfold.

He takes her hands, laying them against his flesh, instantly jolted by the current running through her, causing his skin to tingle. "You have a motor or something?" he teases, sure she is charged somehow.

She nods, jesting. "Think I'm idling."

"Let's try and keep you there," he whispers, pulling her mouth toward his, knowing full well overdrive may prove deadly.

She resists him a little in meeting his lips, the movement extremely awkward to her in this state. Her senses incredibly heightened, the softness of his mouth feels like silk, each warm bead of moisture like water on fire, her internal temperature on the rise.

She leans her head back, breaking the union of their mouths. "I feel like I'm outside my body. Just under the surface," she whispers, disconnected. "It hurts," she laments, letting her eyes settle onto his, mirroring his carnal expression.

"Where's it hurt?" he asks, teasing her lips exquisitely with his tongue. Her hair disheveled and cascading around her face, Tony locks his hands into it holding it out of the way.

She runs her hand across her lower abdomen. "Here. It aches," she replies. "The more you touch me, the harder it aches."

Tony grins, empathizing with the same ache. "I can make it stop."

She presses her lips to his, agonizingly, it hurts so good. "Make it stop," she pleads, pulling her mouth away, remaining only centimeters apart. Her breathing laborious and heavy, sure to expire if there is no release.

Tony prepares her, as well as himself. *Take it easy, take it easy, take it easy,* he rehearses, a reminder to counteract the ravenous urge running through him every time he looks at her, purely intoxicating. He delivers, first just the tip, to which she tenses, gasping and holding her breath. "Easy...easy...easy," he rehearses aloud this time, entering her further with each *easy.* He bears down with his mouth as her fingernails penetrate deeper into the flesh on his shoulders with each new depth. She does not react, fully unaware of her own strength and clueless she has drawn his blood, yet again.

Once he is fully inside her, she sighs a contented exhale, locking her body around his.

"Oh God," he murmurs, his body quaking, her current consuming him. His thick, dark eyelashes pressed together momentarily, soaking up the sensations, the floor surely disappearing beneath. The intensity so great, he barely notices the nicks and scratches left from her exceptional roaming hands and mouth, the pleasure far exceeding any discomfort, fully aware he is as close to the supernatural as he will ever be. He slowly opens his eyes, finding hers, now bewitchingly iridescent, multicolored. He looks around the room in awe as the colors bounce and spin off the remaining mirrors lining his walls, reminiscent of a disco ball. "See what you're doing?" he asks, searching for clarification as if his own eyes may be playing tricks on him.

"I can't see anything," she confesses, her voice smooth and melodic, a most pleasing sound to his ears.

He caresses her face, realizing she speaks the truth, her eyes clearly glazed, unable to track or focus.

"But I can feel every single thing. So sublime," she moans, the corners of her mouth curving into a fully satisfied smile. "Your heart is beating one-hundred-and-fifteen times per minute. Every time you breathe, it takes my breath away. Your hands feel like silk on fire. Your scent." She breathes him in. "Virile, but sweet. Like a cherry lollipop...sex on a stick." She giggles. "Feels like I'm freaking floating on air."

"I'm not so sure we aren't," he concurs, a smooth libidinous chuckle escaping him. He breathes in deeply, causing her to gasp, literally taking her breath away. "Gina, Gina, Gina," he groans, fully willing himself unto her clairvoyant spell, engulfing her mouth with his own.

"You might want to get ahold of something," she warns, her breathing tumultuous, her grip ever tightening, nearing climax.

He smiles eagerly. "Bring it, baby."

CHAPTER 20

Two days later. Vanguard County Courthouse. The place is astir. Amidst the lore surrounding the case and the media blitz, there is no shortage of spectators. Groups rally and shout opinions at each other outside the main entrance to the courthouse. Inside, the sound of well-made shoes *clip-clop* off the tediously tended granite floors, as passersby extend quick nods and smiles, holding phones to their ears or in their hands, their thumbs tapping wildly. Vanguard PD is out in full force beefing up security.

A few familiar faces, Chief Burns and his secretary, Bonnie, scurry through the commotion to the appropriate courtroom. Everybody is seated, waiting on Judge Carter to enter. The energy in the room is strained, quite obvious it's verdict day. Chief and Bonnie spot Tony, sitting in the back as usual, an easy exit. He is bent over his knees, elbows resting on them, absently rocking back and forth, hands fidgeting. He catches Bonnie and Chief out of the corner of his eye. Motioning them over, he makes room to accommodate them both, surely offending the lady to the left of him who actually has to put her purse on her lap to make space. Tony blows it off, used to the disapproving eye roll. Chief, a little more PR-friendly, extends a subtle wave and smile to the woman as he sits down on the other side of Tony. She smiles back, smirks at Tony (who pays her no attention) and nods her head as if she has been vindicated.

"What happened to you?" Chief asks, assessing Tony's bruised cheekbone, split lip and scratches trailing from his jaw along the length of his neck.

Tony smiles, ducking his head. "You wouldn't believe me if I told you."

"What's this, you requesting a transfer to New Orleans? Saw the papers on my desk this morning," Chief inquires. Removing his glasses, he wipes them haphazardly across the stomach of his shirt, attempting to remove the greasy fingerprint he accidentally placed there after his morning bear claw and coffee.

"Only temporary. Need to look into something down there."

"DeLuca?" Chief asks, knowingly, looking through his glasses. Disappointed with the smudge that still remains, he goes back to rubbing them across his shirt. Bonnie huffs, prying the glasses from his hand, dragging the appropriate accoutrement, a chamois, from her purse, efficiently tidying up the lens.

Tony nods, his eyes failing to meet Chief's, his line of sight focused on his hands, rubbing briskly together.

"Nothing more you could've done, Gronkowski," Chief sympathizes.

"Oh, there's a lot more to be done, Chief. Just have to follow the crumbs."

"And your cookie's in New Orleans?" Peering through the lenses, Bonnie approves, nudging Chief with her elbow. "Thanks, Bonnie." She smiles, looking straight ahead, intently focused on Gina at the defense table.

Tony watches the two of them, shaking his head, a low chuckle surfacing.

"Stuff it, Gronkowski," Chief mutters, his vision renewed through the flawlessly clean lenses.

Tony leans back, looking around the room, at Dr. Ryan, Dr. Godfrey, William and Emily Truly, Aubrey Raines, Gina. "You ever get the feeling that things are not the way they seem? People aren't who they appear to be?"

"You still got a hard-on for Dr. Ryan?" Chief's attention is piqued as Judge Carter walks into the courtroom. "Battle axe," he mutters under his breath.

"Didn't you say she transferred here from New Orleans, Dr. Ryan?" Tony affirms. "Battle axe? She's soft as down," he further comments on Judge Carter.

"She would be to you. Total panther," Chief speaks out the side of his mouth, as Judge Carter nears her podium. "Get a few years on ya, then we'll talk."

Tony chuckles, appeased he can rely on Chief for comic relief considering the pressure of the verdict. He leans forward again, forearms resting on his knees, hands beginning to fidget, looking up at Chief Burns.

"What?" Chief says.

"Cougar, Chief. The appropriate terminology is cougar." He shakes his head, grinning.

The sound of Judge Carter's gavel brings immediate silence to the courtroom as all eyes and attention are paid to her. "Bailiff, please call the jurors." She allows them to file in, taking their seats, pulling her reading glasses from the pocket of her robe.

Mr. McVain eyes the jurors, maintaining a friendly smile, yet again fluffing his lavish locks with his fingertips. Aubrey exchanges an apprehensive glance with Gina, who nods her head reassuringly. Dr. Ryan, quite conceivably the most emotionless person in the room, sits astute and pulled together as the scene unfolds.

"Ms. Foreperson," Judge Carter addresses the lead juror. She stands dutifully. "Have you, the jury, reached a verdict?"

"Yes, we have, Madam Judge." She extends several folded sheets of paper to the bailiff, who transports them to Judge Carter.

Judge Carter takes a moment, scanning the documents, double-checking that they remain the same as the official forms reported to her chambers before handing them off to the court clerk for reading. "Will the defendant please rise, along with counsel?"

Gina stands. Aubrey joins her.

The court clerk, a petite woman with a surprisingly resonant voice, clears her throat. "In the case of The City of Vanguard versus Gina Marie DeLuca. As to the charge of first degree murder of Thomas Boyd, verdict is to Count One, we the jury find the defendant, 'not guilty.'"

A nearly uniform sigh rings throughout the courtroom, accompanied by a few gasps. The court clerk has to coerce her lips from curving into a smile. Aubrey grabs Gina's hand, squeezing tightly. Bonnie does the same to Chief Burns. Mr. McVain slaps his hand down on his table, shaking his head, contemplating the fact he may lose his first case. Dr. Ryan remains perfectly unruffled, while Tony and Gina hold their breath, waiting for the other shoe to drop.

"As to the charge of first degree murder of Victor Peebles, verdict is to Count Two, we the jury find the defendant, 'not guilty,'" the court clerk continues.

At this point, Gina's ears maintain function while her mind grows jumbled, confused and disbelieving as she listens to the remaining twelve verdicts, all the same as the first two.

The momentum of the court clerk shifts gears as she nears the last two verdicts. "As to the charge of first degree murder of Trenton Biggs," (the attempted rape of Aubrey Raines with the accompanying DNA in the form of skin), "verdict is to Count Fifteen, we the jury find the defendant, 'not guilty.' As to the charge of voluntary manslaughter of Trenton Biggs, verdict is to Count Sixteen, we the jury find the defendant, 'guilty.'"

This time, nearly uniform gasps chime throughout the courtroom, attended by a few sighs. Tony's chin falls to his chest, recognizing the lesser charge of voluntary manslaughter versus first degree murder, still somehow disappointed. Gina's eyes close, her head dipping in one solitary nod, grateful for the verdicts, acknowledging her fate and fully stunned at the lack of a more stringent outcome. Mr. McVain shrugs, flitting his head to the side, pursing his lips, disillusioned yet appeased by a charge of any sort, sustaining his perfect record.

"Thank you, Madam Clerk," Judge Carter interjects. "Considering your lack of criminal record," she begins addressing Gina, "and the fact you served this city as a peace officer, and from all accounts did a fine job of it, I hereby sentence you, Gina Marie DeLuca to the minimum requirement for voluntary manslaughter per my jurisdiction—two-years imprisonment." She turns fluidly to Mr. McVain. "Your petition to release Ms. DeLuca into the psychiatric care of Dr. Patricia Ryan is denied. "Guards, please take Ms. DeLuca into custody." With a bang of her gavel, she exits her podium and the courtroom.

"Viva Vigilare! Viva Vigilare! Viva Vigilare!" the chant breaks out in finite groups throughout the room, receiving discernable looks, gestures and a few vocal reprimands from attendees who disagree.

Dr. Ryan quickly rises, making her way through the crowded, noisy aisle. She exchanges glances with William and Emily Truly as she passes them, slipping a note into the pocket of Dr. Godfrey's white lab coat prior to walking out the large wooden doors.

Chief Burns pats Tony on the back. "Could've been a lot worse, kid."

Tony nods, remaining seated, still leaning forward, his forearms rest on his knees, his hands clasped together.

"I'll put in a call to corrections. See if we can get her some eyes on the inside," Chief consoles.

Again, Tony nods, speechless.

Chief motions to Bonnie as he stands to leave.

"I'll sit with Tony," she says solemnly. Chief pats her on the shoulder and pushes through the milling crowd.

Bonnie slides closer to Tony. She sits upright, her shoulders a little rounder than usual, her customary large, bold eyes now small and timid, her hands resting numbly in her lap. Neither says a word nor expects such, they simply sit in silence as the crowd flits around them. Mr. McVain makes it a point to track Bonnie with his stare, as he stands from the prosecution table headed toward the exit. Even in her dejected disposition, she is a sight to behold. Her auburn hair cascading against a royal blue dress, matching the color of her eyes. Her fair skin like white chocolate, luscious in its design. She looks up feeling the searing heat of Mr. McVain's glance. He flashes her his best smile, running his fingers through those golden locks. She huffs, darting her eyes away from him, folding her arms defiantly across her waist, which does not help her cause, as it only further defines the voluptuous V, already prominent at the top of her dress. He walks on by, consoling himself with the fact that one victory shall suffice for the day.

Chapter 21

Four hours later. Vanguard County Jail. Gina awaits transportation to the federal corrections facility three hours outside the city limits.

"DeLuca, and Barnes," an officer reads last names from the transport papers rounding the corner to Gina's cell.

"Yep," a rather large man confirms, accompanied by another man of equally paramount stature in federal prison guard gear.

"Bring Barnes up from the back," the officer yells.

"I'm aware my insight may not be wanted or welcomed at this point, but you really think it's a good idea to put me and Barnes on the same transport?" Gina confronts the officer.

Familiar with her and the case, he agrees, "She does make a good point."

"Warden's transfer papers say DeLuca *and* Barnes," the guard speaks up. "If the warden ain't happy, ain't nobody happy." He smiles. "We'll handle it."

"All right." The officer shrugs.

Randall, less than enthused, is delivered to the guards, unaware of Gina's presence.

"Tessa and her mother can finally rest well at night," she deduces, standing on the inside of her cell. The officer slides the door from in front of her.

Randall jumps back, his eyes wild. "I'm not getting on a bus with this crazy bitch," he contends.

Gina shrugs. "I told them it might not be the best idea."

"Seriously," he pleads. "She'll kill me."

The guard pushes into Randall, grabs him by the elbow and leads him toward the exit. "We're the ones armed with AR-15s, and you're worried about her," he scoffs.

A short, white bus with black lettering idles in front of the jailhouse. One guard mans Gina, and the other Randall, loading them into the back of the bus. The original seats have been ripped out and replaced with two long benches running parallel to each other against the sides of the large, white metal rectangle on wheels. Gina's handcuffs are connected to ankle cuffs, further locked down to a large steel ring bolted to the floor underneath her seat. Randall undergoes the same procedure. They sit, facing one another. A driver eyes them through his rearview mirror. The guards load up in front of the massive sheet of steel fencing that separates them from Gina and Randall. One of the guards holds up his index finger, swiftly circling it. The driver gives the clutch a little action, shifting into gear.

An hour into the trip, Randall continues talking incessantly. Gina manages to ignore him up to this point, her head relaxed against the glass of the window behind her. Her eyes take turns closing and opening for intervals, as she takes in her surroundings and attempts to block Randall out. They are far beyond the city limits, the middle of nowhere, to be exact. On a narrow two-lane road, no houses around for miles, fall foliage nears its end, as the trees stand scarecrowed and brown. Her head jerks from side to side in the back of the bumpy bus, too wide to maintain its position between the lines on the confined road, the tires take turns riding on and off the berm. They steadily climb, ascending and descending, the roads winding in their terrain. The guards sit stoic, making occasional eye contact and signals, but there is no conversation, no vocal interplay. She pays close attention to them, something unsettling about their demeanor. A black Sedan comes into view intermittently. One that has been doing so since they left Vanguard. Gina looks at Randall, his lips still moving, totally clueless. She shakes her head.

"You ever been to jail?" Randall asks. "I bet you haven't, being a cop and all," he continues, answering his own questions as he has been doing for the past hour. "Maybe juvy or something? Bet you never did anything you shouldn't do. Were you a good girl?" he inquires jeeringly. "Bet you were a good little girl." He licks his lips with a sly smirk.

Gina stares at him, her expression blank. No sense carrying out a conversation with an invalid she reasons.

"You don't talk much, huh?"

"Maybe you should take some lessons," she replies, her vocal tone jaded and commanding.

He smirks again, pleased with himself for drawing something out of her. "Why don't you break out of those things?" he motions to the chains surrounding her hands and feet. *"Vigilare,"* he says with contempt, "wouldn't let chains stop her." He puffs his chest out with a cocky undertone. "Come on, superhero. Where you at?"

She remains unfazed, looking at him, through him.

"Ooh," he mocks. "You gonna do that eye thing?"

"What eye thing?" she retorts, reprimanding him with her intonation of his fabricated testimony.

He sits back, grinning smugly, letting the air leave his puffed out chest. "How's the shoulder?" he digs, alluding to his handy work.

She darts her glance away from him, instinctively as the bus speeds up, shifting to and from on the bumpy, winding turf. The eyes of the driver in the rearview mirror communicate with those of the guards. He reaches toward the dash, pushing a button that releases harnesses from above the three men. Five-point seatbelts, those found in the speediest of race cars, drop from the ceiling. They assume the position, until the harnesses have locked and secured them. Looking out the window behind Randall, Gina searches for guardrails, of which she unfortunately finds none.

"What?" Randall reads the concern in her eyes, his body now rigid and alarmed.

Momentarily, forgetting her hands are shackled, she jerks her arms up in an attempt to grab hold of the bar above her attached to the ceiling. Met with the force of the irons, her wrists instantly ache. She bears down against her seat, her body tensed, her hands digging into the bench. "Hold on," she warns.

"Hold on?" he quips, pulling against his cuffs, stifling any attempt to hold onto anything. "To what!"

The right front tire of the bus veers across the berm and onto the grass, quickly followed by the back tire, continuing until it runs out of ground surface. The engine screams with unmet acceleration, the tire spinning with nothing to latch onto. The momentum of the bus pulls the right side down, finding the contact it so desperately seeks, unfortunately rocky and unlevel. The steel frame creaks and falters, finally giving way to gravity. Randall screams as his side is the first to make contact with the hard ground below, shattering windows behind him gouge into the flesh of his head and neck. Upside down now, Gina feels the force of the shackles nearly pulling her limb from limb. The bus continues to topple end over end, slamming Gina back against the windows as her side makes contact with the soil below, catapulting Randall's body into the air in her direction, still held fast to the ring in the floorboard of the bus. He screams over and over again, as the bus grates with indentations, windows pop and break, the sound of their shackles clanking and screeching between slack and taut. Gina's mouth grimaces tightly, her body firm and adaptive, her eyes pressed together, waiting for calm.

With one last tumble, the bus rocks slightly, finally coming to a stop on its right side. Randall feels a surge of water surround him as he is pinned on his back. Gina hovers over him, nearly airborne, her hands and feet remain shackled to the opposite side of the bus, her body stooped and crouching to accommodate the irons.

Randall screams and blubbers, the water engulfing him.

Gina opens her eyes, unsure of her own consciousness at this point, every joint and muscle in her body throbbing from the beating of the bus and the shackles. She looks down at Randall who flails about slightly, limited by his cuffs. His body and head fully submerged. Her ears pull her attention from him as the sound of something mechanical calls her in the direction of the driver and the guards. Their harnesses release, dropping each of them to the right side of the bus, as gravity would have it. Unwounded and light on their feet, they stand, clearing what remains of the glass from the front windshield before exiting the bus and making their way around to the back. No words are spoken as Gina hears their footsteps slush up and down. Her vision pulled to the water below as she notices scant red drops splashing into it.

"Shit! Shit! Shit!" she whispers with each drop, feeling her heartbeat begin to pick up its pace. *Just breathe,* she talks to herself, Tony's words from their intimate night ringing in her ears.

The pain from the cuffs pulling against her wrists, accommodating her entire body weight shoots through her, tingling intensely as if she were pressed against pins and needles. The sensation calls out her bodily supply of adrenaline. As direct as a shot to the heart, her transformation arrives. Mind and body fight internally, one attempting to maintain control, the other simply waiting to relish its release. Her back muscles engage, with one sporadic flex, her wrists and arms are free from their chains, the explosiveness causing the links to shatter. She now hangs from the side of the bus, her body taut and dangling by the ankle cuffs still securely intact to the steel ring in the floor. Her mind maintaining by a slim margin, she holds herself up on one arm while grabbing with the other at the steel ring binding Randall's shackles, his body giving out on his fight against the water.

The driver and the guards are at the back of the bus now, banging and pulling on the back door, apparently jammed as they are unsuccessful in their attempt.

Gina pulls against the steel ring; it gives only slightly. Engaging her entire core, her body is nearly parallel to the floor as she grabs the ring with both hands. A guttural yell escapes her lungs, the ring breaks loose. Grabbing at Randall's prison uniform, she pulls him from the water, using the steel ring holding her feet securely to the other side of the bus as leverage. The water, not quite knee deep is forgiving as she leans Randall against the side of the bus, his torso and head now free of the suffocating liquid. She beats his back against the wall of the bus, causing him to stir to consciousness and expel water from his lungs. He looks at her dazed and puzzled.

"Don't look at me," she warns, abruptly. Her ears tracking the footsteps of the driver and the guards sloshing through the water, headed back to the front of the bus.

Randall scans her quickly, his breathing returning, fast and furious. Her eyes are sparkling that same shade of emerald green he witnessed the night at his apartment. She avoids looking at him, focusing on steadying his body.

"Close your eyes, dammit!" She slams him against the wall of the bus. The physical urge to wrap her hands around his neck and lock eyes with him begins to outweigh her mental reasoning.

He squeezes his eyes shut, the jar to his back causing him to find and engage his feet beneath him, propping himself up.

Just breathe, she rehearses again, letting go of him as he takes control of his body weight. Her lungs burn with the deep inhalation, the additional oxygen catapulting through her system filling her muscles with fuel. The power exerted by her legs causes the cuffs to blow apart from her ankles. Quickly reassembling her balance, she flips through the air, landing perfectly on her feet in the water below, her arms autonomically assuming a defensive position as she rounds up. Her head shifts to her left in the direction of the driver and the burly guards. They make quick work of the steel fencing separating them from the back of the bus with a propane torch, the orange flame crackling and hissing as it releases the metal. Her thoughts are interrupted by a distant, approaching sound. *Whoosh! Whoosh! Whoosh!* A chopper, helicopter.

Stealthily, she makes her way to the emergency door at the back of the bus. Turning her back to it, she plants a mule kick to its center, over the lock. The door swings open, clanking, metal against metal. Lurching out of the white box on wheels, cool water splashes up around her. A quick glance up the ravine reveals the black Sedan parked on the berm.

The driver and the guards stop cutting through the steel fencing, swiftly exiting the front windshield in pursuit of Gina. Knee deep in the water, her body prepared to fight, every muscle, every fiber taut as a bow, simply waiting to spring. *Fight or flight,* the words echo through her head, still cognizant at this point, not fully delivered unto Vigilare-mode. The driver and the guards have guns—long rifles—semi-automatic AR-15s with all the bells and whistles. Her feet stay firmly planted, her option chosen by instinct. The chopper charges louder, temporarily clouding her hearing, closing the gap on its distance from the ravine.

The two guards round the corner of the back of the bus, their weapons engaged and in position. Gina pivots, facing them, fully prepared to meet their challenge.

"Now!" a voice yells from behind her, on the bank.

The guards simultaneously pull their triggers, one gun aimed at Gina's left leg, the other at her right shoulder. Her keen, sparkling emerald green eyes catch sight of the bullets as they leave the chambers. She throws herself into a back bend, the bullet meant for her right shoulder whizzes by above her. Within a fraction of a second, her body counter-reacts, straddling the bullet targeted for her left leg as it hisses underneath her.

Randall watches everything in utter awe from the inside of the bus. His hands and feet still shackled, ingenuity certainly not his strong suit. He remains up against the wall, his body beginning to shiver from the cold water.

Midair, Gina's upper back, between her shoulder blades burns as spikes penetrate her skin, burrowing into her flesh. Her entire body jolts from the current running through the tines. She grits her teeth as she comes down into the water, knowing the shock is about to multiply by ten at her contact with the optimal conductor. The pain knocking her swiftly off her feet, she falls to her knees in the water, her body convulsing. Her emerald green stare now choppy and short-circuited, her mind shuffles in and out of cognition between Gina and Vigilare. The surge of oxygen and power running through her, currently without any use, only seems to fuel the shock waves. She is completely powerless.

The man at the controls of the significantly beefed up taser comes into her view—Dr. Bernard Shaw of the white coats, ETNA Division. Reminiscent of her hospital stay, her head turns weakly in the direction of the two guards, hazily identifying them as the two orderlies. She musters up any strength she has left, lurches forward in their direction, stretching her body out for all it's worth. One of the guards meets her attempt with a large utility boot to her chest, knocking her onto her back, fully submerged under water. Her limbs flail about, the current entirely circular now. Her auburn hair scattered and drenched, winding itself in the rocks and moss of the creek bed. The sound of the chopper, a muffled lullaby sings her into a dream. A young boy appears before her, a cascade of light surrounding him, the sound of his laughter quenching that of the helicopter. His arms outstretched, she smiles and meets him, wrapping the boy in her arms. Dr. Shaw holds the trigger down on his apparatus until the last air bubble escaping her lungs surfaces. Randall watches her lifeless body, disbelieving, waiting for her to pop up out of the water. She does not.

CHAPTER 22

Randall's attention is quickly drawn in another direction. *Whoosh! Whoosh! Whoosh!* The chopper is overhead, circling, preparing to land. Dr. Shaw is not surprised by the arrival of the helicopter, as if he expects it. He braces himself against the wind it stirs up, maintaining his station.

The large *black hawk* touches down, its main rotor disengaging, allowing the propellers to slow, eventually stopping altogether. The door slides back, and the look on Dr. Shaw's face quickly changes from one of comfort and expectancy to bewilderment.

The individuals leaping out of the chopper, landing swiftly on agile feet are not his fellow members of ETNA Division. The first coming into contact with the ground below is Emily Truly. Her jet black hair laid back against her scalp in a tight ponytail, she wears black military fatigues, most certainly mission bound. The guards spin in her direction, wielding their long rifles, awaiting Dr. Shaw's command. Aubrey Raines trails behind Emily, her feet barely making contact with the turf below, her body seemingly untethered by gravity. Much in the same fashion as Emily, her blonde hair is slicked back tight to her head, held together by one long, lavish braid, her black fatigues perfectly fitted to her form.

Randall's eyes all but pop out of his head taking her in. She exudes a ray of sparkling emerald light from her glazed-over dark greens, the cast exorbitant and powerful, like a blanket over the whole ravine. Dr. Shaw attempts to order his guards to fire, but his speech does not come. He is frozen in the luminescent glow. The driver and the guards feel it, too, their efforts at any action met with resistance. The light has yet to reach Gina, lying limp in the bottom of the cold, watery ravine, as if the absence of her heartbeat nullifies the connection.

"Emily," Aubrey reprimands, focusing all her energy on emitting the light, her eyes quickly tiring.

"Fine," Emily answers, less than enthused. Her hands at her side, she stares straight ahead in Gina's direction with intense resolve. Her eyes, violet, do not emit any kind of light. She zones out, wiggling her fingers and her toes, engaging their telekinetic energy. Momentarily, Gina reciprocates, still buried under water and unconscious, her body somehow connected, her fingers and toes dexterous.

"Today, Emily," Aubrey warns impatiently, her eyes beginning to fatigue.

Emily inhales deeply, the pressure within her chest prompting a generous squeeze to her heart, causing its pace to surge. Gina's eyes flash open, flooding with the shock of the cold water against them as her heart is pummeled with its first thunderous *lub dub,* quickly keeping pace with Emily's. Her chest rises, her lungs engorged with air. Aubrey's connection complete, her luminescent stare finally feeling the push of Gina's, so powerful Aubrey is catapulted back into the side of the chopper, her eyelids coming to rest in painful relief. The emerald green ray shoots through Dr. Shaw and the guards, releasing them of their frozen positions. The momentum sends them to the ground.

Randall watches from inside the bus in fear and amazement as Gina swiftly rises from the water. The motion so fast, plays in his mind in single-frame snapshots. Her body bowed backward and airborne, sacrificial in its presentation, rises at least a full body length up off the earth's surface. Drops of water disperse from her frame. With a whipping motion, her torso contracts, bowing inward as she lands upright, solidly on sure feet, poised and in full Vigilare-mode.

The guards and the driver shuffle frantically in the direction opposite her along the rough terrain on their bellies, grabbing for their weapons. Dr. Shaw in crab position, his hands and feet in contact with the turf, faces her. He grabs for the little box controlling the current delivered through the tines still gouged into her back. His hands fumbling with the device, searching for the surge button. With the push of the red dial, the jolt is delivered, causing Vigilare to arch her back in pain. The contraction of her muscles simultaneously forcing the barbed tines from her flesh. She catches the shiny metal, blood-tinged spikes in midair with her eyes. They hover, juggling as the volts continue to their ends, hungry to make contact with something, someone. Bearing down with her stare, the silver soon turns emerald green as the spikes change direction on her cue. With flawless precision and speed, the tines bury deep into the chest of Dr. Shaw. His finger held fast against the surge button, delivering to him a duplicate current. His body flops to and fro, resembling that of a fish out of water, until his finger falls limp releasing the dial.

Aubrey, fully recuperated, engages her eyes on the rifles the two guards have in their grasp as they settle onto their feet. Clutching at the guns, their bodies begin following the magnetic pull, their feet dragging in the soil. Looking to one another, they nod, letting go. The rifles spring in Aubrey's direction. She diverts her eyes to the left, the weapons following until they come to a stop, a safe distance from the guards. Releasing her gaze, the guns drop, clanking against the rocky surface.

With the same momentum, stride and poise, Emily and Vigilare run at the two guards, who easily stand a foot taller and doubly outweigh each of them. They meet the burly men with simultaneous flying double chest kicks, using the leverage of their robust bodies to push off into roundhouse position as they land swiftly on their feet. The two women fight in tandem, their moves and deflections perfectly timed, as if controlled by one mind. It is a supreme dance of anatomy and kinesiology, flawless in its execution. The only difference is power, unquestionably in Vigilare's favor. Their bodies taut and flexible, engage and retreat at swift intervals. Not even the men's size is an obstacle, as their agility is metaphysical. The guards and the driver, outnumbering them, outweighing them, out-bruting them, even engaging knives they pulled from the crevices of their uniforms now lay lifeless at the bottom of the ravine.

Emily and Vigilare remain crouched, adrenaline still surging through their intricate systems. Eyeing one another, Vigilare instinctively feels threatened, as she should. Emily lurches at her, and the two tumble through the air, grappling end-over-end, each attempting to assume the dominant position. Emily swings and Vigilare dodges. Vigilare engages and Emily retreats, only to recoup with a countermove. Extended to the ends of their limbs, both arms and legs, pivoting and leaping through the air, scuffling along the rough terrain, the women combat and refrain with power and finesse. Neither is capable of fully submitting the other. Every action superbly executed, every reaction timely and absolute, their conditioning and control equally matched. The sounds of their clothing, sharp and crisp with each follow-through, mimicked and aspired to in many a karate dojo by students wearing perfectly designed gi to promote such resonance.

"That's enough," a female voice rings through their action, accompanied by a blast from a shotgun.

They stop momentarily, both of them on their feet in defensive stances, eyes locked on each other. Their chests heaving up and down, replenishing their oxygen, hearts pounding ferociously, seemingly ready to burst from their ribcages.

"Load up," a male voice orders.

Emily is the first to break eye contact, letting her guard down. She turns swiftly away. Vigilare rests her clenched fists at her sides, her gaze shifting in the direction of the voices. There, in front of the chopper, Dr. Patricia Ryan stands beside William Truly, who holds a shotgun in one hand aimed at the sky.

"Aubrey," Dr. Ryan beckons.

Aubrey obliges, meeting Vigilare's fading luminescent emerald green gaze with her own, fully voiding it. The action causes Vigilare to wince, pressing her eyes together. Opening them, the glow is gone and Gina remains. 'She's in this up to her eyeballs, Gina. I can feel it,' Tony's voice flashes through her mind in reference to Dr. Ryan.

Emily circles the bus, inspecting cautiously as she makes her way to the back entrance. Spotting Randall leaned up against the side of the bus, shivering from standing in the cold water, his hands and feet still firmly shackled, she purposely slows her pace, sauntering toward him through the water, a malignant smile gracing her lips.

"What do we have here?" she says, pleased with her find, a regular gold mine.

Randall watches her fearfully, the whites of his eyes large and protruding, nuzzling his body closer still against the back of the bus frame.

Grabbing the propane torch from the vicinity of the broken metal fence that once separated the front of the bus from the back, she fires it up, causing Randall to flinch, closing his eyes.

"Hold your hands out," she orders.

He peeks through one eye, then the other, swiftly offering up the cuffs, his arms stretched to their limits in front of him. The heat from the flame warms him as it sputters, slicing through the irons, releasing his hands from their confinement. Emily holds the shackle leading to his ankle cuffs. With one swift jerk, she pulls his feet out from under him, dumping him back into the water.

Randall's words garble from beneath the cold, liquid mask, bubbling to the surface. Emily coolly continues cutting through the shackles, freeing his ankles, paying him no attention. Her work complete, she discards the torch. Randall splishes and splashes, gathering his limbs, assisting himself to a standing position.

He sputters, spitting water from his mouth, a thin fog clouds around his body, the cold air meeting the moisture from the water.

His eyes dart from Emily to the front and then to the back of the bus, searching for his most accessible exit.

Emily chuckles. "Told you I'd be seeing you, Randall," she says, the words echoing inside his mind, reminiscent of the same threat he received in the elevator weeks ago.

"You!" he gasps, hurtling toward the back of the bus.

His screams are heard outside the big white metal box, soon followed by silence. Emily emerges from the front of the bus, her body language fully offensive.

"And you call yourself Vigilare...keeper of the night," she spews bitterly in Gina's direction, returning to the helicopter. "You better get a handle on her, or I will, *mother*," she scoffs to Dr. Ryan, loading into the chopper.

Dr. Ryan wards her off with an accommodating nod, her hand rising in testament fashion.

William Truly follows his daughter's lead, rounding the front of the *black hawk,* piling into position at the controls.

Gina remains completely still, dumbfounded, her mind, or internal computer rather, overloaded and attempting to process and compile data.

"There will be time for explanation," Dr. Ryan consoles in her distant and cold manner. "Load up, Ms. DeLuca." She turns, climbing up into the open sliding door, taking her seat next to Emily.

CHAPTER 23

Aubrey extends Gina a genuinely compassionate smile, standing there in front of the chopper.

Gina looks around at the wreckage, her flight instinct kicking up inside her, unanswered as her legs fail to accommodate. Tears press hard against the backs of her eyes, recognizing her life is no longer her own. Maybe it never was.

Whoosh! Whoosh! Whoosh! The propeller on the chopper winds up slowly, the beginnings of a formidable wind.

Aubrey walks to Gina, taking her by the hand, the gust feathering her hair and Gina's, catapulting it upwards. "We have no choice, Gina," Aubrey raises her voice to be audible over the propeller. "They chose us." She sways her head toward the chopper.

Gina gives in, her body on autopilot. The two women load into the helicopter, taking their seats across from Dr. Ryan and Emily Truly. William Truly engages the big bird, steadily putting more space between it and the ground. Emily pulls against the sliding door until it slams shut, barricading them inside. In the navigation seat, a familiar round, happy face emerges, peeking from behind Emily. Scrunching up his nose, his glasses resting at eye level, Dr. Godfrey smiles reassuringly at Gina.

She shakes her head disapprovingly, unwilling to return the gesture.

"Here, put this on," Aubrey instructs, pulling Gina's harness from the ceiling.

Gina gives her a condescending look as if to say, *What's the worst that could happen?*

Aubrey smiles, hooking it around her anyway.

Emily watches the two with full antipathy, her icy stare unwavering.

The atmosphere in the chopper is silent for miles. Gina looks out the window. They head north and west.

"The man, in the alleyway, by the dumpster," Dr. Ryan begins. "It is as Emily testified. He raped her three years ago and left her for dead. Do you know she laid behind that dumpster all night and half of the morning, before someone found her?"

Emily doesn't react, her expression stone cold, looking straight ahead as if she has completely detached from the memory. Gina refuses to pay Dr. Ryan any attention, continuing to look out the window. Her ears perked, however.

"You should know how it feels to watch your child suffer and not be able to do anything about it," Dr. Ryan pokes Gina's emotions, causing her to turn her eyes in her direction, full of questions and quickly connecting the dots. "Your visions. The little boy... Braydon."

With the pronunciation of his name, Gina mouths the word, *Braydon,* with renewed recognition, remembering him as her own. Vivid snapshots flash before her—Lon's excitement in finding out they were pregnant, Braydon's birth (painfully blissful), the first time he clutched her finger in his tiny hand, his first words ('Bou Bou,' reminding her of Boudreaux's happy, panting face), proud yet fearfully waiting for the bus to arrive on his first day of school, armored with his Superman backpack, family dinners, bedtime stories, his big blue eyes and gorgeous dark, curly eyelashes matching his hair, just like his daddy's, his laughter, his sweet little body laying lifeless beside Lon's on their bedroom floor.

Gina lunges forward at Dr. Ryan, her anger bridled by the harness crossing her body, hooked into her seat below.

Emily smirks at her, satisfied with her discontent.

Dr. Ryan holds her hand out, defensive and sympathetic. "That was before I knew you. Before any of us knew you." She settles her hand in her lap, continuing, "Dr. Godfrey was called in on your case. From the coroner's office."

"I was dwelling in New Orleans at the time," Dr. Godfrey confirms from the front seat.

"He and I go way back. To my West Point days," Dr. Ryan confirms, looking suspiciously at Gina, aware she knows all too well about her connection to West Point.

Gina remains flat in her affect, neither confirming nor denying Dr. Ryan's suspicions.

"He had his own private lab," Dr. Ryan continues, referring to Dr. Godfrey. "Your body was delivered to him for autopsy, upon his request." She crosses one leg over the other, leaning forward intently, her elbow resting on her knee. "That thing you do with your eyes. The sparkling emerald green light. Dr. Godfrey saw hints of that in the blood encircling your bodies—you, your husband and your son. The combination. He passed it off as antifreeze, knowing it was anything but. Something happened that night, Gina."

"Brianna," Gina corrects, remembering her birth name.

"Gina," Dr. Ryan amends sternly. "Brianna Castille died that night. On her bedroom floor in New Orleans."

Emily rolls her eyes as if the drama is unnecessary.

"When you woke hours later, with the help of Dr. Godfrey, you were reborn Gina DeLuca."

"Vigilare," Emily chimes in mockingly with a spooky intonation. Dr. Ryan stifles her with a reprimanding glance.

Gina looks out the window, disbelieving and done with the conversation.

"The mixture of your blood," Dr. Ryan continues.

"O-negative," Dr. Godfrey confirms.

"Your husband's," she waits for Dr. Godfrey to chime again.

"AB-negative."

"And your son's."

"B-negative," he finishes.

"When infused back to you, gave you renewed life." Dr. Ryan looks at Gina intently. "Aren't you the least bit impressed?" She proceeds in her mildly excited manner, too reserved to fully inspire. "You are the only one of its kind."

"That we know of," Dr. Godfrey adds.

"And when exposed to oxygen, it gives you supernatural strength. Power beyond that of the human realm. That luminescent emerald glow on the hardwood floor of your bedroom now resides within you. Because of your husband and your son, you have the ability to do things unparalleled. And they are alive in you, literally, in your veins."

She has Gina's attention now as she looks to her from the window.

"Every breath, every heartbeat, every empowered move, possible because of them. It can't be wrong, Gina."

"My husband," her voice breaks, causing her to gather herself before continuing. "Lon and Braydon. Pure hearts," she says, her hand finding its way to her chest. "I've killed fifteen people, that I know of. How many more?" Her body language intense. "You think that would make them proud? And if I am this way because of them, why am I *avenging* others? What about the bastards that killed them? When do they get a visit from Vigilare?"

"Eight," Emily quickly corrects her. "You've killed eight rapists and pedophiles," she exaggerates the labels. "You don't get to have all the fun." She smiles, looking at Aubrey, who turns her head away to the window, slightly ashamed.

Gina nods, fully catching her drift. "And if I'm the only one of my *kind,* how do you explain these two." She flicks her arms at Aubrey and Emily.

"If you would be patient, I was getting to that," Dr. Ryan replies, annoyed. "Aubrey was the first, after you." She motions to Aubrey, urging her to speak.

Aubrey begins, her glance finding its way back to the window. She talks with a distant tone. "I was in New Orleans, on Spring Break. Mardi Gras. My goal to get wasted and wild. Do it up right. My neck was weighed down with beads, if that tells you anything," she says, condemning herself for flashing her chest in exchange for the four-cent plastic beads in traditional Mardi Gras fashion. "Stupid." She shakes her head, still punishing herself for her adolescent actions. "My friend and I fell in with some locals. Boys, of course. We accepted as they provided us round after round of anything and everything. Merciful, really, to be completely shit-faced. Complete consciousness would have been even more damaging." She stops.

"Dr. Godfrey found her the next morning just before sunrise, in the gutter, outside his lab." Dr. Ryan looks to Aubrey, who continues staring out the window. "Nearly torn limb from limb. Not a shred of clothing left on her body. Her blonde hair saturated in her own blood. They took turns with her. Virginity stolen. Her face and physique bruised and marred beyond recognition."

"I couldn't leave her lying there, the poor thing," Dr. Godfrey adds empathetically. "Her pulse was so weak, she had lost a lot of blood. Surely a goner." He turns around farther, his mouth curving into a smile as he makes eye contact with Gina. "Then I remembered, I had a living, breathing marvel in my lab—Vigilare. You saved her."

"My blood," Gina concludes. "You transfused my blood to Aubrey." She shakes her head, the information a bit much to wrap her mind around. "Why can't Aubrey be Vigilare? If you have her, why do you need me? I was happy with life as Gina DeLuca, Detective."

Emily bites down on her lip, her head shaking scornfully. "Ingrate." She hastily pulls the neck guard from her fatigues, revealing a crucifix hanging just below her collarbone. The shiny silver pendant catches Gina's eye, momentarily piquing her memory—Lon's exuberant face, mirroring hers after opening the small silk-lined jewelry box.

"What the hell is your problem?" Gina bears down on Emily's frosty stare. "You wanna be Vigilare? Go ahead. I didn't sign up for this shit!"

Emily says nothing. If looks could kill, Gina surely would be deceased.

Dr. Ryan pats Emily's leg, which she pulls away. "That was the plan, initially."

"I was the test dummy," Aubrey offers up flippantly.

Dr. Ryan sends her a disparaging look, gathering herself. "After Dr. Godfrey saw how Aubrey responded with the transfusion of your blood, he called Mr. Truly."

"Dad," Emily corrects. "You can call him your husband. Could you be anymore uptight?"

"Emily," William Truly speaks to her, his tone deep, reprimanding.

Dr. Ryan presses her head between her hands, wearing thin from the constant interruptions. "Anyway. After Emily was hospitalized, that morning, when she was found behind the dumpster." A hint of emotion reflects in her eyes, an uncanny occurrence. "She couldn't maintain her blood pressure. She has the rarest blood type, AB-negative. After several transfusions, and a general shortage of blood, I called Dr. Godfrey. He told me about you. And Aubrey. It seemed crazy, unreal." She looks at Emily, scanning her with an affection only a mother would recognize. "When it's your own, you're willing to believe in anything. Imagine, your child supernatural, forever untouched by the pain, the tragedies that accompany life as we know it as humans." Dr. Ryan leans forward in Gina's direction, her body language full of adoration. "What you have, Gina, it's a shield. You're resilient to anything mortal. Superior in every way. The perfect defense. Nobody can hurt you, physically, without your immediate retaliation and triumph. I wasn't trying to take anything from you. Certainly didn't want to hurt you. I simply wanted what you possessed, your gift, for my daughter. For every daughter."

"So, you propose to clone me?" Gina asks, her voice soft and understanding, yet morally concerned. "My blood? Where does it stop? How many others are there?"

"Nobody's playing God here," Dr. Ryan defends. "We've cloned nothing, simply transfused your blood into two individuals, who may have died otherwise, and who now have the power to make the world a better place, a safer place in the meantime."

"ETNA. That's what they were after. My blood," Gina whispers.

Dr. Ryan nods her head.

"If they know, who else knows? And how many others do we have to fend off? And why did Dr. Shaw act as if nothing was extraordinary about my case? And why were you so suspicious and noncompliant during the investigation?" Gina rambles, questions attacking her mind faster than she can process them.

"When nothing is as it seems, you create the perfect defense," Dr. Godfrey answers. "You knew nothing of the truth, providing you with integrity in your testimony. Obviously, that translated to the jury in their generous verdict."

"With all due respect," Gina begins, knowing she speaks to the man who saved her life. "Are you sure you simply didn't tell me the truth because I would have rebelled. I wouldn't have gone along with any of this. In my sane mind, as Gina DeLuca, I know it's not right to go around baiting people to kill them. And maybe I wanted to die, and stay dead, with my husband and my son." She thuds her hand against her chest passionately.

Emily shakes her head. "I told you she doesn't deserve this power. She's got no heart. I tried to tell you that when I was training her. Can I please do us all a favor? Two seconds, that's all I need to open this door and boot her ass out."

"If you want it so bad, take it," Gina challenges.

"She can't," Aubrey defends. "It doesn't work that way. Dr. Godfrey, Dr. Ryan and Mr. Truly planned this for almost three years," she turns to Gina relaying the significance of the elaborate plan. "They took good care of you, Gina." The first time Aubrey has spoken against her.

"I don't understand. It doesn't work what way? You...you and her have the same powers. I saw them, back there at the ravine," Gina ponders.

"You're the center. They're support, if you will. Their primary powers to serve you. They don't function independently," Dr. Ryan explains.

Emily huffs, tormented by the fact.

"I'm a little telepathic. I can reach you, mind to mind, speaking through the eyes of course. Mine sparkle like yours. Same DNA and like color, Dr. Godfrey says," Aubrey assists, waiting on Emily to elaborate. She does not. Aubrey continues, "And Emily's kinda telekinetic. She reaches you, body to body. She can make you mimic her every move, if you're so inclined. Her eyes don't work like yours, though. Different DNA and color."

Gina's expression emits a bit of gratitude and sympathy, realizing the burden placed on the young women. Not unlike her, but akin in the complicated scheme. None of them actively choosing their roles, with little control over the outcome. "When you trained me?" she questions Emily.

Emily looks away, refusing to answer.

"Your martial arts training," Aubrey explains. "Emily and Mr. Truly trained you. Some real hardcore, Navy Seal's shit." Aubrey smiles with enthusiasm. "It was amazing to watch. You and Emily. Pushing and challenging one another. Neither of you willing to give up. Both carrying a deep-seated desire to be the best. Just like at the ravine. It never gets old. Watching the two of you, your bodies cohesive. Always mesmerizing. Better than the ballet."

"Why can't I remember any of this?" Gina reasons aloud. "Flashes...snapshots, that's all I get."

"Extensive psychotherapy and hypnosis," Dr. Ryan explains.

"Quite possibly reversible," Dr. Godfrey adds. "We needed a clean slate. A new beginning, if you will."

"A robot," Gina quips.

"Bottom line, *Ginger*," Emily begins, referring in slang to Gina's hair color. "There'll be no victims here. Either you're in or you're out. Your choice." She folds her arms over her chest, eyeing Gina, knowing exactly how she would like her to opt.

"Choice?" Gina scoffs. "I'm dead to the world as Brianna Castille. And a fugitive no less, as Gina DeLuca, after that little showing at the ravine." She looks out the window.

"Come on, *Ginger*," Aubrey says playfully, poking fun at the hostility between her and Emily. "All families have some level of dysfunction," she continues, looking around at the motley crew in the chopper. A lingering silence follows.

"Alright. I'm in," Gina confirms. Looking from the window, she adds, "On one condition. The two men..."

"Lifers at the Louisiana State Pen," Emily interrupts, confirming the whereabouts of the two men who murdered Lon and Braydon. *"Alcatraz of the South,"* she further elaborates on its infamous nickname.

"Done," Dr. Ryan endorses.

Gina leans forward in Emily's direction, her hand nimbly swiping the crucifix from around her neck.

Emily smirks with understanding and mutual respect, force, a concept she easily identifies with.

Gina holds the broken necklace and pendant securely in her hand, a tangible connection to her past.

Off in the distance, a desolate, spartan compound is visible. Buildings made of iron and stone hide in the foothills of rugged, mountainous terrain. A dwelling most suitable for a Vigilare.

CHAPTER 24

At the state correctional facility three-hours from Vanguard, Detective Tony Gronkowski waits in his police cruiser for a bus that never shows.

HOURS LATER, ROUGHLY midnight, upon his return home, he shaves in front of his bathroom mirror, capping off a much-needed long, hot shower. His mind busy with thoughts of the past few months—the case, Gina, Vigilare, the absence of her transportation. Preoccupied, he gets a little heavy-handed with his razor, nicking the skin on his jawline.

"Shit," he mutters, rinsing the razor under the steady stream of warm water from the spigot.

The red, sticky substance slowly weeps from the cut to his flesh, running in a thin jagged line around the curve of his jaw and down onto his neck.

"Wooh," he quips, shaking his head. "Ease up on the caffeine, Gronkowski," he reprimands himself as his heartbeat hastens, resonant in his temples, brisk and steady, rhythmic like a drum. He thumps his hand against his chest a few times, agitated with the urgency by which his lungs suddenly require air in large quantities. Feeling faint, he leans onto the sink, breathing with great focus through his nose and out his mouth, attempting to squelch the adrenaline rush to his system. Burying his face under the spigot, he turns the water to cold, splashing it around him.

"Ah, much better," he says, finally feeling some relief.

Returning to an erect position, he presses the blade to his face, his eyes making contact with the mirror. The razor immediately drops from his hand, its plastic surface tumbling off the sink below. His hazel eyes, reflecting colors around them as hazel eyes do, one in particular, sparkling emerald green.

Epilogue

So on it goes, the mission,
Understanding, finally, at last.
The Vigilare assumes her position,
A driving force comes to light in the form of her past.

Internal odds weigh heavily, a constant battle in her mind,
Remedied by visions, haunting nightmares, lurid dreams.
Is revenge truly sweetest? We shall see,
The future holds no boundaries for the supernatural, it seems.

In a world where nothing is as it appears,
Do the eyes, 'the windows of the soul,' hold the key?
Blood flows through good, as it flows through evil,
One Vigilare, two Vigilares? Could there be three?

A red hue emerges,
Where once it was only emerald green.
It rages, free of sparkle, a heavy, hungry light,
Merciless and destructive, arrogant and brutally keen.

To fall from grace,
Such is a divine one's plight.
Be wary of your neighbor,
Tread softly, Vigilare, keeper of the night.

SHOUT-OUTS

TAMMY – My first read. When I sent you the first half—the only half at the time—you said, "I can't wait for the rest!" That fueled the spark, my friend. I think we've done that as long as we've known one another. A little push here, a little push there; challenging each other to grow, evolve. Thanks for the never-ending support and faith. I love ya, Tam!

MOM – "On the road again, just can't wait to get on the road again." Are you ready for another road trip, books in tow? We keep up at this rate, they'll be calling us Willie & Waylon. Ha! I've really enjoyed our time together this past year. Thanks for your unwavering encouragement. I believe I wrote the most laborious part at your house. Nothing like the smell of coffee at Mom's in the morning to get me in the zone! And thank you for listening and nodding your head appropriately at all of my rambling in constructing the plot. And Morgan's rambling, too. That girl's got an opinion about everything (just like her mother...I snicker). I love you bunches!

ANGE-A-BELLE & NETT-A-BETT – I know you thought I was the oddest little sister in the world, when I would go off into the corner and sing and write by myself for hours, but that never stopped you from rallying for me, always. Ange, thanks for the writing breaks aptly filled with delicious treats. I swear you should have your own show on the *Food Network*. And Nett, thanks for the much needed workouts—one, to equally exhaust my physical self as writing exhausts my mental self, and two, to burn off all those delicious treats *Betty* showers us with! Thanks for everything. I love you both, always and forever.

AMY HESS MEAD – My first customer ever. Gives a girl a nice dose of confidence seeing that first order in her *Inbox* (I smile). I'll never forget the feeling it gave me. Thank you for that moment. You've always been a great source of support for me. And I see you fulfilling that same role for your uber talented, respectful, beautiful children. They certainly are something to be proud of, Miss Amy. I love and admire you.

JANET KILGORE – Lovingly referred to as JK. Thanks for being my grammar and punctuation compass. Boy, would I ever be lost in the words (ie. woods... ha ha) without you. As always, I enjoyed your company throughout the editing process, which I might add is a most humbling experience for me. I'm thankful to have such a good teacher. I'll be your "grasshopper" any day of the week! Looking forward to the next one.

STEVE RICHEY – They say, "Don't judge a book by its cover." Unfortunately, I think most people do. And if that's the case, then I have nothing to worry about, thanks to you! Kick-ass job with the cover, Steve. I love it! So thankful to come across you in film class. I hope this is the beginning of a long relationship in pagination and cover design.

SCOTT MCMAHAN – Hey gym rat! Takes one to know one, right? Thanks for all the input, proofing and encouragement. Hopefully the next one will be better than you thought it would be, too!

KIM, CARRINE, & NELL – Have we really been out of school this long? Can't be! I miss you guys. Thanks for your warm welcome last year and for all the help at the book signings. Even though we're all *Moving On* as life does, I think of you often with a smile on my face and a squeeze of my heart. Friends for life. I love you guys!

THE PA POSSE – Nobody is as lucky as I am to have your support. Thanks for all the website hits and Facebook 'likes.' They always seem to come at the perfect time. Just as the monster of doubt rears its ugly head, it never fails, I get a new fan or someone sends me a nice message about how they enjoyed the book, or the music. It is then that I smile and emerge with renewed spirit, squashing that annoying little monster. Your encouragement, your acceptance, your kind words touch my life more than you know. Thank you. Muahs & Hugs!

TO ALL THE INDIES OUT THERE – specifically Shelley Meyer and her staff at *Wild About Music,* Austin, Texas. Love you Shelley! From all of us without big name labels and publishers—thanks for giving us a chance, and an outlet for our work. Forever indebted. Rock On!

FINALLY, MISS MORGAN (MY SWEET THING) – You are too cool kiddo! I am amazed at your awareness and presence of self at such a young age. You make me, and everyone around you so proud. And your wit—awe man, you make me laugh. I loved sitting in Mom's kitchen with my laptop writing *Vigilare*, looking over the top of my screen to see you sitting at the other end of the table peeking back at me over your laptop writing your story. Writing is often a lonely, solitary act, but not with you around. I don't think you even realized it but that spurred me on, just having you there, your presence always uplifting and inspiring. I know your mother did all the work in having you, but I swear I feel like you're my own—I love you that much. I think you've been my biggest fan from day one. Thanks for always believing in Aunt Boo. I know the world holds nothing but great things for you, my little cherub, as you have nothing but the greatest of virtues to offer. I keep you with me always, in the pocket of my heart.

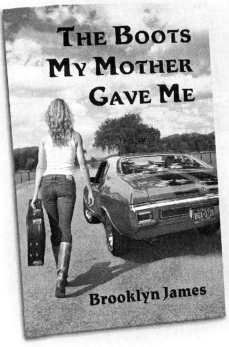